CORPSE WALKER

The Night Parade

Book 1 of

The Infernal Artifacts Collection

The Infernal Artifacts Collection
Timeline Order:

Corpse Walker: The Night Parade (1940s)
Dioscuri: Secrets of the Fey (2002)

CORPSE WALKER

The Night Parade

RALYNN KIMIE

Steely Co. Publishing

CORPSE WALKER: THE NIGHT PARADE Copyright © 2022 by Ralynn Kimie.

All rights reserved. Printed in the United States of America. No part of this book may be used or reproduced in any manner whatsoever without written permission except in the case of brief quotations embodied in critical articles or reviews.

This book is a work of historical fantasy fiction. Names, characters, businesses, organizations, places, events and incidents either are the product of the author's imagination or are used fictitiously. Any resemblance to actual persons, living or dead, events, or locales is entirely coincidental.

For information contact: www.ralynnkimie.com

Paperback 5x8

Second Edition: 2023

Contents

Introduction 1

Chapter 1 3

Chapter 2 23

Chapter 3 43

Chapter 4 59

Chapter 5 77

Chapter 6 93

Chapter 7 111

Chapter 8 133

Chapter 9 149

Chapter 10 167

Chapter 11 185

Chapter 12 201

Chapter 13 217

Chapter 14 239

Chapter 15 259

Chapter 16 275

Chapter 17 293

Chapter 18 309

Chapter 19 323

Chapter 20......333

Chapter 21......345

Chapter 22......363

Chapter 23......379

Chapter 24......389

Epilogue......397

for my grandfather,
Retired LTC John R. Jones of the Army

World War II
Korean War
Vietnam War

The only thing we have to fear is fear itself.

-FRANKLIN D. ROOSEVELT

INTRODUCTION

Pearl Harbor

Black clouds swallowed the blue sky. From beneath the clear ocean surface, flashes of reds and yellows could be seen illuminating the expanding darkness overhead. Translucent and glassy from the water, the light show continued above while sinking further into an abyss. The water was not cold to the touch but boiling hot from the surrounding flames eating away at the sinking ships. Screams and explosions echoed hauntingly in the ears of many before dimming into a constant ring, then deafening to nothing.

The water grew darker as it cooled in the depths, now polluted with debris, oil, and blood. All eight of the present U.S. Navy battleships were damaged, with four sunk in the harbor. Two thousand four hundred and three Americans died during the early morning hours on December 7, 1941. A date that would live in infamy.

CHAPTER ONE

Guam, December 8, 1941
0806 — local time

Captain George McMillin, lids heavy over bloodshot eyes, sank back in his creaky wooden chair. The top edges of the backrest were worn from his palms constantly resting upon it when he'd stand behind his chair rather than sit. Captain McMillin didn't like to sit, but that morning, he couldn't help it. It was the first time in hours he was able to catch a break. The day was dry and hot, and he rubbed the sweat and oils beading on his face with a handkerchief. Nearly four hours passed since he was informed by the Department of the Navy of the attack on Pearl Harbor in Hawai'i, both as governor and overall commander of the garrison in charge of Naval Forces in Guam.

McMillin was compelled to act quickly.

Under extreme pressure, he ordered the evacuation of various civilian populations throughout the island, along with the immediate jailing of all Japanese nationals. Churches, banks, schools, and other public places were to be closed until further notice. McMillin was on high alert since the information reached him, knowing they were not equipped with the proper defenses to stand a fighting chance in protecting Guam from an Imperial Japanese assault should one be headed their way.

He continued to pat his forehead rapidly with the soiled handkerchief. His brown eyes were red-rimmed, and they watered from the pressure of defending the island. He put a cigarette to his lips and fumbled with a lighter as he made several attempts at lighting it. The thumb of his shaking left hand made it nearly impossible to ignite a flame. He threw it back on the desk in frustration, letting the cigarette fall from his mouth.

Guam's guard ship, the USS *Gold Star*, which had sailed to the Philippines to pick up supplies and allowed the crew to buy Christmas presents, had since been directed to remain docked there, leaving behind two hundred and seventy-one personnel and four nurses, most of whom were unarmed, untrained, and unprepared for war.

Out at sea sat only the minesweeper USS *Penguin*, the immobile oil depot ship *Robert L. Barnes*, and two old yard patrol boats.

McMillin sat with two Naval officers. One mentioned the Marine barracks at Sumay.

"How many again?" McMillin asked.

"One hundred and forty-five men," answered the officer. "They're quickly organizing into a company armed with rifles and some machine guns."

"There's also the Guam Insular Force Guard—I believe that's at least an additional two hundred—maybe almost three hundred men."

McMillin sighed as he closed his eyes. He massaged his temples with his fingers.

"The Insular Force Guard only recently underwent expansion in May," he said. He lifted his head from his hands and slowly opened his eyes to look at the officer. Slowly, he began shaking his head. "Most of them have little to no proper training. They're not prepared." His worn wooden chair creaked more beneath his weight as he sat back, fumbling with the cigarette. "We're not prepared."

"There's also the police force," the officer suggested, while the other continued to make phone calls. "That's almost a hundred more."

"They've only got pistols."

"I don't know what you want me to say, Captain."

After making calls for the last several hours to prepare them for what would likely come, McMillin sat dejected.

Defeated before an attack had even started.

In his head, he replayed the United States government's abhorrent decision that it would neither be possible nor practical to defend Guam should there be an attack during the war. Low priority and discarded, his heart sank for his people.

"We're going to be severely outnumbered and outgunned," McMillin said firmly, sticking the cigarette back into his mouth. "But we won't go down without a fight. And we'll give it all we got." Steadying his left hand with his right, he finally managed to light his cigarette. The two Naval officers with him managed to smile as they exchanged glances with one another.

At 08:27 a.m., three minutes after McMillin lit his cigarette, fire rained from the sky as he blew smoke from his mouth. They all thrusted themselves out of their chairs and onto the ground. Scuttling across the floor, the three of them darted in different directions as McMillin shouted orders. A Japanese aircraft from Saipan had attacked the Marine barracks first, and the Battle of Guam began.

That morning, the beauty of the small island full of tropical forests and wooded hills lit up in flashes of explosions and rampant fire as the aerial assault ensued. Planes roared violently overhead as they swarmed Guam with their fury. The Japanese further attacked the Piti Navy Yard, the Libugon radio station, the Standard Oil Company, and the Pan American Hotel.

The island was ablaze.

The minesweeper, USS *Penguin*, managed to shoot down one of the Japanese aircrafts only to be sunk soon after. The USS *Robert L. Barnes* was ignited, the reflection illuminating brightly in the ocean water below. It was quickly captured by the Japanese forces. Throughout the morning and all over the island, the air raids terrorized people and their villages. They were screaming and crying, men and women, noises that were soon drowned out by explosives and death. They reached pitches that were inhuman and choked violently on the smoke.

The attack lasted throughout the day, carrying on into the late afternoon. Fire rained from the sky as the Japanese aircrafts circled the small island of Guam.

Were they gone? Was it over?

There were murmurs of hope. Whispers, begging, and prayer.

Civilians and the military looked to the skies for reassurance. Many of the Chamorro people had fled from their homes and crowded the churches for shelter while they held hands and sat in prayer. Tears were streaming from many faces. Eyes were red, bodies were shaking. Families were huddled together. Parents consoled their children, and couples consoled each other. They waited patiently with water in their eyes, watching from church windows while their world burned around them.

For a moment there was hope, until the sky raged above them the next morning when nine Imperial Japanese aircraft returned.

The same targets were attacked with vigor. In addition, the Japanese further destroyed what was left of several Chamorro villages. The only thing louder than the air raids were the screams that came from the terrified children. It was the screams, the sudden cutoffs, and then the silence that truly haunted the people of Guam. The day was long, but the night would be even longer.

Later on the evening of December 9, a Japanese invasion fleet of four heavy cruisers, four destroyers, two gunboats, six submarine chasers, two minesweepers, two destroyer tenders, and ten transports left Saipan for Guam.

The small U.S. Navy and Marine Corps units fortified their positions and put up their best defense against the Imperial Japanese aerial assault to protect the Plaza de España, but the battle lasted only until the early morning of December 10 when they met a much larger military force led by Major General Tomitarō Horii. The screams and clamor of barbaric combat grew louder inland with the advancement of the Japanese, who were just as deadly on the ground as they were from the sky.

It was a mistake in the Japanese intelligence gathering that caused Japan to overcommit resources and attack Guam with disproportionate force.

In the process of the battle, the Americans suffered losses and casualties of nearly one-third of their entire force, severely overwhelming the four nurses left to care for the ones who remained—most of whom were injured.

From earlier that same year, the Empire of Japan already planned to capture Guam. It was spring of 1941 when the Japanese sent an aircraft to fly photo reconnaissance sorties over the island, and the plans for the invasion were completed by fall. The South Seas Detachment was selected to be the prime unit responsible for executing these plans, made up of the 144th Infantry Regiment and other units detached from the 55th Division. While the South Seas Detachment appeared to the world to be commanded by Major General Tomitarō Horii, the experimental division of Yamata no Orochi, led by Flight Commander Isamu Mori, pulled all strings from behind a well-hidden curtain. Commander Mori had special plans for the Pacific War. Plans that would change the world as humanity knew it.

And he truly answered to no one.

Imperial Japanese Flight Commander Isamu Mori of Yamata no Orochi arrived the morning of December 10 with his beautiful Akita dog, Tadeo, at his side, and a fleet of over four hundred troops at Dungcas Beach, north of Agana, with every intention of conquering Guam once and for all. After they attacked and quickly defeated the small Insular Force Guard, the fleet advanced on Piti, headed toward Sumay, and then finally the Marine Corps barracks, leaving a trail of bodies and a river of blood in their wake.

The air smelled of smoke and burning flesh.

The once-clear sky was cloudy and full of ash.

The small United States units gave it their all and defended the territory with their lives. It was more than McMillin could have asked for.

Only on the governor's orders, did what was left of the U.S. Marines finally surrender. At 05:45 a.m., McMillin ordered the sounding of a car horn three times, which both sides recognized as a sign to cease fire.

They lost.

Past the Spanish San Antonio Bridge that crossed the Hagatna River and across the street of the Dulce Nombre de Maria Cathedral Basilica, the governor himself surrendered at 06:00 a.m. when Japanese troops captured him in the reception room of his living quarters. Still, a few skirmishes took place all throughout the island before the news of the surrender spread and the rest of Guam's forces laid down their arms.

The Imperial Japanese Military force officially defeated the American garrison of Guam on December 10, 1941, with the surrender taking place only a few days after the initial bombing of Pearl Harbor. Twenty-one American military personnel and civilians died during the attack. Thirty-five were wounded. Six U.S. Navy seamen evaded capture, but the rest were to be imprisoned in Japan.

At Agana's Plaza de España, within a beautiful white three-arched gate, Commander Isamu Mori approached Captain McMillin, who was the first American prisoner of war held by the Japanese. The Commander was dressed in a single-breasted tunic with a stand and fall collar, five buttons that ran down the front, and two internal pockets with scalloped flaps. He wore long trousers along with puttees and tapes. His feet were covered with leather ankle boots that had hobnailed hard leather soles with better heel J-cleats. His oddly shaped head was covered by a cap with a neck flap hooked to the bottom and made from four cloth rectangles.

Captain McMillin was already accompanied by Major General Horii. After the two Japanese officials addressed one another, Major General Horii retreated to his own detachment—who had their official landings at Tumon Bay in the north, on the southwest coast near Merizo, and the eastern shore at Talofofo Bay—to give further instructions on their new occupation as Major General

Tomitarō Horii would become the new governor of Guam. Mori circled McMillin like a shark with its prey just in front of a beautiful and elaborate hexagon fountain. While the U.S. Navy Captain stood surrounded by Imperial Japanese officials in the courtyard, he remained poised and unthreatened by Mori's presence, just as he was in Horii's presence despite being stripped of the freedom he once knew—and may never know again. To keep his calm demeanor, McMillin focused on the beauty of Guam, finding himself blessed to be surrounded by the greenery year-round, though disheartened now by how much of it remained on fire and smoking from the battle. But the leaves continued rustling in the wind without a care in the world, and life went on, regardless of the war between humanity. It was something to be cherished. McMillin looked down and noticed a small shrub growing in the crack of the concrete. A small, barely noticeable smile appeared at the corner of his mouth.

Men would always fight, but nature would persevere.

"We surrendered," the former Governor said calmly, returning his gaze to the Japanese Commander standing in front him before glancing down at the Akita that stood proudly beside Isamu Mori. "What more do you want?" While his question was genuine, it was also dismissive. He knew he and the rest of the survivors would be taken prisoner. What he said no longer mattered, as he couldn't bargain for anyone's freedom. McMillin was almost baiting him.

Commander Mori readjusted the military cap on his head as he glanced out over Guam and the Imperial Japanese forces that had invaded. Inhaling the ashy air, he looked back at Captain McMillin and scrunched his brows together. Commander Mori tilted his head challengingly, tucking his chin down as his gaze darkened, brown eyes fading to black till the whites of his eyes all but disappeared. Black beady eyes focused on the American. Captain McMillin did his best to not appear threatened by the sudden demonic change in his appearance, but he was slightly taken aback. Captain McMillin's eyes were shifty, but he kept his expression blank and unreadable. He had heard stories, but he hadn't seen anything like it.

"I think you *know* what I want," Commander Mori said.

Captain McMillin's expression fell with the realization of what Commander Mori sought, and unfortunately, the Commander was quick enough to catch it.

"You just missed it," Captain McMillin said swiftly, collecting himself as he cleared his throat, making an attempt to cover his rather subtle slip up as he hardened his expression. Commander Mori sought Guam's piece of an Infernal Artifact. He couldn't let him know where it was. Captain McMillin glanced away from the

Commander and looked out at the grounds of the plaza that, for the most part, had remained undamaged from the aerial assault. He opened his arms as much as his shackles would allow. "It's not here. The USS *Gold Star*—" he nodded as he pointed out at the sea, "they're guarding it in the Philippines. They were specifically instructed to stay there until after Christmas."

Commander Mori smiled slyly beneath his thin mustache, unconvinced. He tapped his chin with his gloved hand as he shook his head in disappointment while stroking the small patch of scruff.

"You are a terrible liar, Captain." Commander Mori turned away from Captain McMillin and looked around the plaza. He inhaled deeply, and Captain McMillin couldn't help but observe the back of the Commander's head and the way it pressed up into his military cap. "You see, I know much about this plaza—constructed in 1736— during the Spanish occupation when *they* found *it* first. But they did not have the strength to move it far, too many of their men died and they knew too little about it, so I know you didn't move it either. Given your surrender," Commander Mori taunted him, "I don't think you have what it takes to risk the lives of your men in order to handle something you don't quite understand."

"And you think you do?" Captain McMillin asked, raising his eyebrows. It was fruitless to pretend he didn't know what Commander Mori was talking about. Being the governor and commander of the garrison, of course he knew, and Commander Mori knew exactly *what* he was looking for—and he knew it was there.

Commander Mori was in search of one of the Infernal Artifacts known mostly by verbal myth and legend, and he was the last person Captain McMillin wanted to hand it over to. But in the chaos of the surprise attack and lack of preparation, they hadn't thought to protect it. They were in a war between the Allies and the Axis powers, not one of gods and goddesses. Captain McMillin could only stall now.

"I know I do," Commander Mori assured.

Captain McMillin rejected his claims. "You don't know what you're doing."

"You don't know *who* I am, Captain. Or *what* I am."

Captain McMillin tilted his head and narrowed his eyes. Commander Mori did the same as to mock him. He put his gloved hands behind his back as he paced the courtyard. He looked out into the distance, as though to recall a lost memory.

"A long time ago, I had a friend—a mentor, you could say. He told me a story about the Creator and three of his sons: Destiny, Dream, and Death." Commander Mori wrinkled his nose a bit at the mention of his mentor before dismissing it. He held up three fingers as he faced Captain

McMillin again. "Three pivotal parts that make up human life. He told me how Death cast out his scythe, the strongest artifact in the world, across the Pacific Ocean, so that the lesser deities could co-exist and rule cooperatively without one being stronger than another. Guam, Midway, Hawai'i." He inhaled deeply and exhaled sharply, growing impatient as he curled his raised hand into a fist. "Where is it, Captain?" he asked, his eyes still black and beady. "I know you know. The next time I have to ask will not be so kindly."

Captain McMillin had heard many stories regarding the Creator and his sons. They were divine beings with Infernal Artifacts, thought to have come with the creation of the universe. One artifact was on earth, one left with an ancient civilization, and one was never before seen.

Without conscious thought, Captain McMillin quickly glanced toward the Chocolate House. It was a little white structure with small open windows and a tiered rust-colored roof. Commander Mori smiled genuinely as his eyes followed the gaze. He patted the tanned cheek of Captain McMillin harshly, both appreciatively and disrespectfully, as he, his loyal Akita dog, and two Imperial Japanese officials approached it.

It was dark inside the little Chocolate House, aside from the natural light seeping through the open windows. Within it housed two older Spanish coats of arms. With admiration, Commander Mori let his officials know—in Japanese—that the two coats of arms dated back between 1879 and 1895.

"I love *human* history, you know," he said, his words returning to English as he emphasized the word human. Commander Mori was well-spoken and could fluently speak several languages. "I think it's fascinating. People are fascinating. Stupid and without real purpose—but fascinating nonetheless." Like a dance, his feet shuffled along the ground as he carefully observed the two coats of arms before him. While both were exquisite, one was not like the other. To him, it was a sad attempt at hiding something in plain sight, and he was surprised it was still there. Then again, most couldn't contain the power within it.

Commander Mori stood in front of the one on the left-hand side of the Chocolate House. He ran his hand over the Spanish crest and the iron rods that held the piece together, before breaking through it with ease, using his fist. The wall crumbled behind it from the force.

The handle of the scythe was knocked free, clattering against the ground. There was faint black smoke dancing about and encircling the rod that soon dispersed into the air. Commander Mori stepped around the rod, watching as the smoke dissipated. With his gloved left hand, he picked the pole of the scythe up effortlessly and turned it over twice, admiring the long, slender piece of the artifact.

One piece down, two to go.

"That is not for you to touch." Captain McMillin had approached, hands balled into fists in his shackles. Imperial Japanese officials aimed their weapons at him in defense, but they lowered them at Commander Mori's signal.

"He's harmless," Commander Mori sneered. His focus was on the piece of the artifact he now held in his hand. He hadn't even bothered to look up at Captain McMillin when he approached. Commander Mori turned the handle over to grip it with both hands. He closed his eyes and steadied his breathing. He could feel its power and knew the potential of the scythe once all of the pieces were gathered and the artifact was completed. Captain McMillin was of no real threat to him.

"You don't know what you're doing!"

"That's where you're wrong, Captain." Commander Mori opened his eyes and finally looked over at Captain McMillin. "I know *exactly* what I'm doing." Commander Mori pushed past him with the handle of the scythe still firmly at hand and Tadeo trailed behind, following his lead. "Tell the German to meet me in the palace," Mori said to one of his officials. "We must continue with the assembly of the portal—and get me in touch with Captain Kaname."

"But we do not have all of the pieces," replied the Japanese official. Commander Mori clenched his jaw. "We lost the one at Pearl Harbor and then Midway was—"

"Silence!" Commander Mori snapped, his voice roaring above the noises of nature and soft chatter between the military. He held up his free hand to silence the official, and the man obeyed the orders instantly. Commander Mori inhaled deeply, calming himself. He made sure to gather his composure before speaking again. "It is being taken care of," he said, though his voice was still stern, and he waved him away. "Now go."

The official nodded and turned around to leave immediately.

Commander Mori pivoted on his heels, while again admiring the length of the scythe's handle as he turned it in his hand. It was beautifully crafted, gold with ancient runes etched into the body. No one knew just how old Death's scythe really was, but it was at least as old as the universe itself. Commander Mori looked up at Captain McMillin, who simply stared at him in horror. His eyes were wide, mouth left open. He was aghast.

"Why isn't it hurting you?" he asked, both curious and horrified. "I watched that artifact consume men—I watched men die trying to hold that thing and break it free from the arms—"

Commander Mori smiled proudly. He was always pleased to know of the others who tried and failed while he succeeded. It stroked his ego.

"Do you know who I am?" he questioned genuinely, tightening his grip around the body of the broken scythe. Commander Mori observed the Captain, who furrowed his brows as though he didn't quite understand the question.

"Flight Commander Isamu Mori," Captain McMillin responded.

Commander Mori nodded at the practical answer, though it also made him chuckle a little.

The grin on his face made Captain McMillin uneasy.

"Yes, and no. I am known as Isamu Mori, this is true," Commander Mori said, as he paced the floor. He then stopped in his tracks and pointed the top end of the scythe at the Captain. "But what more?"

Captain McMillin's brows pulled together in confusion. He looked around at the Japanese officials who now stood quietly around them. None of them offered any sort of hint as to what Mori was talking about. They all stared straight ahead, professionally. Silent and obedient. Almost robotic, as if only to move when necessary or on command.

"I don't think I understand," Captain McMillin admitted finally, shaking his head. He shuffled in his shackles as he glanced past the Japanese officials at the American personnel being escorted onto the Japanese warships as prisoners.

"Of course you don't. You are, after all, only *human*."

The human mention caused Captain McMillin's attention to be drawn back to the conversation. His eyes refocused on Commander Mori and his heart sank. This was much more than the takeover of a United States territory. The Commander pulled off his uniquely shaped military cap, revealing a bald and unusually elongated head as he placed his cap at his chest with authenticity.

"I am Nurarihyon." Commander Mori's eyes darkened again into a marble black as the whites of his eyes disappeared. A chill ran down Captain McMillin's spine as a wide hellish grin creepily stretched from ear to ear on Mori's face, letting his jaw hang ajar. "And once I gather all of the pieces of Death's scythe, I will bring upon Hyakki Yagyō—the night parade of one hundred demons."

CHAPTER TWO

York, Pennsylvania, February 24, 1942
1003 — local time

It was as normal of a Tuesday morning as any other. Crisp and cold in the middle of winter. Snowflakes drifted from the sky and blanketed the grounds of the surrounding factories. The radio in the toasty Sharp Co. Factory in York, Pennsylvania, currently aired a recording from the previous evening's fireside chat with President Roosevelt *On the Progress of the War.*

The choice of entertainment caused disagreements between factory workers. An older man, thin and missing an eye, groaned about the lack of music. His injuries were sustained during the first world war. He sat back in his chair, frustrated and exasperated.

"I'm tired of listening to this depressing crap."

"Hey! I wanna hear that depressing crap!" A younger worker snapped back from across the assembly line. "I didn't get to hear it last night, so keep it down over there!"

"We have most certainly suffered losses—from Hitler's U-Boats in the Atlantic as well as from the Japanese in the Pacific—and we shall suffer more of them before the turn of the tide," said the president. His voice was loud and stern, properly communicating his self-assurance while crackling through the radio speaker. *"But, speaking for the United States of America, let me say once and for all to the people of the world: We Americans have been compelled to yield ground, but we will regain it. We and the other United Nations are committed to the destruction of the militarism of Japan and Germany. We are daily increasing our strength. Soon, we and not our enemies, will have the offensive; we, not they, will win the final battles; and we, not they, will make the final peace."*

The fireside chats were a series of evening radio addresses given by the president of the United States himself. During the times of uncertainty and despair, it was important to him that he spoke to the American people directly; to properly explain his policies in his own words and to put an end to any and all rumors others may have started— whether intentional or out of misunderstanding—and confront conservative-dominated newspapers. President Roosevelt was an effective communicator over the radio and he spoke with familiarity about the recovery from the Great Depression, the promulgation of the Emergency Banking Act, the 1936 recession, New Deal initiatives, the course of the new World War, and the part the United States of America would now play in it.

While the fireside chats originally aired first in the evenings, many radio stations would often replay the recordings the following morning for the citizens who might have missed tuning in. Hope was important in such a dark time, and the broadcasts not only kept President Roosevelt in high public regard, but redefined his relationship with the American citizens.

The Sharp Co. Factory was particularly at its peak of performance that February morning due to the presence of Miss Dorothea Sharp on the premises—the owner's one and only daughter. Sharp Co. was a primary contractor in the Manufacturer's Association and followed the York Plan. Prior to the bombing of Pearl Harbor and the official entry of the United States into World War II, Sharp Co. had planned long ago to assist in the war pending their country's direct involvement.

Presently, York County's finest men were being drafted, leaving behind women, children, and only the ineligible and incompetent men. At least, that's how many of the remaining men saw themselves—weak, incapacitated, and unfulfilling of their duty to their country. No one wanted to work in a factory while others were laying down their lives and fighting for the freedom of their country and the freedom of the American people.

There were a few young men who worked in the factories who weren't quite old enough. They often naively chatted to one another about how different things would be once they came of age and would become eligible. There were two in particular, Lance and John, who would often exchange smirks and excited comments about the strength they'd bring to the war.

The elder man, Mr. Jensen, who complained about the lack of music, often found them intolerable to listen to.

"You two eager beavers have no idea what you're talking about," he would say, once he'd had enough and his blood came to a boil.

Rather than listen to any wisdom Mr. Jensen might have to offer, Lance would instead cover one eye and mock how Mr. Jensen did his job.

"How can you possibly get anything right, not being able to see?" Lance asked, purposely knocking over the box he had packaged. "I can't see bupkis."

The two boys would break into laughter, while Mr. Jensen would mutter a few expletives to himself and shake his head. While he appeared to be a bitter old man, his expression showed real pain. It broke his heart to have the injuries he sustained from the first World War be made a mockery of.

"Show some respect, will ya?" A blond man in a wheelchair scowled at the two boys. "You have a list of medical ailments longer than Santa's naughty list," he said to Lance, who averted his eyes, "and you—" he turned his attention to John, "probably couldn't even get through the first day of bootcamp." The blond man patted his own stomach to acknowledge the boy's belly. The two boys just rolled their eyes and Lance picked up the contents he had knocked over.

The blond man wheeled over to Mr. Jensen as he passed by. "They're just kids, Mr. Jensen," he assured.

"They don't know any better."

"They're a bunch of yucks." A defeated sigh left Mr. Jensen's lips as he just lowered his head and continued to work. "Please don't defend me, Davey."

He only nodded his head. "If it's any consolation, thank you for your service in the first war."

Mr. Jensen looked up just as Davey wheeled his way back to his spot in the factory line. A small smile appeared at the corner of his lips as he continued with his job.

Some men there, however, very few, believed their work in the factory was just as important and had pride in their accomplishments when it came to aiding in supplies the military needed. Support could be just as important as an active role, if not more so. But many disagreed with that notion. The primary view the people shared was that if you were a man and weren't serving your country in the military, you were a coward, regardless of the reason for it. Legitimate or otherwise. Whether you were physically unfit to do so, unwell, or incapacitated in one way or another, none of it mattered.

Cowardice.

That was the sole label, and no one was proud to wear it.

Fights often broke out in the factory due to many of the employees having something to prove, but no one misbehaved when Dorothea was in town.

Dorothea 'Dot' Sharp was a leading chemical engineer, heavily involved in the secret Manhattan Project, which formally brought together the S-1 Committee eleven days after the attack on Pearl Harbor and gathered the most brilliant minds of the United States. She was an intelligent and beautiful woman, and her striking Bulgarian features caused her to stand out amongst the many blonde-haired and blue-eyed women in Pennsylvania. Miss Sharp's dark brown hair came to her shoulders in perfect ringlets. Her thick, dark eyebrows that matched her large brown eyes were distinct against her warm tawny-colored skin. She was something to look at and turned many heads. Short in stature, she was a petite woman, but she knew exactly how to handle a room.

A good majority of the single male factory workers sought to impress her, being the only 'eligible' bachelors soon to be left behind from the war. They all failed tragically. But better men than them had tried.

She was smart, capable, and beautiful. She could have anyone she wanted.

The thing was, she didn't want anyone.

Every single man, regardless of status, was turned down. Money didn't matter, looks didn't matter. Her focus was on work and the war. She cared about little else.

Her personal assistant, Kitty Nichols, entered the working area with wide yet glaring eyes. The men of the factory made a joke of her, teasing that she was simply a knockoff version of Miss Sharp, as she too had dark hair and dark eyes with tawny-colored skin. But her chin was sharper, and she was much plainer, someone you would easily lose sight of in a crowd full of people, and unfortunately, she had the face of a rat.

Miss Nichols approached the blond paraplegic man at the assembly line. His posture straightened as he worked diligently in his wheelchair. He chewed on his bottom lip as he concentrated, and was in the middle of running his weathered palm over his short, sand-colored hair when Miss Nichols addressed him.

"Howard Davey?" she asked. Her shrill voice could be heard clearly over the noise in the factory, but everyone was too consumed in their own business to have heard her.

"Yes, ma'am?" He didn't look up from his packaging supplies. Instead, he scratched at his scruffy face, and continued on, hardly acknowledging her presence.

"Just ignore her," said Lance from across the factory.

"Yeah, usually she goes away if you just pay no attention to her!" John added.

Howard tried not to chuckle as he stifled the amusement from surfacing to his face. He scratched at his chin again in an attempt to cover up the smirk threatening to escape.

Miss Nichols huffed at the comments made, but didn't look up at the two snickering teenage boys.

"Miss Sharp would like to see you in her office," she said quickly.

The factory immediately went dead silent. All eyes were now on the two of them as Howard lowered the items in his hands. He slowly looked up at her with his brilliant blue eyes as he sat back in his wheelchair. Murmurs streamed throughout the workspace of people questioning what on earth Miss Sharp could possibly want with him. He could hear Lance and John both whispering their comments about it.

Howard gripped the rims of his wheelchair and was careful to not bump into Miss Sharp's assistant as he followed behind her. He kept his focus straight ahead rather than looking at his colleagues as he passed them. They watched from their stations, whispering to one another as Miss Nichols and Mr. Davey passed each of them. His heart pounded aggressively in his chest.

CORPSE WALKER: THE NIGHT PARADE | 31

"Alright, back to work," Miss Sharp said as she clapped her hands together. She had come out of her office after noticing the silence. Immediately, the factory workers followed her instructions and the production noise began to pick up once more. After all, no one wanted to disappoint her.

"Productivity tends to increase while I'm here," Miss Sharp said, looking over at Kitty. "Daddy always makes comments about how he wants me to stay here rather than play around with my chemistry set in Manhattan." Miss Sharp rolled her eyes.

Howard stopped his wheelchair in front of her just as she turned to face him. He looked up at her, though it wasn't very far up from where he sat. She stood only a little higher than five feet and he could see the reflection of his bright eyes in her dark brown ones.

"Howard Davey?" Miss Sharp asked with skepticism in her voice as she looked down at the clipboard in her hands before glancing at him.

He furrowed his brows into a slight frown.

"Yes, ma'am?" he asked, apprehensive.

Miss Sharp crossed her arms over her chest as she tucked the clipboard beneath her arm and arched a brow.

"Not Corporal Hayden Dáithí?"

His eyes widened as his heart sank.

"I—I—um…" he stammered, unable to find the words to explain himself.

Miss Sharp held up her hand to silence him. Part of him was glad she did, but the other part was now nervous about their meeting.

"Please, come in."

She spun around and walked right back into her office. Heels clicked against the wooden floorboards while the skirt of her dress swished behind her. He looked up at her assistant, but Miss Nichols didn't look at him; instead, she turned away to return to her small desk just outside of Miss Sharp's door. Hayden inhaled deeply and wheeled himself inside.

Miss Sharp closed the door behind him.

A middle-aged man sat in a chair positioned in front of Miss Sharp's desk. Bulky and with a graying crew cut, he was a man Hayden recognized immediately—even without the man turning to face him.

His heart sank further, dropping into his gut.

"When Colonel Richards showed up at my office, indicating that you were someone else, I didn't believe it." Miss Sharp leaned back against her desk. She twisted her body to grab a photo from behind her and held it up for him to see. "But he brought me this." In her hands was a photograph of Hayden in his Service Alphas as a Marine. "I heard a lot of crazy things in my life in my line of work—seen even stranger things—but this? *This?*" She turned the photo around to stare at it. Even he could tell she still couldn't believe what she was seeing. It was well-written all over her face.

Colonel Richards didn't even glance in his direction. "Corporal."

"Sir," he sighed, not looking at him either.

Colonel Richards turned his head. He observed the wheelchair for a second before turning to face the desk again.

"I pulled your corpse from the water three weeks after the USS *Oklahoma* went under," Colonel Richards said, gripping the wooden armrests of his chair as he forced himself out of it. His small green eyes wandered the room as he continued to recall the memory. "Your uniform was mostly burned off. Your body was bloated. Skin, blue and black. You were dead, Corporal Hayden Zachariah Dáithí. Yet here you are, right before my very eyes. Alive and well." He inhaled sharply, looking around with obvious disappointment. "Working *here*."

Miss Sharp's large brown eyes narrowed, giving the Colonel a subtle glare. Under normal circumstances, she wouldn't tolerate anyone disrespecting the work at her father's factory, or even the workers themselves. However, this time she bit her tongue. These were not normal circumstances.

Hayden chewed on the inside of his cheek. The act was up.

"I just wanted to be at peace."

"Ambon in the Dutch East Indies is part of the Japanese offensive now. The USS *Shark* was sunk in the Pacific by the Japanese destroyer *Yamakaze*." Colonel Richards began firing off events at Hayden. "Singapore is now occupied by the Empire of Japan—wait, my mistake. I mean *Shonan*. There were two air raids on Darwin. What else—oh, right—the president signed Executive Order 9066. And this is only a fraction of what's happened this month alone, Dáithí. Why do you get to be at peace when your country isn't? You sit in a factory and pack shipments for war. We are not at peace."

"No disrespect, sir, but I did my time. And if you haven't noticed, I paid for it with my mobility." Hayden's expression hardened.

"You should have paid for it with your life," snapped the Colonel.

Hayden clenched his jaw and looked down.

"What about getting back out there?" Colonel Richards suggested, his tone taking a dramatic turn. "You could do more. We'll promote you to sergeant—"

"I'm in a wheelchair, sir."

"Yeah, I see that—quit bellyaching, Corporal. I got eyes that work, you know. But you're completely missing the point. We could use you. Am I speaking English?" He looked at Miss Sharp with expectation and she nodded. The Colonel swiftly turned back to Hayden. "You were dead, Dáithí. *Dead*. I shipped your corpse back here to Pennsylvania. You should be six feet in the ground. At peace," he mocked Hayden toward the end of his tirade. "But now you're a walking corpse."

Hayden furrowed his brows and shook his head slightly, not wanting to be reminded of it. Not wanting to be reminded of when he woke up in a morgue. He ran his hand over his head and stopped to massage his neck.

"How—how did you find me, anyway?"

Colonel Richards grabbed the newspaper from Miss Sharp's desk and dropped it in Hayden's lap. On the front page featured a news article about the Sharp Co. Factory in York, Pennsylvania. He stared at the picture included, depicting him and several of his colleagues. He remembered that picture being taken. He'd only been working there a week. Hayden sighed and handed it back to the Colonel, further averting his gaze.

"I admit," the Colonel began, acknowledging the wheelchair. "I didn't know you were wheelchair bound, but I'm sure Dr. Susanoo can figure that out."

Hayden tilted his head, eyebrows furrowing again. His interest was piqued.

"Wait, what?"

An older Japanese man with a large scar across his cheek just beneath his right eye entered Miss Sharp's office. He had long salt and peppered black hair that was pulled back into a messy bun high on his head. Hayden tensed in his wheelchair. The Japanese were the reason the United States entered the war. The Japanese were the reason he was sitting in a wheelchair. The Japanese were the reason he died.

"This is Dr. Susanoo," Colonel Richards said, introducing the older Japanese man. "After I recognized you in the newspaper and explained the situation, he requested that we come see you immediately."

"Hello, Sergeant Dáithí," Dr. Susanoo said. He had a strong Japanese accent. But Hayden was caught off guard by being addressed with the rank of sergeant. That did sound good with his name. "It's a pleasure to finally meet you. I am part of Research, Analysis, Verification, and Endorsement of the Nonsensical, or R.A.V.E.N. for short if you will, and we would like to evaluate you."

He cocked his head. "Why?"

"Well, because you were dead," he said simply. Too simply for Hayden's liking. Dr. Susanoo crossed his arms and leaned against the wall beside the door of the office. He looked up at nothing and smiled fondly as he appeared to recount a memory. "The Pearl Harbor Naval Shipyard housed part of an ancient artifact that was moved very carefully—by me—aboard the USS *Oklahoma* to be guarded." Dr. Susanoo pointed at Hayden. "By you, and several other Marines. Unbeknownst to you all, of course. For your safety. I believe its properties imprinted themselves onto you, which is why you're standing here today." He cleared his throat, glancing at the wheelchair. "Excuse me—that was a poor choice of words—why you're here today."

"Is there a problem, Sergeant?" Colonel Richards asked, tilting his head, acknowledging Hayden's discomfort. Hayden tensed slightly at the usage of 'sergeant' again. They were indulging him on purpose.

But he was much too lost in his thoughts to answer and had trouble listening to both Dr. Susanoo and the Colonel as he himself remembered the events of that morning. As he remembered the bombs hitting the USS *Oklahoma*. There was no fondness in his expression. He remembered the pain. The piercing screams ringing in his ears. The flashes of light and the saltwater filling his lungs. With every breath he took, there was only water burning in his throat. Hayden unclenched his jaw and inhaled deeply, almost as if to gasp for air, like he had forgotten how to breathe. He rubbed his face and then the back of his neck.

"No, sir." While Hayden spoke to answer the Colonel, he didn't shift his gaze from Dr. Susanoo.

"Well, the other option would be a dishonorable discharge," Colonel Richards said. "Since you didn't die at Pearl Harbor, this would classify as desertion. Especially with your impersonation as Howard Davey."

"But I sustained injuries that—"

"Have not been reported and documented."

Hayden scowled and sank back in his wheelchair.

"You're trying to ruin my reputation."

"I'm trying to win a war," said the Colonel.

"I know what you're thinking," Dr. Susanoo interjected. "I'm well aware of what the Japanese have done to you and your friends and colleagues. To your country. I understand your hesitation. But I really just want to help." He nodded, a few strands of his graying hair fell in front of his face. "I believe I can get you walking again—and perhaps more than that."

Hayden only blinked. He stared at nothing.

"Actually, I was just thinking this is all gobbledygook," he mumbled as he attempted to go over the R.A.V.E.N. acronym in his head, and Miss Sharp chuckled. The entire thing sounded absurd. However, the Colonel and Dr. Susanoo didn't seem amused with him. Hayden cleared his throat to break up the growing silent tension in the office. "But I did die, and there's no real explanation for that." He sighed as his eyes wandered around the room to each person one by one, before landing back upon the doctor. "I need to know that I can trust you."

The corner of Dr. Susanoo's mouth twitched into a subtle smile, and he nodded.

"Yes." He spoke very calmly, in almost a soothing voice. There was something about the small gesture that Hayden found reassuring even before Dr. Susanoo gave a verbal answer.

Hayden too nodded in agreement.

"It would be nice to walk again... and to be a sergeant," he added quickly, to make sure it was still an offer on the table. He looked over at the Colonel, who arched an eyebrow at him in response.

"Great. It is settled then." Dr. Susanoo clasped his hands together and smiled a full, genuine smile as he straightened himself from leaning against the wall. "Let's get you out of that chair, Sergeant Dáithí."

Hayden smiled to himself. It really did have a nice ring to it. However, his smile soon faded as he didn't quite understand how all of it would work.

He couldn't use his legs.

He couldn't even feel them anymore.

"But how?" Hayden chuckled nervously, unsure of the success and unsure of the answers he would receive. "I'm paralyzed from the waist down. I've been paralyzed since I woke up."

Dr. Susanoo smiled as he grabbed the armrests of Hayden's chair. "Don't let the restrictions of your humanity define you," he said sternly.

"What does that mean?"

Unfortunately for Hayden, Dr. Susanoo didn't answer. Instead, he continued to smile and let go of the front of Hayden's wheelchair.

"I hate how ominous you're being," Hayden mumbled. While he didn't notice, this comment amused Dr. Susanoo.

Hayden's curiosity got the better of him though, despite the lack of verbal response. He shifted his focus between Dr. Susanoo and Colonel Richards. "Alright," he said, officially agreeing out loud. "What exactly do you need me to do?"

Rather than answer Hayden's question, Colonel Richards addressed Miss Sharp instead. "Will you be joining us?" he asked.

Miss Sharp wrinkled her nose with slight disappointment as she looked down through the schedule in her thick black planner. She began shaking her head solemnly. "Unfortunately, I'm needed in Manhattan—tomorrow, actually—for a couple of weeks. There are some things I need to go over with the committee… But if you can hold it off for a bit, I'll be sure to meet you there as soon as I can." Miss Sharp then smiled—a rather wicked smile at that. "You can count on it. I definitely don't want to miss

Project Reaper." She looked over at Hayden and gave him a playful yet dramatic wink to match her grin.

He tensed a little, but tried not to make it obvious.

Project Reaper. This thing had a name? Hayden chewed on his bottom lip as the rest of them continued to talk as though he weren't in the room at all. Ever since becoming wheelchair bound, he had gotten used to being ignored. He rubbed at his neck again.

"We can hold it off," Dr. Susanoo said to the Colonel, before looking at Miss Sharp. "I'd like Sergeant Dáithí to come with us to Harrisburg first to get his information, sign some documents, and run a few tests. Then we can bring him back to Hawai'i for the actual introduction with the artifact…"

Hayden rubbed at his temples before running his palm flat against his short hair as Dr. Susanoo's voice faded away from him. He scratched at the small patch of scruff on his chin. What exactly was he getting himself into? He crinkled his nose, silently cursing himself that he could be bribed so easily when he truly hadn't a clue what was going to happen.

"Are you alright, Sergeant Dáithí?" Dr. Susanoo asked.

Hayden looked up at him and nodded, lowering his hands to his lap, where he fumbled with his thumb. "Yeah, I'm good," he said, more so in an attempt to convince himself that he was. He rubbed at his chin again. "Am I going to have to shave?"

Dr. Susanoo only smiled.

"I'm not sure if it matters," said the Colonel dismissively. "I'd hardly call that facial hair."

Miss Sharp held her planner in front of her face to hide her laugh.

"*Oh*," said Hayden, slightly offended by the remark. His pitch was a little higher than usual. "*Okay.*"

CHAPTER THREE

Hagåtña, Guam, March 1, 1942
0903 — local time

Commander Isamu Mori sat in the governor's palace. Though everyone in the Yamata no Orochi division knew what he truly looked like and what he was capable of, he continued to wear his cap so as to not appear out of place should a citizen accidentally find themselves wandering onto the property. His elongated head seemed to cause discomfort to others upon seeing it bare for the first time, as it was at least two times longer than a normal human skull. Nurarihyon wasn't fond of staring, and he tended to react impulsively to it. He could slip unnoticed into homes, where he would be treated like the head of household, but the governor's palace was not a home, and the people there would notice his abnormalities.

Major General Tomitarō Horii was the new official governor of Guam, but due to his own dislike of Commander Mori and lack of understanding when it came to the work of Yamata no Orochi, Horii remained on the field rather than cooped up in the same building. This left the Commander to do as he pleased without Imperial Japanese supervision. Mori didn't do well under the watchful eye of others, and while the two were able to respect one another publicly, he was pleased with this arrangement.

He leaned over in his seat to fondly stroke Tadeo's head. The Akita Inu was a large dog breed originating from the mountainous regions of northern Japan. They were known for their power, independence, and dominance. While aloof with strangers, they were affectionate with, loyal to, and protective of their owners, which made them great Inugami — a demon that could be created through a greatly feared and cruel ritual. Tadeo was a nine-year-old, ninety-pound, silver brindle who had been with Mori since he was a small puppy.

For nine years, Tadeo would stay at Mori's side in a protective yet calm stance. Well-trained, he was watchful of newcomers and very observant of them but wouldn't move a muscle until Mori commanded it.

Unless of course, Mori was in danger and unable to provide a proper command, but Mori was more than capable of defending himself.

Affectionately, he stroked the side of Tadeo's face with his gloved hand, and his dog nuzzled him back.

An Imperial Japanese soldier approached, and though Tadeo was aware of him, his attention remained on the tenderness of Mori's touch.

"Yes?" Commander Mori asked, raising an eyebrow, though he didn't bother to look up. His attention remained on the dog at his side. His best friend for nearly a decade.

"Dr. Sauer is asking for you," the Imperial soldier said, his head slightly tilted, not looking Mori in the eyes. They never did look him in the eyes.

Mori's chest lifted, his mouth ajar as he sighed.

"Let him know I will see him in a minute—and will you get me a shovel?"

The Imperial Japanese soldier nodded at the request. He bowed and then excused himself from the room.

"What is the point of hiring anyone if they constantly need my help?" Commander Mori said to Tadeo, making tsk noises with his tongue. "Can't people think for themselves?" The Akita angled his head toward the left, then the right, swinging like a pendulum the way dogs did when they listened, and perked his ears. Mori ruffled the fur between his ears and smiled. "Soon, my old friend," he reassured calmly. "Soon."

When Mori got up, he tucked his chin down as he looked at his dog and walked into another part of the palace. The governor's palace was where Captain McMillin surrendered. The Japanese Imperial army had all but taken over Guam by the fourth month of their invasion. Mori now sat where Captain McMillin once did and McMillin now sat with the rest of America's prisoners in a camp located in Japan. Prisoners were still being escorted off of the island. At least the ones who cooperated. Runners were killed on site, and those who fought back were taken to the jungles to be beheaded.

The Japanese were ruthless, and weren't going to be made fools of.

Dr. Sauer was in the laboratory, an area of the palace sectioned off for his work. It was a place Imperial Japanese forces weren't allowed to step foot in unless they wanted to lose it. Mori, escorted by Tadeo, wandered into the lab where a tall, blond Polish man stood with safety goggles attached firmly to his face. Dr. Hans Sauer was a unique man—a human with a hatred for humanity. Only three years ago, Dr. Sauer watched as Nazi Germany murdered his family in front of his very eyes. He saw firsthand how humanity did not bind together but rather turned on itself. Dr. Sauer watched as a man, who didn't look much different than he, murder his sister in cold blood.

Commander Mori found the poor young man in anguish not a year later. Despite the Imperial Japanese being allies with the people who murdered Dr. Sauer's family, he knew Commander Mori was operating to fight a different battle altogether. He knew of his origins and he listened to his intentions. Dr. Sauer was now dedicated to the cause of bringing forth the night parade of one hundred demons.

"Hans," Commander Mori said, alerting him of his presence. Commander Mori then looked down to see a tangle of disconnected wires. He frowned.

The tall Polish man turned around, pushing the goggles up onto his forehead so he could see both Mori and his dog. While normally he was a conventionally attractive man, deep red lines remained around his green eyes from the pressure of the goggles. He had a slight look of surprise, but he always looked somewhat surprised. He rarely got any sleep since arriving in Guam. His eyebrows were so blond, you could hardly tell he had eyebrows at all, and his eyes bulged out of his head when he worked for too many hours straight. The laboratory appeared to strip him of his youth.

"Commander Mori—yes—" Dr. Sauer walked around the counter to the first piece of the scythe in their possession that Commander Mori had fetched from the Chocolate House in December. It remained disconnected from his experimental machinery.

"Why isn't anything connected to it?" Mori asked, observing the wires on the table beside the handle that led to nothing, no longer inserted into it like he had left it.

He picked up a loose wire and looked at Dr. Sauer. "Is it broken?" He dropped it back onto the table.

Dr. Sauer sighed, pulling the goggles down from his head, he ruffled his blond hair.

"It's draining my life force." He took off his glove, revealing the decay of his arm. "It did this to me when I separated it. How are your agents supposed to bring the other two back here when it can't be touched by humans without killing them?"

"Perhaps I don't intend for all of my agents to return alive."

Dr. Sauer's expression faltered.

Commander Mori grinned, and it was followed by a laugh.

"You *Germans* are so serious." He patted Dr. Sauer's cheek harshly, and Dr. Sauer flinched both from the word and from the pat. "I'll be sure to send word of the discovery and bring our agents home safe then, hm?"

Dr. Sauer only nodded.

"Now, where are you in the development of the portal?" He looked at the ground. Mori was a short man, but his elongated skull tended to make up for it and gave him a bit of additional height. Tadeo walked alongside Commander Mori, which Dr. Sauer was more than aware of, as he was not fond of dogs or their vicious teeth. The portal that would open up to the Underworld was located on the ground. It was circular in appearance and set in the center of the lab. It had metal panels as a frame that were bolted to the ground. Commander Mori looked up at Dr. Sauer, raising his eyebrows as he awaited an answer.

Dr. Sauer looked down at the Akita momentarily, before his eyes returned to Commander Mori. He then leaned toward the massive iron panels, nodding awkwardly at an angle.

"It's coming along, but we won't be able to do anything without the other two pieces even after I'm finished. I can't even test it. I'll need them eventually—" he paused as he looked at his hand, "—and you, to operate it."

Commander Mori sighed and looked over at his dog.

More demands of him.

"Again, I know." He leaned over to run his fingers through his dog's fur. "Just do what you can, Sauer, with what we have."

"Yes, sir."

An Imperial Japanese officer came to hand Commander Mori a shovel as he headed toward the door of the lab. Mori walked outside of the palace with his dog following beside him in devotion.

"Stay, Tadeo," Commander Mori commanded. His hand lifted to signal for Tadeo to remain where he was and not come any closer. Tadeo stopped. "Sit."

Tadeo obliged.

Many Imperial Japanese officials stood watch around him in silence as Commander Mori began digging in the grass behind the governor's palace. Using his foot to puncture the earth with the shovel, he dug and dug until the hole was about five feet deep, but only less than two feet wide. He wiped the sweat from his brow with a pristine handkerchief as he finished and took a step back to admire his work. He handed the shovel to one of the Japanese officials and tucked the handkerchief back into his pocket. Commander Mori whistled for Tadeo, who came running for him immediately.

Mori knelt before him as he halted at his feet.

"My sweet Tadeo," Commander Mori said, cupping his dog's face. "Your moment has finally come," he whispered. He closed his hands, gripping Tadeo's fur as he kissed the top of his head. "I know you will make me proud."

Repositioning his hands, Commander Mori pressed his thumbs against Tadeo's chest with his palms against his ribcage. With care, he slowly pushed his Akita into the freshly dug hole, hind legs first. Tadeo looked up at him, whining softly as Commander Mori began to fill the hole with dirt cupped in his hands. Tadeo's front paws clawed at the ground, but Commander Mori pushed them back into the hole.

He lifted a finger and raised his eyebrows, tilting his head.

"Now Tadeo," he scolded, "you knew this would be your fate." Commander Mori's voice was stern as he stood up straight. He used the shovel to continue to add dirt into the hole until he buried Tadeo up to his neck. One of the soldiers brought the Commander a pot of water, exchanging it with the shovel. Carefully, Commander Mori poured the water around Tadeo's head, using it to help seal the disturbed earth and making it harder for Tadeo to potentially escape the hole on his own. Commander Mori took a step back as an officer took the pot from him. He and Tadeo kept their eyes on each other. Tadeo's eyes were large and pleading, but Commander Mori remained indifferent.

The following day, Commander Mori brought out a raw steak on a silver plate and placed it down before Tadeo's face. It was close enough for the Akita to both see and smell the food, but regardless of how much he tried, he couldn't reach for it. He whined and struggled in the earth, but his efforts were fruitless. Tadeo couldn't move any part of his body but his head, and that wasn't enough.

Every day after, an Imperial would replace the raw steak with a new one, placed just beyond Tadeo's reach, and every day, Tadeo's anguish and rage would grow with his hunger.

Commander Mori starved him for six days.

On the seventh day, the Commander approached his old friend, dragging a sharp Japanese sword at his side. He took off his cap, and one of the officers came to hold it for him. He wanted to perform this part of the ritual as his true self, Nurarihyon.

Raising his arms, he sliced Tadeo's head clean off. The velocity at which the blade cut into Tadeo was so quick and swift, it jostled the Akita's head toward the steak, where even in death, Tadeo began to chew till the light left his eyes. None of the officers present flinched at the sight. They all remained silent, and they all watched without remorse on their faces. Stern in expression, blankness in their eyes. It was as though his followers lacked souls themselves.

"I would have preferred to do that with the scythe," Nurarihyon noted, wiping the blade clean of Tadeo's blood. He didn't shed a tear for his beloved and devoted friend. Instead, he finished cleaning the blade while another officer picked up the head and placed it in a burlap sack, which would temporarily be buried at a crossroads so that many feet would walk over it.

He picked the base of the Spanish San Antonio Bridge that crossed the Hagatna River across the street of the Dulce Nombre de María Cathedral Basilica. It was near the governor's palace and would have enough foot traffic.

The officer handed the burlap sack to Nurarihyon, and another officer followed him with a shovel in hand. Once the hole had been dug, then filled with Tadeo's head and the rest of the dirt, he sealed it the same way as he had when he buried Tadeo's body—with a pot of water poured over it.

"This is to increase and intensify Tadeo's grudge against humanity as everyone walks over him," he said aloud to the officials standing beside him. Rarely did they engage with him verbally. They were afraid of him, but it was important they didn't appear to be.

Hagåtña, Guam, March 15, 1942
0834 — local time

Commander Mori sent a Japanese official to dig up the dog's head and retrieve it for him. At first, the officer showed fear, which Commander Mori took as disrespect.

"Are you disobeying my order?" he asked.

The soldier refused to look at him. Instead, he shook his head quickly and bowed before hurrying on his way.

Commander Mori pulled out a cigarette and put it in his mouth, but didn't light it yet. Instead, he walked into another part of the plaza. Slipping off his shoes, he began reorganizing and putting the final touches on Tadeo's shrine, where his skull would sit to be worshiped.

The Japanese soldier later found Commander Mori in the kitchen. He outstretched his hand to the Commander, again bowing his head and averting his eyes. Commander Mori looked down at the tattered burlap sack he carried and gently took it in his gloved hand.

He thanked the officer in Japanese and dismissed him. Commander Mori put the bag down on the counter. He took off his cap and placed it down beside it.

Nurarihyon fished a lighter out of his pocket and finally lit the cigarette that was hanging loosely from his mouth all morning. He turned the oven on. Putting the bag on a ceramic plate, Nurarihyon stuck the entire thing in the oven and left it in there as he smoked his cigarette until all the rotten remains burned off of Tadeo's skull. Nurarihyon checked it frequently and cleaned the skull himself once it finished. Tadeo's skull would then be placed in a bowl and worshiped like a god at his shrine. Not only Nurarihyon, but all of Yamata no Orochi would pay their respects.

The ritual for creating an Inugami was both time-consuming and cruel, but worth it to the Commander. The dog's starvation-induced rage turned into a powerful curse that was to be used at Nurarihyon's will to fulfill any of his desires.

Carefully, he brought the skull to the shrine and placed it in the bowl. An officer brought in a large jar, uncapped it, and placed it beside the shrine before excusing himself hurriedly. Nurarihyon lit the incense, closed his eyes, and prayed, reciting his respect for Tadeo, and pledging his own loyalty. Tadeo's spirit slowly manifested, smoking through the eye sockets of his skull and jaw. Nurarihyon opened his eyes, and with his hand, carefully redirected it into the jar. Once full, he capped it. He could see Tadeo's hazy and translucent face, appearing and disappearing.

"Hello, old friend," he said softly, fondly caressing the side of the jar with his gloved hand. Tadeo, his Inugami. Nurarihyon smiled.

Hagåtña, Guam, March 19, 1942
0912 — local time

"I raised him from a puppy, you know. Tadeo." Commander Mori was holding the jar in his hands when he visited Dr. Sauer again. Dr. Sauer looked up at him for a moment, but his green eyes settled on the jar. It looked empty. "Did you know, Inugami can turn against their master and bite them to death?" He fondly hugged the container. "If the dog is loyal to you in life, there's a better chance he will be loyal even in death. I didn't want to kill my best friend, as I'm sure most don't—but now he will be useful in ways he wasn't before."

Dr. Sauer was hesitant.

"What will you do with him?" he asked at last.

"If our agents fail, I will let Tadeo take care of it." Commander Mori looked down at the jar with Tadeo's name engraved onto the side. The Commander gently ran his fingers over the Japanese markings. "They can possess the dead and those who are emotionally unstable." Commander Mori then looked up at Dr. Sauer for a moment, tapping the jar gently with his fingertips. "Are you emotionally unstable, Sauer?"

Dr. Sauer furrowed his brows, unsure of how to answer such a question. He fumbled with the goggles on top of his head. He took them off and put them down on the table with hesitation. "I don't think so—" he answered slowly and hesitantly, gulping hard. "Are you going to let it possess m—me?"

Commander Mori smiled. "Not yet. Maybe not at all. I guess we'll see, won't we?" He finally looked up at him again. "Be good, Dr. Sauer."

Dr. Sauer let out the breath he was holding as the Commander left with the Inugami creation. He could breathe a little easier for now. He turned around, clenching his jaw as he looked at the metalwork of the portal and the single piece of the scythe in their possession. He wondered for how long Commander Mori would be patient. The energy of the scythe was strong, but Dr. Sauer began to doubt that anything man-made could harness it for very long.

Commander Mori first stopped at Tadeo's shrine. He slipped off his shoes and left them near the doorway as he shifted the jar into one arm. Upon approaching Tadeo's cleaned and polished skull, he lit incense and allowed it to burn for a few seconds. He extinguished the flame with a wave of his hand and put it into the burner as he made a short prayer. He then bowed before stepping away.

Putting his shoes back onto his feet, Commander Mori returned to his own sleeping quarters, still holding onto the jar as though it were his most prized possession. In a way, it was. He hadn't parted with it since the manifestation of Tadeo's spirit. There weren't many things that he cared about in the world, at least not ones that were actually alive. Commander Mori didn't find the living to be very useful. They were loud and disobedient, and they thought they were limitless. While Tadeo was one of the few that mattered, he had still been raised with purpose. Animals were also much different than humans. Humans wavered; their loyalties fluctuated. Humans could not be trusted, not fully. Everyone had a hidden agenda. But not dogs. Dogs were loyal to a fault. Feed them, nurture them, and they'll protect you forever. Commander Mori sat down on his bed, still holding onto the jar. He leaned forward and placed it on the ground, keeping the Inugami safe beneath his bed.

CHAPTER FOUR

Harrisburg, Pennsylvania, March 16, 1942
0732 — local time

There were a total of six R.A.V.E.N. offices in the United States, the one in Pennsylvania being north of York County near Harrisburg. Hayden Dáithí sat in the passenger seat of a black 1941 Dodge Custom Town Sedan with Colonel Richards smoking in the driver's seat and Dr. Susanoo in the back. The drive would take less than an hour and the three sat in an uncomfortable silence. Hayden attempted to turn on the radio, but all he managed to hear was a brief news report of Imperial Japan completely seizing Guam before Colonel Richards turned it right back off.

"I can't drive with the radio on," he said. Colonel Richards took one last drag of his cigarette and flicked it out of the window. "Gives me anxiety."

Hayden didn't touch it again. He inhaled and exhaled deeply, silently happy that smoke no longer clouded the car. He rubbed the palm of his hand flat against his crew cut as he stared out the window. Hayden didn't know what to do with himself and began tapping his index finger against the car door. He wasn't fond of the silence and needed more than just the whistling from the wind. However, this would be a far from peaceful car ride with Dr. Susanoo sitting behind him.

"Do you remember what day you came back from the dead?" Dr. Susanoo asked. He had dug his clipboard out from his bag, deciding to make proper use of the time while in the car. "Specifically, the day? How many days have you been alive?"

Hayden scratched at the scruff growing on his chin in uneven patches as he went over the question in his head. But to Dr. Susanoo's dismay, he shook his head.

"Wasn't exactly keeping track."

"Do you remember anything from while you were dead?"

Crinkling his nose, Hayden shook his head again. He inhaled sharply and rubbed his jawline and throat uncomfortably. He pulled at his collar, as if it were choking him.

"Honestly, I just remember waking up in a morgue." He closed his eyes, trying not to think about it. "I'm pretty sure the funeral director was close to spewing when he saw me."

While Dr. Susanoo chuckled, the Colonel glanced over at Hayden disapprovingly, and all traces of amusement immediately disappeared from Hayden's face once he noticed.

He looked in the side mirror at Dr. Susanoo scribbling away.

"How did you do it?" Colonel Richards asked him.

"Do what?"

"York is a small town. You're telling me no one noticed the zombie?" he further inquired, acknowledging Hayden's return to life.

"This is the first I've been back since joining the Marines when I was eighteen," Hayden answered with a shrug. "My bedroom's in the basement of my family's house now. They were a little freaked out, but happy to have me home. And I didn't go nowhere except the factory after I got a job there. Everyone I knew personally thought I was dead. They weren't going to think some disabled man in a wheelchair was me."

"It's true, you don't have a very distinguishable face in comparison to all the other white people here either," Dr. Susanoo added harmlessly while he continued to write. "I couldn't pick you from a crowd."

Hayden frowned at his insult, though Dr. Susanoo didn't see.

"What about the morgue?"

"You think they'd risk going belly up? Who'd want to trust them if there's a chance they might accidentally bury their loved one alive?"

The Colonel nodded.

"Do you really think I'll walk again?" he asked, looking at Dr. Susanoo in the side mirror. As soon as the words left his lips, he regretted it.

Dr. Susanoo stopped and looked up. His brows furrowed slightly, and he leaned back against the car seat. Suddenly, Hayden was unsure whether or not he wanted to know the answer. He pushed the glasses up the bridge of his nose with the back of his pen and stared at the back of Hayden's head.

Finally, Dr. Susanoo nodded after far too much anticipation. He looked back down at his journal and continued writing. "I have faith you will. I'd like to do a few tests first, and once you're cleared, we'll head back to O'ahu and start the trials."

"If the artifact is in danger in Hawai'i, why leave it there? Why not move it somewhere safer to protect it?"

Dr. Susanoo raked back a few strands of his long hair and tucked them behind his ear.

"It is not meant to be moved, Sergeant Dáithí. It was placed there by something greater than man. On Guam, Midway Atoll, and Hawai'i. To leave it there is to keep the natural balance to life."

"And all three were bombed."

Dr. Susanoo nodded sympathetically.

"All three were bombed. Midway, they were unsuccessful, but I believe they will try again, and we'll need you to assist us in protecting it."

Hayden frowned and looked down at his hands, confidence depleting. His thumbnail dug into the corner of his other fingers; his nails were always cut far too short, yet somehow he always thought they could be shorter. If there was space beneath his nails, they were too long.

He was to assist them in protecting the remaining pieces of the artifact, but how?

The R.A.V.E.N. headquarters appeared like any ordinary government building, but with a raven emblem beside the front entrance. It was only once Hayden was out of the car that he felt he could breathe again. Though the Colonel had stopped smoking in the car for most of the ride, the air felt too thin. Hayden's gloved hands fiddled with the wheels of his chair as he observed his surroundings. Even in March, snow still coated the grounds and frosted the surrounding skeletal trees. People were mostly absent from the outside, but it was also below freezing.

Inside, the building was much warmer. Hayden could feel himself defrosting almost immediately. Upon entry, those in the lobby greeted Colonel Richards and

Dr. Susanoo with friendly smiles and often glanced at Hayden in curiosity, but no one was curious enough to stop and speak to him. Part of him was grateful for that. He wouldn't know what to say to any of them.

Behind the restricted doors, two people came to greet them as Dr. Susanoo was pulled away by another official. Colonel Richards stood between them and Hayden.

"This is Sergeant Hayden Dáithí," the Colonel began. "Hayden, this is Agent Elaina Dacua of R.A.V.E.N." The young Filipina woman was petite in stature. Her thick, dark brown hair was pulled back in a high and tight ponytail. The taupe glow of her cheekbones was highlighted beneath the bright fluorescent lighting. To her left stood a man only an inch or two taller than her. Thick glasses sat on the bridge of his nose, and though he wore a suit and carried a briefcase, his light brown hair appeared untamable. It was much like Hayden's on the rare occasion he chose to grow it out. "And this is Dr. Ingram-Zander Stolly," the Colonel said.

Hayden shook both of their hands respectively.

"They're here to assist you. I'm going to check with Dr. Susanoo and see when he'll be ready to get started."

Hayden nodded as Colonel Richards excused himself. He then turned his attention back to Dr. Stolly with curiosity.

"Doctor? You seem kind of young to be a doctor."

Dr. Stolly laughed. "I heard we're the same age, actually. Turning twenty-four this year. Just call me Zander—"

"He's a genius," Agent Dacua interrupted, rather unenthused. She didn't seem impressed by his title and Dr. Stolly looked almost pained at her words as he readjusted the glasses on his nose. Hayden scratched his ear uncomfortably while observing the exchange.

"Not a genius," said Dr. Stolly awkwardly, as he fumbled with the briefcase in his hand. "But I do have an eidetic memory."

Hayden furrowed his brows. "A what?"

"Photographic memory," Agent Dacua said. "Some of us are just born lucky."

Hayden ignored her lucky comment. "Are you not part of R.A.V.E.N. too?"

"Definitely not," Dr. Stolly grinned, though a fair question. "The Republic of Letters, actually. We're known as Intellectuals. We seek to understand beings and happenings that science can't quite explain. While R.A.V.E.N. does the same, more or less, we believe it should remain concealed and even protected rather than be publicly weaponized by the government."

Agent Dacua pressed her lips together and swept her gaze to the side while he spoke. Hayden's focus shifted between the two of them.

"And R.A.V.E.N. thinks it should be weaponized?" Hayden asked, noticing her reaction to his comment.

"Well, of course," Agent Dacua said. "What benefits the country, benefits the world," she said simply.

"Or destroys it," Dr. Stolly scoffed.

Their exchange was interrupted when another agent came to fetch them. He was a little older than the three of them and seemed exasperated with running errands. "Sergeant Kamuela says Dr. Susanoo is ready for you all."

Hayden's ears perked up. "Wait—Kamuela is here?"

The agent paused to stare at Hayden for a moment, then continued down the hallway, not bothering to answer his question.

"Yeah," Agent Dacua said. She tilted her head. "You know him?"

Hayden nodded. "He was a good friend. We were in basic together. We both got stationed in Hawai'i and he was in Kailua when I went to—"

Pearl Harbor.

Hayden had trouble saying it.

Agent Dacua didn't press.

Instead, she smiled and nodded ahead. "Come on, we'll go see him first and then Dr. Susanoo." She then turned to Dr. Stolly. "Please let Dr. Susanoo know of our small detour and that we'll be right up."

He nodded. "Sure thing."

Hayden followed Agent Dacua down the hallway to the elevator. While Hayden mostly kept his focus ahead to watch where he was going, he also looked up at the pictures hanging on the walls. Several historical figures were recognized upon them, but there was no mention of the organization from what he could remember. He'd never heard of it. Perhaps even R.A.V.E.N. wasn't as public as Agent Dacua or Dr. Stolly seemed to claim. Surely he would have remembered if he'd heard of it.

"Is R.A.V.E.N. a newer thing or—"

Agent Dacua looked over at the historical figures on the wall. She pursed her lips together, unsure of exactly how to answer his question.

"Yes and no," she said finally. "They started its formation during World War I, I believe. Though don't take my word for it."

"You believe?"

"I'm at the bottom," she said with a small chuckle. "I'm still kind of new here." She started tapping her foot. "The elevator is taking a little long, don't you think?"

Hayden shrugged, still looking at the pictures. Many of them were decorated war heroes, and many were from Pennsylvania.

Agent Dacua breathed a sigh of relief when the elevator doors finally opened.

Once inside, she pressed the button for the second floor. The ride seemed rather long for only going up one floor.

She led Hayden to Colonel Richards's designated office where she knocked, then opened the door and poked her head in.

"Someone—wanted to see you."

She pushed the door open further and stepped out of the way. Sergeant Charles Kamuela was a Marine with broad shoulders and a smile that could charm almost anyone from miles away. Seeing him again reminded Hayden of when they made a competition out of flirting with women. While Hayden's ocean blue eyes often worked in his favor, Sergeant Kamuela's Hawaiian descent made him easily more popular with the locals back in Hawai'i.

He could connect with them in a way Hayden couldn't. They shared culture and appreciation for their land that Hayden respected, but couldn't relate to.

Upon seeing Hayden Dáithí, Sergeant Kamuela's expression hardened, and his eyes began to glisten. He fell into the chair behind him and rubbed the bottom of his chin while he struggled to find the right words to say.

"I mean, I *knew* you were here for the project, but— seeing you—it's different—I thought you were dead."

Hayden tilted his head slightly as his wheelchair came to a stop in front of his old friend.

"Well," Hayden shrugged. "I mean, technically I was."

Sergeant Kamuela's smile took up half his face, and they both shared a laugh as he got back to his feet and walked around the desk.

"Son of a bitch..." While shaking his head, his smile remained, reaching from ear to ear. "You would be the one to not *stay* dead." He patted his hand on Hayden's shoulder before leaning down to give him a hug. "It's good to have you back."

Hayden hesitated. "It's good to be back, I think." He tilted his head, crinkling his nose slightly. "But congratulations on making Sergeant."

Sergeant Kamuela grinned. "I heard I wasn't the only one."

Hayden shrugged. "Well, I mean only if the trials work."

The two men were a little caught up, nearly forgetting that Agent Dacua was still standing there.

"My apologies, Agent Dacua." Sergeant Kamuela said. His acknowledgment made Hayden look over at her too. She smiled awkwardly at the attention. "Do you mind if I take him up to Dr. Susanoo?" he asked her.

She shook her head and shrugged. "Be my guest." Agent Dacua looked down at Hayden. "Good luck," she said softly, patting his shoulder. "It was nice to meet you. Hopefully I'll see you later."

After she escorted herself out, Sergeant Kamuela leaned against the Colonel's desk. He crossed his arms and looked over at Hayden.

"Are you ready for this?" His tone had changed.

"Honestly? I'm a little nervous—but Dr. Susanoo thinks he could get me walking again." Hayden looked down at his chair.

"And maybe even more than that."

Hayden frowned. "What do you mean?"

Sergeant Kamuela's eyebrows scrunched together in both confusion and concern. "What exactly were you told about Project Reaper?" he asked.

Hayden shrugged. "Not much—but the name isn't exactly growing on me if I'm being honest."

"Well, you came back from the dead, Dáithí." Sergeant Kamuela shrugged too. "I mean, who knows what else you might be able to do. But these people? R.A.V.E.N. and the Republic of Letters? If anyone's going to figure this kind of shit out, it's these people." Sergeant Kamuela patted Hayden's shoulder as he straightened his posture. "Come on, let's get you to Dr. Susanoo."

While seeing his old friend made Hayden feel better, Sergeant Kamuela's words only increased his anxiety. He knew the Colonel and Dr. Susanoo wanted him back in service, but doing what, he wasn't sure. He was even less confident now than he had been during the car ride to Harrisburg in the first place.

Sergeant Kamuela brought him to Dr. Susanoo's office on the third floor and a nurse prepared Hayden for the physical exam. She took his measurements, his pulse, and asked him for any changes in medical history.

"Aside from the obvious resurrection and paralysis of my lower legs, no."

She gave him a sarcastic, lip-tight smile. "Sergeant, I'm just trying to do my job."

"I know. Sorry."

"Height?"

"Sixty-nine inches."

"Weight?"

"I don't know, maybe about one-eighty."

Dr. Susanoo came in while the nurse was finishing up the end of the form. He had a tray of seven empty vials and began setting up his workspace to draw Hayden's blood.

"I haven't had the chance to check his eyesight," the nurse said as she handed Dr. Susanoo the file. He waved his hand and dismissed it.

"It won't matter. Thank you."

She nodded and excused herself from the examination room. Dr. Susanoo took a seat beside Hayden and pulled the mobile cart between them.

"Those all for me?" he asked, looking at the empty vials.

"Yup. Blood doesn't make you queasy, does it?"

"No, sir."

"Good. Then let's get started." Dr. Susanoo took Hayden's arm and began examining his veins as he had him make a fist. "Normally the nurses would do this, but given the unique circumstances, we agreed it would be best if I handled it," he explained, and Hayden nodded. Dr. Susanoo wrapped the band around his arm and allowed him to relax his hand.

"Can I ask you a question?" Hayden asked as he watched Dr. Susanoo prepare the needle.

"You just did," he replied without looking up.

"Well then, can I ask you two more?"

Dr. Susanoo chuckled. "What is it you're interested in knowing, Sergeant Dáithí? I'll do my best to supply you with satisfying answers."

"What am I needed for—exactly? What is Project Reaper?"

"As I mentioned back at the Sharp Co. Factory," he began as he inserted the needle into Hayden's arm, and to his surprise, Hayden didn't even flinch. "I believed the energy from the artifact imprinted itself onto you, which is why you came back to life. Theoretically."

Hayden nodded as he stared at the needle. "Has this happened before?"

"Not exactly. Not from the artifact, anyway." Dr. Susanoo inhaled, then sighed. He filled one of the vials, then another. "If I may ask, where were you born?"

"Pittsburgh."

"What brought you to York?"

"Peace."

Dr. Susanoo only smiled. "You really want peace, don't you?"

Hayden shrugged. "People take it for granted."

Dr. Susanoo cocked his head at Hayden's curious answer and then nodded.

"The world works in mysterious ways, Sergeant Dáithí. While your situation is unique to you, there was once a man who was known to be impossible to kill in battle. He was believed to be protected by the High Spirit. You may know of him—George Washington. He actually should've died here in Pennsylvania—during the Battle of the Monongahela—when he had not one but two horses shot out from under him. Four musket-ball holes were found in his coat." Dr. Susanoo held up four of his fingers with his free hand for emphasis while the other steadied the vial. "But nine diseases, Indian snipers, and even a British cannon shot all failed to take him down."

Dr. Susanoo shook his head. "No, you did not *survive* death, Sergeant Dáithí. You died and came back to life. It's not the same. It's remarkable." He changed out the filled vial for another empty one. "I believe the artifact chose to save you for a reason. You may not think so, but you are important to this war. Perhaps because you may be the only person capable of stopping them."

"Stopping who? Japan?"

Dr. Susanoo continued changing out the vials until he was finished. He slowly pulled the needle out and discarded it safely—but not until after he taped up Hayden's arm. It took him a while to answer because he wasn't quite sure what to say.

"Flight Commander Isamu Mori," he answered finally. "He runs an experimental division behind Imperial Japan's military forces known as Yamata no Orochi. To them, he is known as Nurarihyon. And I believe his goal is to unleash Hyakki Yagyō." Dr. Susanoo stopped talking for a moment. He paused as he was packing his things. But even his hands had stopped moving. "It is the night parade of one hundred demons."

Hayden's eyes widened, and he sat back in his chair while Dr. Susanoo stood up.

"The—the—" he laughed awkwardly. Not to be disrespectful, but because he was unsure if he could believe what he was hearing. "The—th—" he couldn't stop stuttering.

Dr. Susanoo nodded. "One hundred demons. He wants to unleash hell upon earth and end humanity."

"And I'm supposed to stop him? Me?" Hayden jabbed his finger into the center of his own chest as he continued to laugh nervously. He rubbed his right palm against his hair and slid it down to the back of his neck before his hands both dropped into his lap to meet one another. "That—that's—that's a lot of pressure."

"You've already encountered him once, Sergeant."

That shook him from his nerves. He frowned, looking up at Dr. Susanoo curiously.

"I did?"

Dr. Susanoo nodded as he stood up.

"He's the Japanese flight commander who targeted the USS *Oklahoma* and killed you the first time." Dr. Susanoo pat Hayden's shoulder. "I'll see you in Hawai'i."

CHAPTER FIVE

York, Pennsylvania, March 21, 1942
0948 — local time

Máiréad Dáithí Quartermaine was on edge ever since Hayden told her who came to see him at work back in February: Colonel Richards and Dr. Susanoo. The two of them barely spoke since it happened and when they did, only words of contempt were exchanged. To Hayden, she was being unreasonable, but to Máiréad, she was acting rationally as a mother who was blessed to have her son back from the dead.

Hayden's mother was a young, elegant Irish woman. She kept a clean home and made holding everything together during a war seem effortless. A blonde hair was never out of place on her head, clothing always without any wrinkles to be found, and her makeup was perfect every single day. She was normally calm in demeanor, understanding, and affectionate. It was only Hayden's desire to re-enter the war that gnawed at her core and put her off balance.

Hayden sat outside, bundled in a jacket as he watched his little brother, Finley, shoot hoops with his worn basketball. Finley was only six years old, but tall for his age. Chubby, too.

In the wind, snow fell from nearby trees and settled on the already blanketed grounds. Máiréad was outside with them, but the two didn't speak, and she didn't look at Hayden. Her focus remained on their puppy. Her hair was neatly pulled back, bangs combed nicely over her forehead, and as always, not a single strand of blonde hair was out of place—even with the rustling of the cold wind.

Hayden finally could not take the silence any longer.

"You're being unreasonable," he said loudly, his breath visible in the air. Hayden glanced at her before his eyes landed back on Finley. Their mom continued to ignore him as she entertained the undersized Husky pup with a rope toy. "They think they can get me out of this chair," he continued, gripping onto the armrests of his wheelchair. "They think they can get me walking again and you don't want me to go."

"Because I see the risks, Hayden." The puppy continued to growl playfully while tugging at the rope Máiréad held tightly to. She glanced back at him. "Would

I love for you to walk again? Of course. Do I think it's worth the risk of you dying? No."

"Who said anything about dying?"

Máiréad scoffed, shaking her head.

"You're going back into war, Hayden. People die. You died." Máiréad tugged the rope out of the dog's mouth and threw it into Hayden's lap. She let herself into the house and the door slammed shut behind her. The dog, a pure white Husky puppy, jumped at him and pawed at the rope toy.

His stepdad, Gabe, witnessed the commotion as he came out of the garage, and even Finley stopped playing with his basketball. Only the dog seemed oblivious to the happenings around them, too preoccupied with the toy she desperately wanted in Hayden's lap. Hayden, of course, kept it out of her reach.

"I have to go," Hayden said as Gabe approached him. He sounded almost apologetic.

Gabe finished wiping his hands with the rag and tossed it over his shoulder. He was a burly, bearded man with a face hardened by the pains of war. But despite his intimidating appearance, he was as friendly as they came. He motioned toward Finley to keep shooting his hoops as he walked toward Hayden. There was a limp in his step. His own war injury sustained from World War I.

"I know," he said. He grabbed the toy from Hayden and threw it far into the yard. The Husky puppy bolted after it. "You don't have to convince me—and don't worry about your mom. She'll come around before you leave." He nudged Hayden's shoulder with his elbow. "Hey, you know she supports you."

"Yeah," Hayden said with a sigh. "I know. It's just the way she shows it."

"She's as stubborn as you. Where do you think you get it?"

Hayden raised his eyebrows and tilted his head as he grinned. Gabe had a point there. Still, he only had a few days left before R.A.V.E.N. would come for him and he'd be boarding a plane back to Hawai'i.

The last time he'd been there alive, he was drowning. Swallowing mouthfuls of saltwater that burned at his throat while the searing hot ocean water burned him alive. He may not have remembered death itself, but he remembered dying. The flares gleaming overhead from the bombs striking the ships. The explosions. While deaf to the noise, he could see the flashes of reds and yellows from beneath the water, till it grew murky with debris, oil, and blood. He remembered the dead bodies breaching the surface, absent of movement or the desperation of air. The rain of fire. The start of war.

That was something he'd never forget.

CORPSE WALKER: THE NIGHT PARADE | 81

Tension remained in the air throughout their house. Máiréad cleaned around Hayden and barely looked at him or acknowledged his presence. Gabe did his best to support him and assisted in packing his things for his trip back to the Hawaiian Islands. The two of them were going through his old military things, as he had been instructed to pack everything from his service in the Marine Corps.

In the box, he discovered the utility uniform he'd been wearing on December 7 of the previous year. It was tattered, worn, and burned. Most of it had been destroyed. He ran his fingers along the burned edges of the uniform.

"Well, this one's crummy," Hayden commented, a daring smile crossing his face as he looked at Gabe, hesitant and trying to gauge a reaction. But Gabe snorted and shook his head. They shared the same sense of humor.

"You're a knucklehead," Gabe scoffed in disbelief.

Hayden, of course, meant no disrespect to all those who died during the bombing. It was still very raw for him, as he had lost many friends during the surprise aerial attack. The country being dragged into another world war was a serious subject and not to be taken lightly. Lives were in danger. People were dying. But humor was just his way of handling things.

"That's not funny, Hayden."

Hayden looked up to see his mom standing in the doorway.

His arms lowered, the uniform resting in his lap.

"Mom... I have to go—I—"

"I know," she finally agreed as she nodded. "I don't want to fight anymore. I've run out of gas. I get it. But if Gabe helps you pack your things, you're bound to forget something." She clapped her hands together as she approached the boxes. Her eyes were red-rimmed, but she didn't cry. "We're going to make sure we get this right and that you come home safely this time."

"Why did you keep this?"

Máiréad froze. She glanced down at the uniform her son was holding and chewed on her bottom lip. Gently wetting her lips with her tongue, she tilted her head and slowly extended her hand to touch the material before retracting.

"It was the last thing you wore when you were alive," she answered quickly and in one breath. She sniffled softly and wiped her cheeks before returning to the box, ignoring it from then on. "We'll get these cleaned and pressed, and I'll have them packed for you before you leave."

"Thanks, Mom."

Gabe got up to check on Finley, leaving the two of them together.

"When they brought you home, I didn't want to believe it. My son?" she said while folding clothes and shook her head. "No, not my son. That couldn't be my son. I'd heard on the radio—and I knew where you were—and I'd gotten the telegram, but I didn't believe it. It took me a week after you actually came home." She dropped her hands into her lap, upset by the memory. "Then the mortuary called and said by a miracle you'd reawakened. I was flipping my wig, I was so upset." She nodded, glancing over at Hayden. "I was furious. How dare they play such a sick prank? And at a time like this?"

Hayden listened intently, his fingers still fumbling with the burned edges of his uniform as he looked down at it again.

"But there you were, alive, and I—well—I didn't question it because I didn't want you taken away again." She sniffled again and wiped her cheeks with the handkerchief she kept in her breast pocket. "I just—I want you to know that no matter what happens, you can always count on your mother." She forced a smile before clenching her jaw. "Just promise me you'll come home, okay?" she asked as she turned to face him again. Her hands covered his, which were still clutching the damaged uniform. "And not in a casket this time."

Hayden inherited his mother's bright blue eyes, but there was a bit more obvious care and concern reflecting in hers. He knew why she wanted him to stay, but at the same time, she understood why he had to leave. The war mattered to him. *Once a Marine, always a Marine.*

It took Hayden a few seconds, but eventually, he nodded.

"I promise," he said.

Máiréad smiled, and continued to assist with packing his things, setting aside his uniforms to be professionally cleaned.

His remaining days at home seemed to blur as they passed much sooner than he liked. He hadn't even been home for very long. Then again, after he came back in the first place, he hadn't intended on leaving ever again. It was the whole reason for the creation of Howard Davey. To be with his family. To be at peace.

Hayden spent as much time as he could with his little brother, Finley. The two of them would shoot hoops together outside in the lane of their driveway, and Hayden would jokingly tease him that he was getting a little chunky.

"You were bigger than him at his age, Hayden, don't you forget that."

"Quit busting my chops, old lady!" Hayden shouted, glancing up at the kitchen window on the second floor of their home. Máiréad was watching the two of them, and she smiled from where she stood.

Like the child of innocence he was, Finley would laugh it off and run away with the ball, down the lane to the backyard, past the garage. On occasion, he'd even throw the ball into his treehouse in the backyard and climb up so Hayden couldn't reach him. Finley held the basketball and looked down over the edge at his brother stuck in the wheelchair below.

"That's cheating," Hayden would declare from the ground, and Finley would just taunt him from above.

"Not if your legs work!" he shouted and snickered.

"*Oh, okay.*" Hayden raised his eyebrows, feigning his offense. "I'm gonna get you for that, fatty."

York, Pennsylvania, March 27, 1942
2126 — local time

"Hayden?"

Hayden looked up to see his brother standing in the doorway. He was dressed in his pajamas, but his eyes were wide.

"Yeah, bud?"

Finley pursed his lips together as he stepped into his older brother's room. A portion of their walk-in basement had been remodeled when Hayden had returned home, as he could no longer access most of the house due to the stairs. His mom and Gabe were looking into a single-story home, but Hayden was fine with the arrangement. Even if it was particularly chilly that winter.

"I'm scared."

Hayden frowned as he sat up in his bed.

"Of what?" he asked, and patted the side of his mattress. "Come're, sit."

Finley kept his eyes lowered as he trudged slowly into the bedroom. He climbed onto the bed, but still he didn't look at his brother. He continued to look down, and stared at his hands in his lap as his fingers fumbled together.

"What's up?"

"You're leaving tomorrow," he started, his voice was soft and while he occasionally turned toward Hayden's direction, Finley never quite managed to look up at him. When he got close, he would quickly avert his gaze again. "What if you don't come back? I hear Mommy and Daddy talking about it at night sometimes."

It was a reasonable fear. In fact, it was one Hayden had in the back of his head too. Not coming home. Dying for good. He inhaled deeply, his chest expanding and collapsing with the large breath. He wasn't entirely sure what to say.

Finley remained looking at the ground.

Hayden leaned toward him.

"Between you and me, I'm scared too."

Hayden could see the teardrops dripping onto Finley's hands. He reached over to grab his hand and wiped them away with his thumb.

"I don't want you to go," he whispered, his voice cracking. Finley stared at his brother's hand, watching his thumb rub against the back of his.

"Finley, you mean more to me than I have the vocabulary to express. But I have to do this. I have to go."

Hayden watched as his little brother's back rose and then fell, with very jagged breaths as he began to cry. He grabbed Finley's arm and pulled him close. Finley gasped for air as he gripped Hayden's shirt. His eyes were red and full of tears. His lashes were wet, face damp and blotchy.

"Come on, Finn," Hayden tried to say light-heartedly, trying to keep himself from falling apart as his eyes began to well with tears. "You gotta take care of Mom for me." Finley hugged him tighter. "I'm counting on you, okay? See that she and Gabe are alright through this." He could feel Finley nod into his shoulder. He managed a meek 'okay' in response between his gasps for air.

Máiréad came in to say goodnight and saw Finley curled up against Hayden. Part of her was happy to see her two boys getting along, but another part of her knew that she would mourn this moment. She mouthed a 'goodnight' to Hayden, who smiled in return, and she shut the door.

York, Pennsylvania, March 28, 1942
0502 — local time

Early morning the next day, Gabe came into Hayden's room to retrieve the sleeping Finley and put him into his own bed for a little while longer. Máiréad came down to help Hayden finish any last-minute packing and prepare him for his flight. Quickly, the time was coming for Hayden Dáithí to leave Pennsylvania for the second time. Sergeant Charles Kamuela had arrived early in the morning to accompany Hayden back to Hawai'i, to make sure the flight was as smooth as possible, and to see that his old friend was comfortable.

Colonel Norman Richards had made the final call, believing Hayden would be best to go back with an old friend, someone he both knew and trusted when it came to returning to the place of his death.

Hayden said his goodbyes to his family, and his mom stood there with her expression hardened to stone so that no tears would fall from her eyes. It was always important to her to be strong for her sons, and she had to pull Finley away from Hayden, who had refused to let go of his arm.

"I don't want him to die!" Finley screamed, fighting against her. There were tears streaming down his sleepy face.

"Remember what I said, alright?" Hayden told his brother.

Finley's bottom lip quivered as he gave him another hug. "I can't do it," he whispered.

"Of course you can," Hayden reassured.

Gabe gave Hayden a nod goodbye and helped Máiréad bring Finley into the house. Sergeant Kamuela had started down the driveway toward the car with Hayden's luggage in hand but stopped when he realized Hayden hadn't been following him.

"They're going to be fine."

Hayden nodded. "I know, I'm just… I never thought this would be happening again. I didn't think I'd leave again."

Sergeant Kamuela stuck his hands into his pockets and leaned against Hayden's suitcase. "You've more moxie than I got," he admitted.

Hayden rolled his eyes.

"Man, I'm serious." He hit Hayden's shoulder with the back of his hand. "If I died, if I fucking died, and by some miracle, I got a second chance at life, the last thing I'd be doing is walking right back into this minefield. This is war. I'd find a pretty little thing who wouldn't mind taking care of me and settle the hell down. But not you." Sergeant Kamuela shook his head. "That's selfless, man."

"Or maybe I just don't know how to say no."

"Well, and that too."

Hayden scoffed.

Sergeant Kamuela laughed. He stood up and acknowledged the car.

"Come on, we're gonna miss the flight."

He stuck Hayden's luggage on top of his own in the trunk before helping Hayden into the passenger's seat. Wheeling the chair to the driver's side, he loaded it into the back seat and got into the driver's seat.

"Back to Hawai'i," Sergeant Kamuela sighed.

"Holy mackerel, you make that sound so appealing," Hayden said sarcastically, looking over at Sergeant Kamuela. "This is gonna be a gas."

"I'm not even gonna lie to you," Sergeant Kamuela said as he started up the car. "It's fucked up over there."

Hayden sighed, staring out at the dead trees still covered in snow. "I really hope this works," he uttered under his breath.

"Me too." Sergeant Kamuela gripped at the steering wheel. "It's crazy, right? Project Reaper. Never in my wildest, and I mean my wildest dreams, did I ever think any of this shit could be possible at all. I mean, I've seen Miss Sharp's program on the telly, and her work is revolutionary—and she's not bad to look at—" Hayden rolled his eyes at Sergeant Kamuela's commentary, "but

CORPSE WALKER: THE NIGHT PARADE | 91

this? Coming back from the dead? I'm no schnook. This is going to change everything."

Again, the pressure upon him was building. Hayden's thumb tapped against the handle of the door while Sergeant Kamuela turned on the radio. The host recapped Joe Louis retaining the World Heavyweight Boxing Championship after knocking out Abe Simon in the sixth round at Madison Square Garden, then jazz filled the automobile: "A String of Pearls" by Glenn Miller and His Orchestra. Music had died down with many musicians going into the war, but jazz and swing were in full effect. The tune was smooth and upbeat, and likely good for the families of servicemen and women.

Hayden looked out at the snow-covered grounds as Sergeant Kamuela continued to talk about the aftermath of Pearl Harbor. Part of him wanted to listen, but another part of him didn't want to know what he had missed. He focused on the thin, boney trees. It hadn't snowed recently, so much of the snow that covered the branches had since fallen to the ground. Winter was beautiful when the snow was fresh. But as time went on, it melted into spring, tainted and browning from the mud. He stared at the brick buildings that sat right at the roads, the women on their front porches saying hello to neighbors as they eagerly checked the newspaper, and Hayden turned his head as they passed an old brick post office, briefly thinking of the telegram his mom had received.

Back home, Máiréad consoled Finley. She rocked him back and forth, not letting him go. Her chin was tucked down, hand stroking his brown hair.

"You said he wouldn't leave again," he mumbled into her shoulder.

"I'm sorry, baby," she said softly, rubbing his back. "But the country needs him more than we do right now." Máiréad steadied him to look at her. His eyes were lowered but eventually, he looked up. "But he'll come back, okay?" she whispered. "He'll come back."

Finley nodded as he sniffled. He wiped his runny nose with the back of his hand, and Máiréad then cleaned it with her handkerchief. She looked up at Gabe who stood in the corner with their Husky. He nodded once, and she gave him a small, half smile.

"We have to be strong for him," Finley declared, forcefully wiping his flushed cheeks with his hands.

Máiréad smiled and nodded, then gently tapped the tip of his reddened nose with her index finger.

"That we do," she said softly.

CHAPTER SIX

O'ahu, Hawai'i, March 28, 1942
1402 — local time

If there was one thing Hayden Dáithí absolutely did not miss about Hawai'i, it was the stickiness of the Hawaiian heat. He suffered greatly from island fever while stationed in Hawai'i, and felt trapped by living on such a small land mass with the sameness of the summer weather day after day, year after year. With the sun blazing at the center of the sky in the middle of the day, the heat and humidity engulfed him the second he rolled out of the plane and into the airport. It was unbearable. Complaints tickled the back of his throat far too much for him to keep it to himself

"How can it be this hot in March?" Hayden asked while tugging uncomfortably at his sweater. He wiped the sweat and oil beading on his forehead with his sleeve as he rolled them both up to his elbows, mentally kicking himself for wearing a sweater to Hawai'i. Sergeant

Kamuela just shook his head and laughed as he fumbled with a cigarette.

"You enjoy freezing your ass off in Pennsylvania?" he asked, tucking the cigarette between his lips as he fished out a lighter from his breast pocket.

"Well, I would if I could feel it."

Sergeant Kamuela grinned and hit Hayden in the shoulder.

"You're such a crumb, Dáithí." He shook his head, twirling the lighter between his fingers. "You want one?" he asked, pointing to the cigarette. Hayden made a face of disgust, crinkling his nose and curling his lip.

"I still don't smoke."

"Right, I forgot. You're one of them boring Marines." Sergeant Kamuela spoke out of the corner of his mouth as he lit his cigarette.

Hayden stared at the burning end.

"I hate cigarettes."

"Well, at least it's probably not gonna kill you," Sergeant Kamuela chuckled, blowing smoke into the air and away from the two of them.

"Ha ha." Hayden rolled his eyes.

Upon further observation, Hayden noticed Sergeant Kamuela was right about one thing. It was different there than he remembered. The energy of the islands had clearly shifted since the bombing. He could feel it. While people still smiled, it seemed forced. Looking into their eyes, there was a reflection of sadness—and with good reason. The bombing was aggression, and the people paid the price.

Hayden didn't notice until his return just how large the Asian population was on the islands. He noticed Sergeant Kamuela seemed tense as he walked beside Hayden, whose brown eyes were observing the people around him.

"Did you hear about the executive order?" Sergeant Kamuela asked without looking down at him.

Hayden shrugged. "I don't think so? Well. I mean, Colonel Richards mentioned one when he met me at the factory, but he didn't exactly elaborate on anything."

"Does he ever really elaborate on anything?" Sergeant Kamuela asked. Hayden tilted his head in consideration as he raised his eyebrows. That was true. "The Navy's already been removing Japanese citizens from Terminal Island near Port of Los Angeles," Sergeant Kamuela continued. "There's talk about them being moved into internment camps." Hayden noticed Sergeant Kamuela's eyes were fixed on a group of Japanese men.

Hayden sighed. "So basically we're turning into Nazi Germany."

"Hayden…" Sergeant Kamuela grabbed the handle of Hayden's wheelchair to stop him. He turned him around. "Japan attacked *us*."

"Yeah, did you hear yourself? *Japan*. Not our own people."

"It's hard to distinguish between Japanese nationals and United States citizens. It's better to be on the safe side, don't you think?"

Hayden was haunted by his initial hesitancy with Dr. Susanoo for being of Japanese descent. He sighed. Of course, he tried to justify it in his mind with the actions of Imperial Japan, the horrors he endured during the bombing, and the losses he had to live with—but he couldn't categorize people that way. He knew it wasn't right.

"It's not forever—besides, it's not really happening here in Hawai'i." Sergeant Kamuela walked behind him and pushed Hayden's wheelchair toward the terminal where they'd wait for their bags to arrive. "They take up like one-third of the population. So honestly, it's just not really possible. It's unrealistic and all."

Hayden looked over his shoulder. "I can wheel myself, you know."

"Yeah well, hopefully soon you won't even have to do that."

Hayden kept his head turned to the side before glancing up at Sergeant Kamuela behind him. "Hey, careful. Don't drop ash on my shoulder."

Sergeant Kamuela flicked his cigarette away from him. The corner of his lips pulled into a subtle smirk as he just shook his head.

Hayden didn't really know what to think about the anti-Japanese activity they were surrounded by. The fact that the Japanese population was so prevalent in Hawai'i made the treatment of them much more obvious. It was something he'd been mostly sheltered from while back home in Pennsylvania. In the area where he lived, the Asian American population was mostly non-existent. There were definitely no Japanese people from what he could recall.

But in Hawai'i, it was a different experience. He could see up close how they were being treated—with people throwing their garbage at them, spitting at them. While he tried not to pay any attention to it, ignoring it didn't help the situation either. Not when it was right in front of his face.

In the car on the way to base, Hayden tensed in the passenger seat as he noticed an elderly Asian man on the street getting attacked by U.S. military officials. He started cranking down his window abruptly as he told Sergeant Kamuela to stop the car.

"What are you gonna do?" asked Sergeant Kamuela, putting the car in park. Hayden, of course, ignored him.

"Hey! Cut it out!" Hayden shouted out of his window. "Leave him alone!"

The two officials ignored him, though. The Japanese man was on the ground, his face bloodied. He tried to block their kicks from his abdomen. Hayden felt sick.

He started opening his door.

"Kamuela, get my wheelchair."

"What—what exactly do you think you're gonna do? Roll over them?"

Hayden clenched his jaw as he glared at Sergeant Kamuela.

"Someone has to do something!"

Sergeant Kamuela grabbed the sleeve of his sweater.

"Dáithí, you're fucking paralyzed!"

"Then you do something!" Hayden smacked the dashboard of the car with his palm in frustration.

"Alright! Don't snap your cap."

Sergeant Kamuela got out of the driver's seat and slammed his car door shut before running over to the elderly man to make sure he was alright. The military officials were walking away by the time he got there.

"Stupid Japs," one of them muttered.

Sergeant Kamuela helped him get to his feet and dusted the old man off.

"I should report you for that!" he shouted after them, but they ignored him. "You alright?" he asked, steadying the man. While he nodded, the old man didn't make eye contact. He quietly thanked Sergeant Kamuela and went on his way.

When Sergeant Kamuela finally got back to the car, he shut the door and started it back up.

Hayden was still tense from the situation.

"Why did you hesitate?" Hayden asked.

"That's not my business to interfere."

But that answer clearly wasn't good enough as Hayden waited for more.

Sergeant Kamuela sighed, putting the car back into park. His hand dropped from the keys and rested at the bottom of the steering wheel. He stared straight ahead, not bothering to look at Hayden. "They killed our people, Hayden."

"They killed me too, Kamuela. I just got lucky." Hayden glanced over at him. "The Kingdom of Hawaii was illegally overthrown and a lot of Hawaiians died. Do you hold that against me?" he asked sincerely.

Sergeant Kamuela looked over at Hayden before he shook his head and rolled his eyes.

"Don't be silly."

"But I'm white."

"It's not the same."

"Why not?"

Frustrated, Sergeant Kamuela gripped the steering wheel for a minute before relaxing his hands. He rubbed his forehead and sighed, dropping both his hands into his lap. "You can't condemn people for the wrongdoings of their ancestors."

"Where'd you hear that?"

"My mom used to say that to me when I was a kid. You know I got a lot of family here and my brothers wanted to hate everyone who wasn't kānaka maoli—Hawaiian by blood. But hate breeds hate." Sergeant Kamuela's voice softened toward the end of his words. "Hate breeds hate," he repeated to himself.

Hayden lifted his shoulders as he glanced at his friend.

"She's got a point." He raised his eyebrows.

Sergeant Kamuela made a face and grumbled to himself. "Well, she'd like you." He looked down at his hands before looking back at Hayden. "You know, now I'm starting to reconsider how happy I am that you're back in the land of the living." His eyebrows raised quickly, looking like a deer in headlights. "Too soon?"

Hayden laughed. "What a fathead."

"Let's get you walking again so I can stop questioning my morals."

"Oh, that's the only reason, huh?"

Sergeant Kamuela grinned as he started the car back up so they could continue on their way. The R.A.V.E.N.

office on O'ahu was located in Kailua on the Marine Corps base and was where Dr. Susanoo was waiting for him with a piece of the Infernal Artifact. Hayden was glad he wasn't going back to Pearl Harbor just yet.

"Have you ever seen it?" Hayden asked. "The piece of the artifact?"

Sergeant Kamuela shook his head. "After the attack on Pearl Harbor, they kept it under lockdown. I mean, a lot of security. The higher-ups weren't saying much, but they knew the Japs—*Japanese*—would come back for it after what happened on Guam and they keep thinking there were spies all over the place. But honestly? I can't say that I really want to see it. I mean, the whole thing is crazy—I'm not that intrigued. Or stupid."

"What do you mean?"

"The artifact is Death's scythe, Hayden. His *scythe*. The actual thing that Death *himself* carried. The myth is that it was broken into three pieces by Death himself and hidden on Guam, Midway, and Hawai'i."

"Which is why I came back from the dead."

"I'm told it's the working theory—but I don't really know." Sergeant Kamuela shrugged. "Dr. Susanoo can answer more of your questions better than I ever could. It's not really my area of expertise, y'know."

"And what is?"

"Dames," Sergeant Kamuela said with a smug grin and a quick rise of his eyebrows. "Dames are definitely my area of expertise."

"You're so doll dizzy." Hayden chuckled and rolled his eyes.

"Anyway," Sergeant Kamuela continued, "they hid it because they think Orochi will come back for it."

"Orochi—right. Mori's division."

Sergeant Kamuela nodded as they went through the entrance of the Marine Corps base. Both of them showed their identification to the guards at the gate before proceeding further. "Apparently moving it isn't very easy, though. It kills people. Drains their life force. Only Dr. Susanoo's been able to properly handle it." He glanced over at Hayden. "We'll get you settled in for tomorrow. You excited?"

"I feel like I'm going to spew."

"Yeah, I don't blame you. But you're back from the dead. What's the worst that could happen?"

The last time Hayden was anywhere near the artifact, he died. He was blown out of a ship, boiled alive, and drowned in the hot water of the ocean. Intentionally going into the same room with it again, possibly even interacting with it, was weighing on him heavily. The only thing that was a driving force behind his curiosity was whether or not he could have the chance to walk again. He'd already been given a second chance at life. He figured this had to be false hope.

"I could die again?" he finally suggested.

Sergeant Kamuela pained a smile as they drove into a parking lot near the barracks.

"You won't," he assured.

Sergeant Kamuela parked the car and got out to set up Hayden's wheelchair. Near them, parked another car. Hayden would recognize her anywhere.

As Sergeant Kamuela came around to the passenger's side to help him out, Hayden acknowledged the woman across the parking lot as he got situated in his wheelchair. Though he hardly needed to, as Sergeant Kamuela's focus was already on her. "That's my old boss," Hayden said as she was gathering her things from the front seat. "Dorothea Sharp."

"Damn, what a dish—" Sergeant Kamuela raised his eyebrows as she got out of the car, one slender leg after the other. "I've seen the informational programs of her with her dad on telly, but I've never seen her up close." Sergeant Kamuela tilted his head to the side. "I woulda stayed in the factory if I were you, fathead. If I got to see that every day."

Hayden scoffed and hit Sergeant Kamuela in the chest with the back of his hand.

"Boys," she said, acknowledging them with a closed-lip smile as she shut the car door behind her.

"Miss Sharp," Sergeant Kamuela said with a nod and subtle, yet playful smile as she turned to leave the parking lot. He didn't take his eyes off of her.

Hayden raised his eyebrows as he looked up at his friend in disbelief.

"You're whistling dixie if you think you've got a chance with her, man."

Sergeant Kamuela scoffed and shut the car door. "You're a real pain in my neck."

After they too exited the lot, Sergeant Kamuela spent the next hour helping Hayden get situated in the barracks before reporting back to his commanding officer. The racks were all in the squad bay. There were two rows, with an aisle down the center barely big enough for his wheelchair to roll down comfortably. Sometimes his knuckles would accidentally hit the frames at the foot of the beds. Each bed had a small wooden footlocker, and everything else needed to fit comfortably beneath their rack.

It was a lot more cramped than he remembered.

O'ahu, Hawai'i, March 29, 1942
2114 — local time

Dr. Susanoo found Hayden alone in the squad bay, sitting in bed, reading through local newspaper articles about the latest attempted attack on Pearl Harbor.

"Unsuccessful, thankfully," Dr. Susanoo said, spotting the headline.

"They were trying to disrupt the salvage and repair efforts," Hayden replied.

"No reported casualties, though?"

"Not this time. But it has everyone's guard up."

Hayden's mind flashed to the attack on the elderly man near the airport, and his stomach churned.

"Are you doing alright?" Dr. Susanoo asked, looking down at the articles scattered before Hayden.

Hayden didn't look at him. "More or less," he answered quietly.

"Worried?"

Less than three feet away, Dr. Susanoo sat on the bed across from Hayden.

Still, Hayden didn't say anything. Instead, he just gathered up the newsprints and photographs that were scattered across his bed and his lap.

"What if it doesn't work?" He put them on the seat of his wheelchair that was now at his bedside. For a second, he froze, staring at the chair that he relied on for his mobility. "Or what if I die for good this time?"

"I have faith you won't."

A small smile formed on Hayden's face, recalling Sergeant Kamuela assuring the same thing.

"Have you done this before?" he asked, lifting his gaze to look at the elder Japanese man.

"Well, no," Dr. Susanoo said, chuckling to himself. "But I believe it will work."

Hayden thought about the elderly man being beaten by the military officials while observing the scar under Dr. Susanoo's eye. "You know a lot about me, but I don't know much about you."

Dr. Susanoo tensed his shoulders.

"If I'm being completely honest, there's not much to say."

"The scar says otherwise. I'm sure there's a story behind it." It was a very deep scar from what Hayden could see. But he wasn't going to press unless the doctor would willingly tell him. There was one thing he couldn't stop thinking about, however, and he couldn't stop himself from asking. "How exactly do you know Mori?"

Dr. Susanoo sighed, placing his hands on either side of him to grip the thin mattress of the bed. "I figured this would come up." He nodded. "There was a time when he and I knew each other well. A long time ago. I'd been cast out by my sister, and I needed a friend."

"So you were friends?"

Chewing on his bottom lip, Dr. Susanoo shook his head. He traced a few strands of his long black hair out of his face and tucked them behind his ear. "No, I don't think we ever were. Not really, anyway. Wrong choice of words. He used me for my knowledge. I'd boast in his presence. You know, show off, and he let me. He'd feed off of it. Encourage it. I was young, stupid, and arrogant."

"My mom would say the same about me."

Dr. Susanoo smiled. "You're young, maybe, but I see qualities beyond that. I think you have a fear of failure—which could work in your favor, or be your downfall. Don't be so worried about what could go wrong, hm? Try to focus on what could go right."

"I don't want to disappoint—"

The corner of Hayden's mouth twitched. Fear of failure. Fear of disappointment. He could see how that could happen.

Dr. Susanoo sighed as he began opening his journal.

"What we're about to do has never been intentionally done to a human before, and with that said, unfortunately, I can't guarantee it'll work. But the artifact brought you back to life." He handed Hayden a tattered old map of the Pacific Ocean. There was a scythe drawn over it, connecting Guam, Midway, and Hawai'i. He pointed at it, tracing the scythe with his finger. "Death saved you, Sergeant Hayden Dáithí. And I know it was for a reason."

Hayden stared at the rough scythe scratched onto the map. He clenched his jaw, goosebumps crawling across his skin. He could feel it again. Drowning. He could feel the floor drop from beneath him. The heat of the water. He closed his eyes, his eyebrows scrunching into a frown.

"You remember, don't you? Dying."

Hayden nodded slowly, hesitantly. He looked up at the ceiling and inhaled deeply, but couldn't focus on anything in particular. He exhaled through his mouth. He stared at nothing. He closed his eyes again and let go of the map to massage at his temples as he steadied his breathing.

He felt a warm, heavy hand on his shoulder briefly.

"I'm sorry."

"For what?" he asked, not bothering to open his eyes.

But Dr. Susanoo didn't answer his question. In truth, he wasn't certain how. He felt responsible for the bombing. He felt responsible for Isamu Mori. He felt responsible for Yamata no Orochi. But how could he say that?

When no answer came, Hayden finally opened his eyes. Dr. Susanoo was gone. But the map remained resting in his lap. Hayden took another careful look at it and the way each island was connected in the perfect shape of the scythe. He began to remember that morning on the USS *Oklahoma*, but the flashes of red quickly stopped him. He folded the map and tucked it under his mattress before going to bed.

He would have a long day tomorrow—assuming he'd survive it.

CHAPTER SEVEN

Oʻahu, Hawaiʻi, March 29, 1942
0746 — local time

Dressed in his service uniform with the help of Sergeant Kamuela, Hayden wheeled himself into the facility where he would knowingly come face-to-face with the artifact that brought him back to life. He stopped in the hallway and tried to rub the nerves out of his face and neck. His face was smooth now, clean-shaven. While his hair was growing longer up top, he kept the sides cut short in an attempt to represent some semblance of a regulation haircut. There was a little bit of tonic in his hair, but only to keep it from branching out in every other direction but the one he wanted it to go in.

"You doing okay there, Sergeant?"

Hayden looked up from his hands. Agent Elaina Dacua stood before him. Her dark brown hair was no longer tightly pulled back in a ponytail like it had been when they first met, but instead it was hanging loosely in waves over her shoulders. He had to admit, only to himself of course, the former hairstyle made her look a little uptight. She looked better this way. She appeared friendlier, and a little more approachable than her former look. Perhaps that was on purpose.

"Uh yeah," he said with a nod. "You look more relaxed," he added, acknowledging the subtle change in her appearance.

She was about to smile at the fact that he noticed, but Agent Dacua's eyes averted as Miss Sharp walked past the two of them. Miss Sharp had a cheery bounce in her step, as always. The skirt of her pale pink French dress swished with each step she took. Her dark brown hair was always smooth, perfectly resting against her shoulders, and upon her head was a headband of a complementary color that matched her dress. Miss Sharp always looked immaculate. There was never a moment where she looked anything less than perfect. It was evident that everyone around her always noticed. Every head turned as she passed.

Miss Sharp looked at Hayden and crinkled her nose with a playful wink as she pursed together her bold red-painted lips.

"Hayden," she said with a tilt of her head before glancing at Agent Dacua and continuing on her way. There was something in the way that she said his name that made his stomach twist. It was likely because the tone she used indicated she was hinting at the fact that Hayden had initially lied to her when he first went to work for the Sharp company. He sucked in air deeply through his nose, causing a slight whistle.

"She always looks like she just stepped out of a fashion show, doesn't she? Always just perfect. Every single damn day." Her voice sounded irritable. She certainly wasn't making a comment out of admiration. Agent Dacua crossed her arms, making the three-quarter length sleeves on her top slide back to her elbows. Hayden looked back up in time to notice Agent Dacua roll her eyes.

He ignored it.

"Will I see you inside?" he asked as he fixed the cuff of his own sleeve, deciding to change the subject.

Agent Dacua's eyes widened as she looked down. She almost forgot she was in his company rather than standing in the hall by herself.

"Oh, no," she said quickly, immediately pushing her annoyance to the side. "I'm not allowed in there. I'm not cleared for that level yet, unfortunately. I believe Dr. Stolly will be assisting Shark—*Sharp*. Sharp." She gently pounded her chest with her fist as she cleared her throat and corrected her obviously intentional mistake. Her hand then moved to fumble with the roll collar along her v-neckline while the other fumbled with the unpressed box pleats of her brown skirt. "And Dr. Susanoo will be there. You'll be fine."

Agent Dacua reached down to rub Hayden's shoulder with a bit more fondness than the last time. "Good luck," she whispered.

He nodded a 'thanks' as she left him in the hall alone.

The longer he sat there, the more it appeared like a hospital. Between the bright fluorescents and the strong scent of chemicals, it was all too much. Hayden rubbed at his nose as he breathed, trying to get the chemical smell out of it before wheeling himself toward the door. Just as he was about to reach for it, Dr. Stolly opened it for him from the inside.

"There you are."

"Ran into Agent Dacua," Hayden said as he wheeled himself into the room.

"Did you?" Dr. Stolly glanced around outside as if to look for her. "She's looking very pretty today—not that she doesn't look pretty every day. Not that she—" Dr. Stolly furrowed his brows, and started rubbing the back of his neck as he stepped into the room behind Hayden and closed the door. He pushed his glasses up the bridge of his nose awkwardly.

Hayden grinned at him.

Dr. Stolly frowned. "What?"

"You like her, don't you?" he teased.

Dr. Stolly immediately got defensive as he tensed. "No."

"Yeah, *alright*." Hayden laughed and nodded sarcastically before turning his attention to the others in the room with them. Dr. Susanoo, Miss Sharp, and Colonel Richards were among them—along with a handful of other people Hayden didn't recognize, nor had ever seen before. The room was much larger than it appeared, but they filled in a small section of it. The remainder of the room was sectioned off by a wall made of safety glass.

As Hayden rolled further in, a few people tried introducing themselves to him, but he couldn't hear them as his ears began to ring. Louder and louder till his whole head was pounding from the noise. Hayden shut his eyes and covered his ears as he tried to silence it. The ringing shifted into a migraine as he added pressure to his skull from between his palms.

"Cover it!" Dr. Susanoo shouted, and with the use of a mechanical claw, a black cloth dropped over the blade of the Infernal Artifact on the other side of the glass. He rushed over to Hayden, whose eyes were still shut tight. Black veins glowed in his face and seeped toward his eyes in a repetitive cycle. His hands were putting so much strain on his skull that his entire body shook, fingernails digging so deep into his skin, he was close to drawing his own blood. The nether energy ripped through his veins and seared like hot magma, burning through his body, over and over. His eyeballs felt heavy and enlarged. Hayden was scared that if he opened his lids, they'd explode out of their sockets.

"Sergeant Dáithí—" Dr. Susanoo hesitated for a moment, before he grabbed hold of Hayden's wrist, gently trying to tug his hand down from his head. "Sergeant Dáithí..." he said again softly. The shaking of his body soon slowed before coming to a stop altogether, and Hayden hesitantly pulled his hands down from his ears. He opened his watering eyes and looked at Dr. Susanoo kneeling in front of him. "Are you sure about this?" Dr. Susanoo continued. His eyebrows were etched together, which made the scar in his cheek more defined. His long black hair was always pulled back into the same bun, with a few loose salt and peppered strands hanging in his face.

Hayden frowned, staring at Dr. Susanoo.

His jaw was clenched tight.

"What was that?" he asked and looked around the room. Everyone was staring at him, but he hardly noticed that. It wasn't what he was looking for. Hayden finally spotted the black cloth covering the artifact on the other side of the glass. He could see its shape still, with a faint ring emitting from it. He tilted his head curiously. "Was that the—" Hayden looked over at Dr. Susanoo.

CORPSE WALKER: THE NIGHT PARADE | 117

Dr. Susanoo nodded, not taking his eyes off of Hayden. "I think it's reacting to you—and its own energy that lurks within you. The cloth is laced with vulcanium—but—" Dr. Susanoo sighed, still observing Hayden. "Can you handle it, Sergeant Dáithí? I don't want you to experience unnecessary pain. I—I don't want you to—"

"Die?"

Dr. Susanoo finally looked down.

Hayden took a couple of seconds; his eyes wandered to the Colonel, to Miss Sharp, Dr. Stolly, then back to Dr. Susanoo. Everyone else in the room fell to the background like white noise. He didn't see them, and he didn't care to. There was a lot to process, a lot to file through in his thoughts, but he had already considered the consequences. Finally, he nodded.

"I can do this."

Dr. Susanoo nodded, patting Hayden's arm as he stood up straight.

"Then let's get you set up."

Hayden was guided into another room where a nurse helped him change into a hospital gown and handed him a pair of shorts to wear over the adult diapers placed in front of him. Hayden couldn't believe his eyes. He stared at the diaper for a minute and blinked several times before looking up at the nurse in disbelief.

"Are these really necessary?" he asked, looking back down at the giant diaper.

Being in a wheelchair had certainly brought a new set of challenges to Hayden's life, but going to the bathroom on his own wasn't one of them.

"Dr. Susanoo is afraid you might become incontinent," she said bluntly.

Oh.

"Permanently?" His lips parted slightly at her straightforwardness before clenching his jaw again when she didn't answer. "Well, better safe than sorry, I guess," he resigned. The nurse only shrugged, appearing unbothered by Hayden's reaction.

"You do this often?" he asked.

"Yes. A job's a job."

Chewing on his lower lip, he nodded, and they got him changed. He was then brought to another set of doors, where he shifted himself onto a cold metal chair bolted to a mechanical track deep in the ground.

"Good luck," the nurse said.

Hayden nodded and stared at the two metal doors in front of him as she left him alone. Those two words were beginning to make him feel uneasy. *Good luck.* While everyone who said it meant well, it no longer felt that way. 'Good luck' was beginning to feel more like an omen than a wish.

"Are you ready, Sergeant Dáithí?" Dr. Susanoo's voice came from a speaker system overhead.

Hayden nodded again, keeping his focus ahead. Within seconds, the chair he sat upon propelled forward on the track and the doors opened. The black vulcanium-laced cloth remained draped over the artifact, and the metal doors closed shut behind him. Once Hayden had been brought only a few feet away from the stand, the moving seat came to a halt. Hayden could see Dr. Susanoo, the Colonel, Dr. Stolly, and Miss Sharp standing on the other side of the glass. Each of them watched Hayden with expectation.

On the bright side, the extra onlookers with whom he was unfamiliar appeared to have cleared out of the room. At least he wouldn't have much of an audience if he did die. Or shit himself. *Silver lining*, he supposed.

Hayden exhaled deeply as he stared at the black cloth and attempted to mentally prepare himself for the direct exposure to the artifact that he was about to have. There was a faint ringing beginning in his ears again, but not as loud as when he had first entered the room. It was tolerable this time.

"I will need you to grab it, alright?" Dr. Susanoo instructed. The mechanical claw came down from a hidden door in the ceiling and hovered above the cloth.

Unsure if they could hear him, Hayden nodded again to indicate that he understood. "We will begin—now."

The metal claw grabbed the cloth and slowly lifted it, revealing a very old and slender blade, nearly three feet in length. Immediately, the pounding in his skull returned as the ringing increased in volume. Hayden pressed his palms against his temples as the ringing in his ears deafened him. His veins scorched the tissue in his face as they blackened again and blood clouded his eyes.

"Hayden!" Dr. Susanoo shouted into the amplifier. "Grab it!"

While he continued to grip at his skull, Hayden's body began to bloat. His skin changed color to splotchy blues, greens, and various shades of black. Colonel Richards looked away, reminded of how Hayden's body appeared when he had pulled him from the harbor.

"It's killing him," Dr. Stolly whispered to Miss Sharp, whose hand steadily gripped the lever of the mechanical claw. They both exchanged looks of terror with one another.

"Dr. Susanoo?" Miss Sharp asked, looking over at him. Her eyes were widened, brows brought together. Her voice was shaky. "Sh—should I cover it? He's—he's dying—"

But Dr. Susanoo held his hand up to silence her.

"Sergeant Dáithí—" he said, clear and stern into the microphone. "You came back from the dead. Thousands died, Sergeant Dáithí, but *you* came back! Do not let the limitations of your humanity define you."

Hayden groaned from the pain. His eyes were bloodshot and turning black. His dark veins again protruded from his face as they ran up toward his sockets with a vitriolic rage of their own. The sight was horrific.

His left hand shook vigorously as he reached out to grab the blade of the scythe. As soon as his hand wrapped around it, the contact created an energetic explosion that even those on the other side of the glass weren't protected from. The four onlookers flew backward from the energy blast while Hayden remained where he was. He stood up from the chair with ease, hand still holding onto the blade. The energy flowed from it through the veins in his arm, blackening as they bulged and faded back to normal the further they ran up his arms. What was once excruciating pain felt numb. Hayden couldn't feel anything.

Dr. Susanoo was the first to scramble to his feet, while Dr. Stolly made sure Miss Sharp was alright. She got up quickly and went right back to the glass.

"What's happening?" Miss Sharp asked, her hands touching the glass. "It didn't break. How did we—" A smile brightened on her face when she noticed Hayden was standing.

The Colonel got up, shaking his head in confusion, and finally looked back at Hayden before looking at Dr.

Susanoo. He and Miss Sharp both waited for an answer as Dr. Susanoo kept his gaze locked on the view before them. His mouth was hung slightly ajar as he stared at Hayden intently, wondering if Hayden was at all aware of what was happening.

"His body's figuring out what to do with the energy," Dr. Susanoo said finally.

Colonel Richards frowned. "But why's his skin—"

"Disintegrating?" Dr. Susanoo answered, finishing the Colonel's question. Hayden's skin was still discolored, flaking away with every second that passed. The right side of his ribcage was beginning to peek through as the fabric of his medical gown burned away. Dr. Susanoo turned to Colonel Richards and looked him square in the eye. "Because Sergeant Dáithí is dead."

Hayden's eyes were completely pitch-black now. His blue irises were nowhere to be found; a faint white color rimmed the darkness that resided where his baby blues typically did. The wispy smoke that encompassed the blade now encompassed him. The veins in his arm continued to blacken repeatedly and protruded further before normalizing as the nether energy traveled through them and into his body. The bones in his right forearm were beginning to emerge as his flesh rotted away.

"Physically, Sergeant Dáithí died during the bombing of Pearl Harbor."

"So he's like a zombie?" Dr. Stolly asked, writing notes down.

"No. Zombies are completely different. Zombies are just reanimated bodies." Dr. Susanoo furrowed his brows and tilted his head condescendingly. "What kind of intellectual are you?"

Dr. Stolly's eyes widened, taken aback by his comment. "Hey! That's not nice. I was just asking. We've never exactly encountered something like this before." Dr. Stolly glanced at Hayden.

Dr. Susanoo's brows created a crease between them as he stared at Dr. Stolly. He blinked once, then twice, still staring at Dr. Stolly with heavy judgment and concern just as Hayden collapsed. The blade clattered to the floor, attracting everyone's attention.

"Quickly, Miss Sharp," Dr. Susanoo said, hands in the air. "Cover it and let's get him."

Using the claw, Miss Sharp dropped the cloth back over the blade and returned it to the stand while the other three ran to assist Hayden. The Colonel and Dr. Susanoo went to him immediately, while Dr. Stolly went to grab Hayden's wheelchair. The coloration of Hayden's skin had returned to normal, appearing just as alive as anyone else in the room. The black tint that soiled his veins had all but completely disappeared.

Dr. Susanoo checked Hayden's pulse and looked up at the Colonel.

"He's fine."

"Did I do it?" Hayden mumbled, his eyelids fluttering as he moved in and out of consciousness. Though the pounding in his head and the ringing in his ears were both gone, his lids still felt heavy. His head felt heavy.

"You did a lot more than that," Dr. Susanoo assured. "How are you feeling?"

"My legs hurt," Hayden groaned. He opened his eyes, and the black had faded. They were a clear blue once more. "But it's good to feel them again."

Dr. Susanoo and Colonel Richards helped Hayden get to his feet. Miss Sharp watched from behind the glass. She clasped her hands together and tucked them beneath her chin as she smiled again at the sight.

"Guess you won't be needing this," Dr. Stolly said, his hands still gripping the handles of the wheelchair.

"So you are shorter than me." Hayden straightened his posture a bit, acknowledging their height difference. Dr. Stolly frowned and Hayden grinned. Hayden stretched, before looking down at the burns in his hospital gown. It was singed in several places. "What happened?" he asked as he stuck his hand through one of the holes.

"You don't remember what happened when you grabbed the blade?" Dr. Stolly asked curiously.

CORPSE WALKER: THE NIGHT PARADE | 125

Hayden rubbed at his aching thigh, before taking a few steps as he walked in a circle. While he couldn't believe he could walk again, he contained his excitement rather than appear giddy like a small child. Hayden shook his head. "I reached for the blade and I blacked out." Hayden looked back down at the burned gown.

"So, now what?" Colonel Richards asked Dr. Susanoo.

"We'll run trials and see what exactly Sergeant Dáithí is capable of," Dr. Susanoo said with a nod. "I have it all in my notes."

After further inspecting his hospital gown, Hayden looked up at Dr. Susanoo and noticed a faint glow surrounding Dr. Susanoo's skin, similar to the black smoke that encompassed him earlier, but much brighter. Much lighter. It was almost blinding, the brighter it got.

"Dr. Susanoo?" Hayden said, acknowledging the glow. "Are you good?"

Dr. Susanoo tilted his head and furrowed his brows before looking down at his hands. He flipped them over and back again, before extending his arms to examine it further.

"No—no, no, no!" He began shaking them vigorously, as if he would shake off the effects by doing so. "No! I'm not ready! Not yet, Amaterasu!"

"What's happening?" Dr. Stolly asked, exchanging glances with Hayden.

Hayden just stood with his jaw hanging.

"It appears my sister's forgiven me for my transgressions," Dr. Susanoo said, exasperated. "I never thought this day would come." He frowned. As his skin brightened, the age and imperfections began to fade, including the very defined scar across his face. The bun on his head was no longer messily put up, but done perfectly. He was youthful now. Ageless. Free of his corporality. Dr. Susanoo reached to grip Hayden's shoulder as he began to disappear. It was strange to be staring at the young Japanese man who now stood before him rather than the elder one with the defined scar. Dr. Susanoo now lacked any and all flaws. "Sergeant Dáithí, may you always find light in the darkness," he said sternly, eyes wide. "Be well." He nodded.

Hayden reached out to grab Dr. Susanoo's wrist, but as Dr. Susanoo bowed to him, he vanished. Hayden's hand went through thin air.

"What the hell?" Colonel Richards looked around frantically after Dr. Susanoo had completely disappeared. "Where'd he go?"

"Hang on—*Amaterasu*. Isn't that the Japanese sun goddess?" Dr. Stolly asked as he took a step back. "I have to make a phone call."

"What is going on?" Colonel Richards followed Dr. Stolly out of the glass room.

Hayden and Miss Sharp exchanged glances through the thick glass. Her hands were cupping her mouth and her already large brown eyes were unusually widened in surprise. He walked outside of the glass wall and entered the other room to meet her at the control panel of the mechanical claw.

"Did you know that was going to happen?" he asked, pointing at where Dr. Susanoo once stood.

Her hands were still at her mouth. Eyes still wider than he'd ever seen them. She shook her head.

"I guess I could've assumed you didn't," he continued, acknowledging her shock. "Given the state of things. But I came back from the dead and a man just disappeared in front of me." Hayden pointed at the glass. "I don't know what to think—or believe anymore." He reached up to rub at his temples.

She chuckled nervously and chewed on her bottom lip. Her hand moved to fix her hair and she crossed her arms over her chest.

"I'm just as confused as you are."

"No offense, Miss Sharp, but you're one of the smartest people in America—so that doesn't make me feel better at all."

She laughed nervously and sighed.

"Do you think he's coming back?" Through the glass, Hayden looked back at the last place Dr. Susanoo stood.

Miss Sharp pursed her bright red lips together and shook her head.

"I don't think so, Hayden."

Hayden rubbed his face and sighed.

"He mentioned his notes? He had a journal of some kind that he always kept with him—" As Hayden started looking around, he spotted his military uniform that was folded on the table next to the control panels.

Miss Sharp nodded before she shrugged. "I've seen him with it, but he didn't have anything with him this morning. I'm sure Dr. Stolly and I can figure something out, but honestly, I don't even know where to begin with the trials without Dr. Susanoo. I'm a chemical engineer. This is all still really new to me. The—the—uh—supernatural stuff. Spirit world, I suppose one could call it. The Underworld. I don't know..." Her voice trailed off.

Hayden didn't like that word—or any of those words.

"Well then, let's go find where Stolly wandered off to," Hayden said as he turned away from Miss Sharp and took off the hospital gown to change. He pulled his forest green shirt over his head quickly and started buttoning up his service uniform. Hayden pulled at the front of his pants as he tried to adjust himself. The diaper was riding up uncomfortably, but he couldn't exactly take it off yet. At least not in front of Miss Sharp. "He mentioned he had to make a phone call."

"Maybe he's calling the Republic of Letters?" Miss Sharp grabbed her briefcase. "Come on. I think I know where he went."

Hayden stopped and turned around, adjusting his pants again. He nodded toward the blade. "Shouldn't we lock that up?" He could feel his veins tickle, but it was bearable this time.

"You need security clearance to get in here," she said, waving her hand dismissively. "Almost no one has that high of clearance. It's well protected. I wouldn't worry about it."

He nodded and followed her out.

Hayden trailed along down the hall and to the right, past everyone else who was going about their day as if nothing happened. No one really acknowledged him, nor cared that he could now walk, but many of the military personnel acknowledged Miss Sharp. Perhaps they didn't have a clue who he was. He was still invisible. Wheelchair or not. Dead or not.

Or perhaps Miss Sharp just cast a very large shadow.

"I see you're popular everywhere," he noted, as many men tipped their hats to her and greeted her with smiles. Their desperate desire for her attention was almost sad.

"Truthfully, while sometimes it gets old, I do like the attention," she said, speaking over her shoulder as she walked. "Makes things a bit easier for me."

"In what way?"

"Well, it took me a long time to get men to take me seriously in my field of work, so I weighed my advantages as a woman and began playing to those strengths." She shrugged as she used her weight to pull open a door. "May as well use what I got."

Hayden shrugged too. "Can't argue with that."

Upon entering the R.A.V.E.N. communications room, Dr. Stolly was standing between a giant printing machine that took up half of the entire floor space and a dark brown wooden desk with a landline phone sitting on top of it. There was a typewriter pushed off to the side, and Dr. Stolly held a paper in his hands.

"Listen to this," Dr. Stolly said just before he began reading off of the paper. "Susanoo is a wild, impetuous Japanese deity associated with the sea and storms." He looked up at Miss Sharp and Hayden. "He's basically a god."

Hayden rubbed the back of his head, hand moving down toward the back of his neck. "He said Ama— Ama…" He struggled to remember the name.

"Amaterasu?" Dr. Stolly asked.

"Yeah—Amaterasu—she forgave him. Forgave him for what? Did she send him here?" Hayden frowned and chewed on the inside of his cheek as he looked at Miss Sharp. "To the—land of the living? Did she make him human? I didn't think I'd ever say those words in that sentence…"

Miss Sharp hesitated to answer, avoiding his eye contact.

Dr. Stolly didn't know much, either.

"Unfortunately, there's still a lot we don't know," Dr. Stolly admitted.

"Do you, by chance, know where Dr. Susanoo left his journal?" Miss Sharp asked.

Dr. Stolly rapidly blinked behind his glasses and shook his head. "I haven't seen it. But I have to go back to Philly. This is bigger than we ever imagined."

"Well, no shit. Gods? And—and Death's scythe? I can't even wrap my head around it and I came back from the dead."

"No offense," Dr. Stolly began, "but I'm a lot smarter than you."

"A lot shorter too," Hayden mumbled.

"Alright, enough." Miss Sharp held up her hands between the two men. "This isn't a pissing contest. Listen, we need to find that journal if we want any chance at stopping Commander Mori and Yamata no Orochi."

As if on cue, alarms began blaring as red lights flashed in the hallway and throughout the building.

"Security breach! Security breach!"

The sound of a human stampede thundered in the hallway and shook the entire building as though the footsteps competed with the screeching alarms.

Miss Sharp and Hayden exchanged glances.

"The artifact!"

CHAPTER EIGHT

Hagåtña, Guam, April 11, 1942
1109 — local time

Commander Isamu Mori's division, Yamata no Orochi, named after the legendary eight-headed and eight-tailed dragon, grew rapidly on the small island of Guam in the wake of Japan's hostile takeover. The division was founded at the prime of Nurarihyon's friendship with Susanoo many years ago and it sprang to new life near the end of the first world war in 1918. It was a group Nurarihyon wanted to lead with Susanoo, and together they would bring the end of humanity, but the desires each of them followed had diverged down two very different paths. While Susanoo was playful in his chaos, he meant well, not harm. Nurarihyon, on the other hand, was eager and spiteful. Passion brought them together, but their disagreements about humans drove them apart.

Still, Nurarihyon was clever in his learning. He was young when they met. Young, and while he lacked the proper knowledge to do what he was capable of, he was manipulative and cunning. Susanoo opened his eyes, and Nurarihyon knew how to work him in ways that flew right under his nose for centuries.

Nurarihyon would always smile fondly at that fact as he would think back on all he went through to get to where he was. Even if it wasn't what Susanoo intended, Susanoo still played his part in all of it. A very critical part, too. Without him, Nurarihyon wouldn't have gotten this far. Before they met, he wasn't even sure where to begin with his quest to bring about the night parade of one hundred demons. Hyakki Yagyō would end the world as they knew it, and he was so close, he could taste it.

"Our dispatched agent has sent notice that while the mission failed, Susanoo has disappeared entirely."

Nurarihyon's thoughts were interrupted by the bad news.

He slowly turned around, his bare feet shifting against the ground as he did. The soldier who came to deliver the news seemed apprehensive, and for good reason. The young Japanese man fiddled with his cap and tried to avoid staring at Nurarihyon's elongated head. In truth, many of the soldiers hated when he didn't wear his cap. Perhaps it was the reminder that he wasn't actually human that they hated most.

"What do you mean he *disappeared*?" Nurarihyon raised his eyebrows toward the end of his sentence, his curiosity piqued by the words.

The Imperial Japanese soldier bowed his head to continue avoiding looking at him directly. "Well, he— uh—he vanished, sir." He threw his hands up in the air as if to ask for surrender. "The working theory is Amaterasu forgave him and he's a god again. So he's not here in this realm. He isn't on this plane. He's gone."

Nurarihyon made a 'tsk' noise with his mouth, his tongue clicking against the back of his teeth, as he shook his head. He made the same noise, again and again. He picked up the cap in front of him and adjusted it on his head to step back into his role of Isamu Mori. He let out a disappointed sigh through his nose.

"And he didn't even stop by to say goodbye." Commander Mori turned back to face the shrine created for Tadeo. He watched as the incense continued to smoke. "I guess that means he can't interfere with my plans."

The Imperial soldier chewed on the inside of his cheek. Hesitantly, he started again, "Well, actually—"

Commander Mori scowled, narrowing his eyes as he turned around. "What else?" he snapped, and the soldier tensed where he stood. He flinched, as though he were afraid Mori would hit him.

No, Mori would do a lot worse than that if it came down to it. Still, for the time being, he kept his composure.

"Apparently there was a survivor—well, not really a *survivor*. He couldn't be called a survivor, I guess. He died. Technically speaking." The soldier frowned at his own words as he tried to put together a more comprehensible sentence and took a step back from Commander Mori before he continued to speak. Just to be on the safe side. Commander Mori took note of his movements, but was focused on his words. "When we—when we bombed Pearl Harbor, one of the casualties...he—um—he came back to life. Our intelligence tells us he died and came back to life."

Commander Mori grew impatient and took a step toward him as he tilted his head and raised his eyebrows. "And?"

"The exposure to the artifact... apparently enhanced him, in some way. He could be potentially threatening to your plans. Susanoo was working with him, but we don't know how far along things had gotten—"

"He *could* be?" Commander Mori's brows were still raised as he probed for more information. What was Susanoo doing with this man? Who was this man? "He is, or he isn't." Mori demanded clarity.

CORPSE WALKER: THE NIGHT PARADE | 137

The soldier shook his head as he shrugged. "It wasn't specified, sir. We don't yet know what exactly he's capable of—if anything—aside from resurrection."

"Then I'm not worried," Mori said dismissively as he returned his attention back to Tadeo's skull. "When will the blade of the scythe be retrieved from Hawai'i?"

"I was told it should be soon," the soldier assured.

Commander Mori nodded in approval. "Good. What about Midway?"

"That, I'm not sure."

Commander Mori tilted his head down. "Well, we still have time, but I would like all pieces in my possession as soon as possible." He reached out his gloved hand to stroke Tadeo's skull fondly. "I have waited centuries for the parade—" he admitted, though mostly to himself. "What's a little longer?"

Commander Mori was old, but patience was not lost on him. Slowly, he looked over at the soldier who waited to be dismissed.

"What about the Americans? The ones who fled."

"We're still searching for them."

"Search harder," he growled. "It's an island," Commander Mori muttered under his breath as he waved the soldier away.

They had received word that there were at least five Americans still somewhere in the jungle on Guam. Five.

That was five too many. Five who escaped, and had no intentions of surrendering. While Commander Mori himself was not threatened by their presence in Guam, the Japanese had a reputation to protect, and it was in jeopardy. As long as there was American life in Guam, Imperial Japan would appear as just another country, and one that couldn't even do a proper takeover of another territory. They had to be feared.

Commander Mori looked back at Tadeo's skull.

Hagåtña, Guam, April 15, 1942
1344 — local time

A few days passed without another message from their secret agent. Nurarihyon stood in the courtyard without his cap, proudly displaying his elongated skull, feeling less and less as though he needed to keep his true form hidden. Other pieces of his demonic appearance were beginning to show; his lips thinned and his teeth spaced further apart as his confidence grew in the night parade.

Tadeo's spirit was shifting in the wind above him. Nurarihyon raised his hand and pointed at the Japanese official directly ahead of them. Tadeo's translucent head tilted as he looked at his owner, and Nurarihyon nodded

CORPSE WALKER: THE NIGHT PARADE | 139

in encouragement. Tadeo sprinted through the air, leaving a trail of gray smoke as he ran right into the official, who shook violently as the demon dog took possession of his body.

Once he stopped convulsing, Tadeo cracked his neck as he adjusted in new human form. He looked at the ground through human eyes, then at the hands of his new host body. It was foreign.

"Can you walk, my old friend?" asked Nurarihyon, watching the official from where he stood. His brows raised, eyes bulging with curiosity.

Tadeo looked at him through the official's dark eyes. He tilted his head, as if not understanding what his master was saying to him. He stared at Nurarihyon intently, now narrowing his eyes.

"Tadeo?" Nurarihyon furrowed his brows, awaiting a response.

The man looked down at the ground again, hands still outstretched as he wiggled his fingers and shifted his feet against the dirt.

Something wasn't right.

"Tadeo…" Nurarihyon said again, growing slightly impatient with the silence he was greeted with. It was disrespectful.

With the Japanese official fighting against Tadeo, the dog had trouble binding to the man's body. His dog face temporarily split from the human host before binding again, and then split once more. The man looked at Nurarihyon and let out an inhuman growl before charging at him. Nurarihyon outstretched his arm with his hand open wide as he shoved Tadeo back, sending the human body into a trunk of a nearby tree, splitting it from the force.

"How dare you!" Nurarihyon snapped, enunciating each word as he approached his dog. "After everything I've done for you, you choose to disobey me?"

Tadeo sat up in a daze. He reached to rub the back of the human's head, but Nurarihyon was having none of it. Without even touching him, Nurarihyon outstretched his arm again. Tensing his hand around the body in front of him, Tadeo and his human body began to choke, his eyes turning a bloodshot color of red while his skin purpled.

"I—I—"

Nurarihyon raised his eyebrows and tilted his head. "What was that?"

Tadeo gasped for air. "I'm—I' m—" he wheezed.

Nurarihyon released him.

"I'm sorry," he uttered as he collapsed against the tree again, his hands rubbing at his throat. He didn't have a moment to be surprised by his own voice—not his voice, the man's. "He is rejecting me."

Nurarihyon narrowed his eyes, staring at the body at his feet. "Perhaps we need a host who is already de—"

"Nurarihyon—"

He cut himself off as he turned around and inhaled sharply.

"What now?" he scowled at the Imperial Japanese officer who had interrupted them. The officer's eyes grew wide. He backed away and lowered his eyes. They all feared Nurarihyon, and his appearance only heightened their fear and obedience.

"I—I'm so sorry to interrupt, sir," he said, "but we found activity—for the Americans who escaped capture. We believe one has radio communications."

Nurarihyon clenched his fists so hard that his knuckles cracked. Radio communications meant they could potentially contact Americans or their allies for rescue. Nurarihyon scowled at the news. The soldier took another two steps back, eyes still averted, while he looked at the ground. He was careful to not look at the soldier at Nurarihyon's feet, either.

"Find them!" Nurarihyon snapped. He looked back at his dog, still sitting on the ground, before continuing. "Torture any Chamorro natives who may be hiding them, and when you succeed, take them all to the jungle for execution."

142 | RALYNN KIMIE

The soldier's eyes widened. "Execution?" he asked. "We aren't taking them prisoner?"

"They escaped. They had their chances to be held prisoners. They will not make a fool of Japan," Nurarihyon said sternly. "We, instead, will make an example of them for their decisions."

"Yes, sir."

As soon as the Imperial guard left, Nurarihyon addressed his dog, "Tadeo, get up." His voice and instructions were stern and clear.

Tadeo obeyed without question, despite the fighting of the human soul actively working against him. Every now and then, the face of the dog spirit would temporarily split from the human host when the soul of the soldier tried to force him out of the body. This only lasted a second or two before binding again. Fortunately for the Inugami, the longer he was in the body, the stronger he was becoming when it came to total control of it. He shifted his feet and cracked his knuckles. He looked down at the ground, embarrassed by his failure.

Nurarihyon inhaled deeply, searching within himself for forgiveness. It wasn't his Tadeo who betrayed him, it was the soldier. He approached Tadeo and lifted his hand to stroke the side of Tadeo's new human face and beneath his chin, hooking it with his index finger. "We need a dead host, hm?"

Tadeo looked down, averting his now-human eyes.

"Look at me, Tadeo."

His dark brown eyes looked up at his master. He nodded reluctantly. His eyes were red and watering. "I'm sorry I've failed you."

Nurarihyon shook his head, not taking his eyes off of him.

"Loyalty is hard to come by, my old friend." Nurarihyon's words were meant for comfort. He continued to stroke his cheek. "You did not fail me, Tadeo. You are still adjusting to this form. You will get stronger," he assured with a nod. "I promise. I will help you get stronger."

"Yes, master."

Nurarihyon removed his glove to reveal an old, frail-looking hand covered in paper-thin skin with long fingernails that curled over. He gently scratched beneath Tadeo's human chin, and Tadeo's spirit was freed from the body. The host soldier dropped to the ground, and Tadeo remained free in the air. The soldier coughed on the ground, his body burning like it had been lit ablaze. He rubbed at his throat, and slowly looked up at Nurarihyon, who was staring down at him. The soldier quickly scrambled to his feet, somewhat discombobulated with the occurrences that had just transpired.

"You were fighting my Tadeo," Nurarihyon said as he circled the soldier and returned the glove to his hand.

"Fighting my Tadeo and then attacking me." He kicked behind the soldier's knees, forcing the man to drop back to the ground with an immediate thud.

"I'm sorry!" he cried, nearly kissing the ground. "It wasn't on purpose. I didn't know what was happening. I didn't know I was—"

"Being possessed?"

The soldier sighed in defeat. He stared out at the grass before him, unable to find the words to defend himself.

"I was fighting for my life," he came to admit. "I thought I was dying."

"You should have." Nurarihyon kicked the soldier in the center of his spine, causing the man to fall forward from the blow and land face-first into the ground. He barely missed the roots of the nearby trees that likely would've broken his nose or chipped his teeth upon impact.

Nurarihyon looked up at Tadeo, whose dog form perked his ghostly ears and tilted his head. He watched as Tadeo looked down at the man, and then back up at him. Tadeo seemed to feel somewhat remorseful. "I am a merciful man," continued Nurarihyon, as he placed his gloved hand to his chest. "But if you attack me again, fighting possession or otherwise, you won't have a life worth fighting for." Nurarihyon extended his hand to Tadeo, who nuzzled his fingers. He then excused the soldier, who didn't waste a second scrambling away, not even fully returning back to his feet. Nurarihyon turned his head to watch the man pathetically crawl away, making a few attempts to get up, only to fall back down in his hurry.

He sighed and shook his head. "It's so hard to find good help these days," he said to Tadeo, looking back at his one true best friend. "Humans are pathetic and worthless." He gently stroked the underside of Tadeo's snout, just above his neck. "Soon we won't need to deal with them at all, will we?"

The night parade of one-hundred demons would change everything. He was excited for the future. To watch the demons walk the earth.

Humans didn't deserve the earth.

Humans were the ones who destroyed it.

Humans destroy everything.

They were their own plague, and they would cause their own downfall.

Hagåtña, Guam, April 17, 1942
1329 — local time

Another few days passed without word from their agent. Commander Mori paced the laboratory as Dr. Sauer fumbled with something at his workstation.

Commander Mori then lifted his cap to run his gloved hand over his head before placing it back down securely. His facial structure shifted slightly between the human-passing flight commander and his true demonic look.

An Imperial soldier entered the room. Both Commander Mori and Dr. Sauer looked over at him upon entry. He bowed his head almost immediately. The Commander and Dr. Sauer exchanged glances before Commander Mori waved his hand, giving the soldier permission to speak. He already knew it wasn't good news just by his body language.

The man was stiff and hesitant.

Even before he spoke, Commander Mori sighed.

"Sir, there has been another mission failure."

"It's just one thing after another, isn't it?" Commander Mori clenched his jaw as he began collecting a few items from the lab. Though Commander Mori was mostly talking to himself, Dr. Sauer couldn't help but take it as a jab at him as well. The Commander waved the soldier away, and he left quickly.

Commander Mori headed for the door after him.

"Where are you going?" Dr. Sauer asked. His blond hair was tousled, glasses slightly bent in the center and likely needing repair, but Dr. Sauer didn't exactly have the time to go to the eye doctor for another pair.

"To Japan," Commander Mori replied without turning around as he grabbed his coat from the rack. "I have something I need to take care of that I evidently need to do myself." It was becoming clearer to Commander Mori that others could not be relied on. "If you want something done right, do it yourself, correct?" he asked, wondering aloud if that was the proper saying. Not that he cared enough to wait for Dr. Sauer to correct him if he were wrong. With his cap still firmly on his head, he looked back at Dr. Sauer. "I won't be long. Please do not deliver me any bad news when I return."

Dr. Sauer nodded, even though it was something he had absolutely no control over.

"I'll do my best, sir. Be safe."

Commander Mori shook his head.

"I don't need your well wishes, Sauer. No one will harm me."

Nurarihyon was a powerful Yokai. He was mysterious, but supreme, and everyone respected him—especially in Japan. More importantly, however, was the fact that almost everyone *obeyed* him. There were very few beings who had the strength to resist Nurarihyon. And in Japan, among humans, those brave opponents were almost nonexistent.

But it wasn't exactly fear that caused everyone's obedience. People just lacked their own free will to choose otherwise. Humans were sheep to Nurarihyon. If he would miss anything about humans after the parade, it would be their faith to blindly follow. It would be their small brains needing others to think for them because they lacked the sense to think for themselves. Mori took one last look out of the window near the door. The Imperial Japanese military stood outside. He wouldn't have gotten as far as he did if it wasn't for them, and not because they were remarkable.

While their help was not great, their numbers were.

CHAPTER NINE

Marine Corps Base Hawai'i, April 21, 1942
0746 — local time

Hayden settled on his bed in the squad bay. His arm was tucked beneath his pillow while he stared up at the ceiling, going over all of the events that occurred only a few weeks before. His mind was still in the midst of trying to process that his legs worked, and every so often, he'd catch himself shaking his leg or wiggling his toes just to make sure it hadn't been a dream. Everything until that moment had been full of insanity, so out of this world, that even he had a hard time believing it to be his reality. He came back from the dead, he could walk again, and a man disappeared right in front of his eyes. No, not a man. A god. Hayden furrowed his brows. Dr. Susanoo was a Japanese god. What did that even mean? What did any of this mean? He exhaled deeply and ran his hand over his chest while his other shifted beneath the weight of his head.

Turning on his side, he looked down and noticed a piece of paper sticking out from beneath his mattress. Furrowing his brows again, he remembered the map Dr. Susanoo had left behind. Hayden sat up and reached for it. However, it was more than just the map. The map itself was sticking out from being tucked into the pages of Dr. Susanoo's journal. He readjusted himself in his bed as he flipped it open. A note was attached to the page of the map that fell into his lap.

I believe the artifact is still in grave danger, and it isn't wise to keep my journal anywhere near it. Should they come for me, I will leave it with you and hope you find it. Only you will have the means to protect it.
Be well, Sergeant Dáithí.

Hayden frowned. There was a gentle sadness that overtook him for a brief moment, knowing he would never see Dr. Susanoo again. He flipped through a few more pages, but most of it was written in formulas, codes, and languages he didn't understand. Upon hearing footsteps behind him, he shoved the journal back under his mattress and turned to see the Colonel. Hayden cleared his throat.

"Colonel Richards?" he said as he scrambled to get up.

CORPSE WALKER: THE NIGHT PARADE | 151

"You can sit." Colonel Richards said dismissively. Just as Hayden started to sit down, the Colonel handed him an envelope. "You can go back to your small-town Pennsylvania life now and be at *peace*," he spat.

"What?" Hayden frowned again as he opened up the letter. "Dishonorable discharge?" he said, reading it out loud as he looked up at the Colonel. "What? Why? I came back. You wanted me to come back, and I came back!"

"You also faked your death."

"I didn't fake my—"

Colonel Richards cut him off. "You didn't report that you came back to life and paraded under the guise of Howard Davey. It's a dishonorable discharge for desertion." Colonel Richards jammed his finger into the letter in Hayden's hands. "You're lucky you're getting off with this. You ought to be arrested. Now pack up your things and get out of my sight." Colonel Richards didn't wait for him to say another word. He made it clear that the conversation between the two of them was over.

Hayden stared at the paper. The lettering of the dishonorable discharge seemed to mock him. He tightened his fists as he scowled. His eyes flashed black. Dark green smoke flickered around him, taking subtle shapes of translucent beings. Part of his body turned invisible as rage seared through his veins.

"Whoa."

Hayden looked over to see a corporal standing there, jaw dropped, as his sandwich hit the floor, falling in an open splat. The translucent spectral beings that surrounded him quickly disappeared as his body wavered back into sight.

"Do it again," the corporal urged, his eyes lighting up.

Hayden scowled still. He grabbed the journal from beneath his mattress and left the barracks, pushing past the corporal without another word. The corporal shouted after him to wait, but he didn't listen. Hayden hurriedly passed several people outside as he searched for Dr. Stolly or Miss Sharp.

"Dáithí!"

Hayden turned around to see Sergeant Kamuela. His eyes were bright, a smile flashing at the sight of his best friend standing on his two feet. He was animated, his entire face lit up. "You can walk! It worked!"

For a moment, Hayden stopped in his tracks and looked down. He could walk. It was amazing, the things people took for granted every day. Mundane things such as walking. He had only been walking again for a couple of weeks, and his time in a wheelchair seemed like a faint memory.

Still, the experience of it humbled him. He could walk again. He could run. He hoped he'd never take that for granted ever again.

Hayden smiled as he approached Sergeant Kamuela, who was still looking at his legs. "Yeah, it's been pretty great." He nodded, shifting on his feet.

Sergeant Kamuela's gaze finally rose to meet his. "Do you know what else you can do?"

Hayden thought about what had just happened only minutes ago in the barracks. He frowned slightly as the corporal's surprised yet intrigued face flashed in his memory and his exclamation for him to 'do it again' as if he were a dancing monkey putting on a show. Hayden wasn't entirely sure what he had done in the first place—or how. He shrugged his shoulders.

"Not quite," he said finally.

Sergeant Kamuela frowned, tilting his head slightly. "Dr. Susanoo didn't start the trials?"

Hayden's expression faltered. "Wait—you haven't heard?"

"Heard what? I've been so busy—"

"Dr. Susanoo's gone."

"What do you mean, *gone?*" Sergeant Kamuela frowned again at his words, then a skeptical smile slowly crossed his face. "This is a joke, right? When's he coming back? We need to get you out there! In the war!"

"No, he's *gone,* gone. He's not coming back, Charlie."

"What? This doesn't make any sense. Did he go back to the Japanese? Did h —"

"No! No, he didn't betray us." Hayden looked around. He tugged on Sergeant Kamuela's sleeve as he pulled him to the side, away from anyone else. He lowered his voice. "Dr. Susanoo was a god."

Sergeant Kamuela laughed. "You're messing with me, right? That doesn't make any sense."

"I came back from the dead, Charlie. Nothing makes sense."

Sergeant Kamuela tilted his head in acknowledgment.

"Got a point." Sergeant Kamuela snaked his arm around the back of Hayden's neck. "Come on, let's go grab a drink."

Hayden fumbled with the journal in his hands as he pulled away from him.

"You know, I really need to find Miss Sharp or—"

Sergeant Kamuela's ears perked up.

"Miss Sharp?" He looked around as he began straightening his shirt. "She's something pretty, ain't she?"

Hayden nodded in agreement as he shrugged. "Yeah, she is. I guess. You shoulda seen all the guys at the factory trying to get her attention. It was hilarious."

Sergeant Kamuela laughed. "Bet they have fun with that. I can't even get her attention."

"I warned you."

"Have you tried?" Sergeant Kamuela asked.

Hayden scoffed. "I don't need that bruising my ego. I know what I can get."

"Are you really turning down a challenge, Hayden Zachariah Dáithí?" Sergeant Kamuela tilted his head as he arched a brow.

"Full name now, huh?" Hayden rolled his eyes.

"Come on," Sergeant Kamuela said, hitting the center of Hayden's chest with the back of his hand. "It can't hurt to try."

"Uh yeah, it can. And we work together."

"Come on."

"She was my boss," Hayden said, tucking the journal under his arm.

"Even better."

"No."

"What are you two doing?"

Hayden turned around to see Agent Dacua standing behind him. Her hair was down again, resting against her shoulders.

"You look taller," she noted with a soft smile.

"Well, that's what standing up will do for you." Hayden shrugged and tilted his head. "You should try it."

Sergeant Kamuela snickered behind him. Agent Dacua narrowed her eyes before her smile broadened. She simply shook her head, her hair rustling gently.

"Someone thinks he's funny," she noted.

"Oh, I know I'm funny."

Agent Dacua shook her head and continued on her way through the parking lot.

"So that's why you don't care about Miss Sharp," Sergeant Kamuela said. Leading with his head, he moved to stand in front of Hayden and walked backward to remain in front of him.

"What? That?" Hayden looked back to acknowledge Agent Dacua. "Agent Dacua?" He shook his head and rubbed the back of his neck.

Sergeant Kamuela raised his eyebrows, insinuating something that wasn't there.

Hayden laughed as his eyes grew small and he scrunched his nose. "Oh, no, no, no. Nope. Dr. Stolly likes her and I'm not getting in between that. They can have each other. I have bigger things to worry about." He readjusted the journal tucked beneath his arm. "But speaking of, I need to find him or Miss Sharp."

Sergeant Kamuela raised a finger. "I pick Miss Sharp."

"Of course you do." Hayden extended out his arm before them. "Find her then, you bloodhound."

Sergeant Kamuela adjusted his cap, and he gave Hayden a toothy grin.

"It'd be my pleasure."

Pua's Tiki Bar, O'ahu, April 21, 1942
2055 — local time

They found Miss Sharp in a small bar not too far from the base. Hayden had no idea how Kamuela managed to find her, but he didn't question it either. The thing with Sergeant Kamuela was that he had a way of getting almost anything he wanted, when he wanted it. And if not when he wanted it, it would happen in the near future. It wasn't that Sergeant Kamuela was particularly bright—or gifted, as he'd put it—or wealthy enough to buy his way through things. Most of the time, he just had luck on his side.

Most of the time.

Sergeant Kamuela of course didn't waste a minute and made a beeline to Miss Sharp the second he spotted her. But even then, this time, his luck seemed to work against him when it involved Miss Sharp. Her attention was immediately directed to Hayden as soon as he approached the two of them.

"It's good to see you up and walking about," she said, looking down at his legs before lifting her gaze to meet his.

Hayden chuckled, shaking his head.

"Everyone's got jokes." He turned slightly toward the front door to acknowledge the stairs leading up to the entrance. "But I did notice this place isn't wheelchair accessible."

Miss Sharp's expression fell slightly as she nodded her head. She pursed her red lips together for a moment. "Most places aren't, unfortunately." She took a deep breath and looked up at Hayden with her large brown eyes. "Sergeant Kamuela said you have something for me?" she asked, as Sergeant Kamuela dismissed the man sitting beside Miss Sharp and took his seat at the bar.

Hayden nodded, pulling the journal into his hand from being tucked beneath his arm. "I found this under my mattress. I think maybe Susanoo went to find the map he left behind and just left me his journal." Hayden shrugged.

"Well, it makes sense he thinks you'd be the best person to protect it, given your abilities—and situation," she said, looking at the note Dr. Susanoo had left behind.

"You mean my dishonorable discharge?" Hayden asked plainly.

Both Miss Sharp and Sergeant Kamuela frowned.

"Your what?" they spoke in unison before glancing at one another. Sergeant Kamuela smiled at her, and Miss Sharp frowned back.

"Yeah, desertion."

"You didn't tell me about this," Sergeant Kamuela said. His tone, expression, and overall demeanor had changed from the charming one he had been trying to work on Miss Sharp, to serious and somber.

"It happened right before I ran into you. Colonel Richards dropped it off." Hayden rubbed at his temple. "I had a lot on my mind—and the—the—" he just acknowledged the journal rather than saying anything further aloud.

"He's a dick," Sergeant Kamuela said.

"Literally."

"Colonel Dicks," the two men said as they laughed.

Miss Sharp rolled her eyes as she muttered something about boys being boys under her breath. "This will be so helpful," she said to them as she looked down at the journal. "Dr. Stolly and I have been running in circles trying to figure out exactly what kind of trials Dr. Susanoo had planned for you."

"You guys weren't let in on it?"

Miss Sharp sighed. "We were, and we weren't." Hayden and Sergeant Kamuela exchanged glances with one another as Hayden took the empty seat on the other side of Miss Sharp. "Dr. Susanoo said the plans were... unsafe. He didn't want to put either of us in danger, so he kept a lot of the information to himself. Everything was handled on a need-to-know basis."

"He did mention not thinking his sister would forgive him," Hayden said, and Miss Sharp nodded.

"His sister?" Sergeant Kamuela leaned forward on the counter to join the conversation. "What—is she a goddess?" he asked, before waving the bartender down to order a drink for himself and for Miss Sharp.

Miss Sharp and Hayden exchanged glances with one another and shared a smile before they both looked back at Sergeant Kamuela.

"What?" he asked innocently. "I'm just trying to keep up." He then thanked the bartender as he placed two drinks down on the counter before Sergeant Kamuela.

"You didn't get me one?" Hayden asked, feigning offense.

"This is only for people with jobs."

Hayden raised his eyebrows. "*Oh, okay*. You crumb."

"Fathead," Sergeant Kamuela snickered.

Deciding it was better to be on the safe side, the three of them eventually moved to a table in the corner to be away from any prying eyes and ears. Miss Sharp was nose-deep in Dr. Susanoo's journal, fascinated by all of his notes and drawings that documented his work dating back for centuries. His journal was a record that could be dangerous in the wrong hands.

Commotion arose in the bar that pulled her attention from the pages.

Military police swarmed Pua's Tiki Bar.

Several of the patrons wondered aloud what was happening as they verbally asked one another, and then the police. What were they doing there? There were no unruly drunks, and everyone was having a merry time.

Four cops approached the table in the back of the bar. Two remained at the front door, and two were working their way toward the back exit. Sergeant Kamuela noticed them first. He gently kicked Hayden's shoe beneath the table.

"Sergeant Dáithí?" one of them asked.

"It's Dáithí," Hayden corrected as he turned around just as Miss Sharp looked up. She quickly closed the journal and slipped it into her purse before gently cupping her drink with her hands, hoping none of them had noticed. Hayden's expression softened at the sight of the policemen. "Yeah?" He shifted in his seat to face them.

"You're under arrest," the cop said. With his finger, he acknowledged Hayden to get up and turn around, and Hayden obliged without protest.

He got up from his seat and turned to face the table. Sergeant Kamuela and Miss Sharp exchanged glances with one another as the police officer bound Hayden's wrists and cuffed them behind his back.

"What's going on?" Sergeant Kamuela asked the officers as he also got to his feet. "What are you doing?"

But the officers barely acknowledged him.

"This doesn't concern you, Sergeant."

"Excuse me, officers, do you know who you're arresting?" Miss Sharp asked as she too stood up and moved around the table, standing between the police and the doorway. "He's part of a special division working with the Marine Corps—"

"We know what we're doing, Miss Sharp." The officer seemed as though he didn't want to give her any orders. His expression was twisted into one that showed both concern and reluctance. "Please, step aside," he instructed kindly.

She sighed, looking at Hayden as she stepped out of their way. Her eyes were sullen, but Hayden didn't look at her as the police escorted him outside. Miss Sharp looked over at Sergeant Kamuela who slowly shook his head.

"I'm guessing you guys didn't see the newspaper from this morning," said the bartender as he brought one over to them from the counter. "To be honest, I didn't even recognize the Corpse Walker, and he was sitting there right in front of me." The bartender mumbled something about the lights being too dark as he waved his hand overhead and trudged back to behind the bar.

"Corpse Walker?" Miss Sharp said, reading the headline aloud. "A lab in Japan littered with the imperial flag was raided by U.S. troops—found to belong to... Dr. Susanoo." Her heart sank. "Bringing to life his own

CORPSE WALKER: THE NIGHT PARADE | 163

Frankenstein monster, we're led to believe he plans to do significant damage to the United States of America through his Corpse Walker."

"Frankenstein?" Sergeant Kamuela scoffed. "Frankenstein was the doctor, not the creature. Who wrote this article?"

"First of all, you're a square," Miss Sharp said, not being able to ignore his comment. "Secondly, you're completely missing the point."

"Well, what exactly are they saying? Are they calling him a terrorist?" Sergeant Kamuela asked, looking down at the article from over her shoulder. "Dr. Susanoo?"

"This is unbelievable," she said, tracing Imperial Japan's flag with her finger. "None of this is true. It can't be."

Sergeant Kamuela rubbed at his chin, still looking at the article. "I wonder if that's why the Colonel gave Dáithí desertion. So he wouldn't have to deal with it. Deal with—*this*. There's no way he didn't see this."

Miss Sharp blinked rapidly. She tucked her hair behind her ear. "But Dr. Susanoo wasn't a terrorist," she exclaimed as she shifted through the newspaper articles. "Dr. Stolly has known him for quite some time. We would've known this a long time ago if he had any ties with the Empire of Japan. His loyalty was to us, not to them. His history with

Mori—he wanted to fix everything. They weren't on the same side. I know—I know this for a fact."

"Where is Stolly anyway?" Sergeant Kamuela asked.

Miss Sharp frowned, caught off guard by his question. "I don't know, but that's beside the point, too." She pointed her finger at the newspaper article. "I know this is wrong. He wasn't a terrorist."

"I'm not who you have to convince," Sergeant Kamuela said.

Miss Sharp looked down at the paper, her expression sullen. She stared at the pictures of Dr. Susanoo and Hayden. "You're right, but I have to prove their innocence."

"Good luck," Sergeant Kamuela mumbled, slumping down into the seat.

"Oh, I won't be needing luck."

Sergeant Kamuela tilted his head in observation as Miss Sharp's expression changed from pouty to determined. He watched as she folded up the newspaper and tucked it into her purse. She grabbed her drink and downed the rest of it. His eyebrows rose in surprise.

"My kind of woman," he said, awestruck.

Miss Sharp placed the glass back onto the table and looked over at him. She was fighting back a smile that threatened to surface at the corner of her lips.

CORPSE WALKER: THE NIGHT PARADE | 165

"Boys…" she teased softly with a slight shake of her head. She nodded toward the door. "Come with me, Kamuela."

"Oh, I've been waiting for you to say that," he said, scrambling to his feet.

Miss Sharp immediately fished the newspaper out of her bag and smacked his shoulder with it. "Oh, stop it," she said. "Your friend was just arrested. Have some compassion."

"It was worth a shot," Sergeant Kamuela said, shrugging. "Where are we going?"

CHAPTER TEN

The United States Marine Corps shipped Hayden Dáithí back to Pennsylvania like cargo on a steamship. The entire trip took nearly three weeks, as it—and he—had been deemed 'low priority'—especially in comparison to the raging war of the world. It was the intent of the government to keep him under the radar, as he was now considered precious cargo, despite not being treated as such. Now that there were newspapers printed and reports being given on him, his whereabouts needed to remain a mystery before he fell into the wrong hands.

Though he had been arrested, Hayden was kept in the medical facility at the R.A.V.E.N. base in Harrisburg rather than in a cell. His room was padded and white, and he spent most days in a straitjacket aside from the couple of hours they needed each day to draw his blood. His face was scruffy, his blond hair grown and unkempt. But

Hayden tended to pull away from anyone attempting to shave his scruffy face or trim his hair.

On his first day in the facility, a nurse came in to explain they would take exactly a hundred milliliters of blood every day, which went well over the weekly limitations. However, due to his new and unique genetic makeup which had been altered, rearranged, and revitalized by Death's scythe, the frequent blood loss didn't have lasting effects, if any at all.

The nurses were always kind to him, more or less. There was even a nurse who would bring him a newspaper on occasion, typically at least once a week. But the basis of their kindness seemed to stem from fear rather than compassion. Sometimes they had stories about the 'Corpse Walker,' but most were just fictionalized tales by people he'd never met before. At least until he came across the story told by the corporal who saw him in the barracks. That one was true—and perhaps the most spine-chilling. Hayden couldn't really remember what happened, but it was terrifying to read from another's point of view.

'Spirits manifested around us—around him—waiting for orders as though he'd awoken those who died in combat,' the article read.

It was safe to say that the majority of the other nurses didn't seem to be kind to him because they were genuinely nice. They were kind to him because they were afraid of what he might do if they weren't. If he moved a little unexpectedly, they'd flinch.

"What's wrong?" he asked Alice, the nurse currently tending to him. She was a slender woman, small in frame. Her blonde hair was always neatly pulled back. She often wore a bright red ribbon in her hair and not much makeup, but she didn't really need it either. He had only readjusted himself in the chair, yet she flinched as though he raised his hand at her.

"Nothing," she answered meekly.

"You're afraid of me, aren't you?"

Her eyes lifted, but not enough to look at him.

"Is everyone?" he asked.

She lowered her eyes. Alice nodded very subtly, before quickly gathering the blood bag and the materials she'd used to be disposed of outside of his room. She stopped at the door and turned to look at him, though her eyes still refused to meet his.

"We all are, to some extent," she said quietly. "We don't know what you are."

Before he had the opportunity to say anything, she let herself out and locked the door behind her.

We don't know what you are.

Hayden rubbed at his arm where Alice had punctured it with the needle. He peeled the bandage off and tossed it on the floor. He looked at the backs of his hands, then his palms, then back again. Her words echoed in his brain.

We don't know *what* you are.

He was pale in color still, the fleshy tone of a white male. There was still the pinkness of life in his fingertips.

They don't know what I am—what am I?

He closed his eyes, remembering what Dr. Susanoo had said.

Sergeant Dáithí is dead.

Harrisburg, Pennsylvania, May 29, 1942
0746 — local time

Hayden sat back against the wall, looking up at the extremely bright interior of his new home. At least it was clean, he supposed, and they fed him three meals a day. He could sleep whenever he wanted and as much as he wanted, aside from the blood draws and meal times, but boredom crept in. With boredom, he spent too much time in his own head.

"What do you do with all of my blood?" he finally asked a nurse one day.

While holding the needle in its place in his vein, the nurse paused. She was short and chubby, while the majority were tall and thin—aside from Alice, who was both short and thin. Her strawberry blonde hair was pulled tightly back, and she always wore unique earrings that resembled fruits. Every day Hayden saw her, the nurse's earrings revealed a different fruit. Today they were strawberries. She glanced up at him and scrunched her eyebrows together as though she were looking for an answer in his expression. Hayden raised his own eyebrows in curiosity.

"Um," she started off, which didn't sound very promising to him at all. "I don't really know how to answer that, Mr. Hayden."

Definitely not promising, though he was mildly amused that she always called him Mr. Hayden. It was likely she didn't know how to pronounce his surname. Most people pronounced it wrong.

"I'm not following," he said.

"Well, look." She acknowledged the blood in the bag. "Do you see how dark your blood is? It's practically black. It's bright red upon drawing, but it seems to just…"

"Die?"

"Almost immediately," she said, nodding. "We keep drawing, hoping for a good sample, but we can't seem to get one."

"Well, what's it for? What would it be used for?"

She shrugged. "Truthfully, I don't know, Mr. Hayden. I'm just here to draw your blood. They don't really tell us much else."

The nurse went back to work when Hayden nodded and turned away, as it was clear she couldn't answer any of the questions he had. She curiously looked over at the pile of newspapers and acknowledged the one on the top of the stack.

"Is that one true?" she asked. The one at the top was the one regarding the man in the barracks. "They publish a lot of stories about you—but that one's from a Marine stationed in Hawai'i."

Hayden sighed, and when he didn't answer nor look back at her, she didn't press. She knew better than to do so.

Time seemed to stand still in the medical facility. He didn't see outside of those four walls. There was a bathroom but not much else, and eventually, they stopped stuffing him into a straitjacket altogether when they realized he wasn't going to do anything. Nevertheless, he never actually got to leave the room. It felt like he hadn't seen Dr. Stolly or Miss Sharp in months, and the only news he got about the war was from the papers that were infrequent and far in between.

In the outside world, the battle of Midway began.

Marine Corps Base Hawai'i, June 5, 1942
1011 — local time

Dorothea Sharp smoothed her thick brown hair as she fixed the headband on her head. She inhaled deeply and sat back in her chair, before smacking the surface of her desk with her palms in frustration.

"Zander, we've been at this for months!"

Her hands closed into tight fists that she continued to gently pound against the edge of her desk. She shut her eyes and crinkled her nose.

Dr. Stolly had his head in his hands, rubbing his temples for a minute as he stared blankly at the text in the journal. "I don't know what you expect me to do. I said I need help. I can't read Old Japanese." He took his glasses off, dropped them on the table, and rubbed his eyes. "I'm not a genius, and apparently, neither are you."

Miss Sharp cocked her head and raised her eyebrows.

"Excuse me," she said, "you don't have to be rude."

He rubbed his temples again. "Sorry."

"This just isn't my line of work," she admitted quietly.

"Is it anyone's?" He sat back in his chair and grabbed his glasses before rubbing out the smudges with his shirt. He stood up and returned his glasses to his face as he paced the floor, something he often did to help him think.

"Dr. Susanoo's." Miss Sharp sighed, she then began shaking her head. "But we are still not bringing in the Republic of Letters."

He turned around. "They could help!"

"We don't know who we can trust," she said, fixing her headband again, despite it not being out of place. "We're in the middle of a war!"

"I thought R.A.V.E.N. was all about sharing knowledge with the world?" Dr. Stolly said with a mocking tone as he sat back down.

Miss Sharp rolled her eyes. "Technically, I'm not part of R.A.V.E.N. and have no interest in sharing anything."

"That's a surprise."

She shrugged.

"My business is with the Manhattan Project. Fermi and his team achieved the first self-sustained nuclear chain reaction, you know." She rubbed her neck and beneath her jaw. "But I don't want it to come to that." Miss Sharp placed her hands calmly on the desk she sat at, and looked up at Dr. Stolly. "Look, getting frustrated with one another isn't going to solve anything. Dr. Susanoo must have known that sooner or later, his sister would forgive him and that he would disappear."

"Or he just hoped. We don't know how long he's been a mortal. Wasn't he originally arrested for terroristic threatening? Because he knew what Nurarihyon was planning?"

Miss Sharp nodded. "R.A.V.E.N. bailed him out, but now look where we are." She shook her head. "Even still, he left this book to Hayden. If we can't even figure it out, how was he supposed to? We helped Dr. Susanoo. If anyone is going to figure any of this out," she said as she picked up the journal and flipped through the pages. "It's us."

"We don't have the resources, Dot. Not without the Republic or R.A.V.E.N. It can't just be up to you and me. We need help."

"I'll get the resources. I'll get whatever it is we need." She straightened her posture. "But it has to stay a secret."

Dr. Stolly sighed, then nodded. "Alright, I yield," he said, pushing his glasses up the bridge of his nose. "No Republic of Letters and no R.A.V.E.N.—I promise."

"Thank you."

"I guess that means I'm learning Old Japanese in the meantime."

"How long do you think it'll take you?"

"I don't know—as much time as you can get me, I guess. I don't really need to learn how to speak it, so that'll save time. Reading it though—" he looked over the characters. "I mean, some of these are Chinese characters—"

"You know Chinese?"

"I was learning. I thought it could be useful."

"You're a square." Though it was a joke, and she did half smile, her smile faded quickly. "Do you think we're going to win this?"

Dr. Stolly looked up at her from where he sat, chewing on the inside of his cheek. He looked away for a moment to scan the room and to look down at the journal. He pursed his lips together as his expression grew into one of concern. "I honestly don't know, Dottie. I don't know what's going to happen. With the war, with Nurarihyon, with Sergeant Dáithí. I mean, we're going up against demons. Nurarihyon is known for being elusive. He is literally the demon that cannot be caught. But maybe with this—" he turned to a page depicting a strange weapon neither of them had ever seen before. "Maybe this will help. But we need to know what all of this says first before we create anything. There's not really much room for error." He pointed at one of the characters. "I'm pretty sure this is 'summon.'"

Miss Sharp pursed her lips together and clenched her jaw as she looked at Dr. Stolly. "We have to get him out of there. Hayden's just rotting in that cell after everything Dr. Susanoo did to help our military and R.A.V.E.N.—"

"We will, but there's no point until we know what we're doing. Things are at a high right now. It'll calm down and we'll have a better chance when it does."

She nodded and grabbed her jacket.

"Where are you going?" Dr. Stolly asked as he started to stand.

"We need somewhere to work if we're going to do this by ourselves," she said as she put on her jacket. "I'm going to see what's available before I have to go back to New York." She pulled her hair from beneath the collar of her jacket to let it rest on her shoulders. "Are you going to be okay?"

Dr. Stolly shrugged. "No one's coming after me. I might head back to Philly, though."

Miss Sharp raised an eyebrow and started crossing her arms.

"Not for help," he clarified. "But I may need to do some further research. I can only do so much from here without certain texts."

"Fine. I'll meet you there then. I'm going to make a stop in York as well."

"For what?"

She gathered up the local newspapers regarding the Corpse Walker. "I'd like to talk to Hayden's family. Kamuela has their address."

"You don't think that might put them in danger?"

"They deserve to know," she said. "They already lost him once."

178 | RALYNN KIMIE

He nodded as she kissed his cheek and gave him a hug. "Be careful, Zander. And I'll see you soon, alright?"

"Yes, ma'am."

"Don't call me ma'am. You know how that makes me feel."

"You aren't even old."

"But I feel old!" Miss Sharp said dramatically as she flung open the door. "I could be someone's mother."

"I can't imagine you as a mother," Dr. Stolly chuckled.

"Honestly, me either." Miss Sharp shook her head at the thought. She waved him goodbye and went on her way. Dr. Stolly looked at the journal and sighed. He had no idea how he was going to pull off learning Old Japanese in such a short amount of time.

Harrisburg, Pennsylvania, June 6, 1942
0746 — local time

"Are you holding my son hostage?" Mrs. Quartermaine threw the newspaper at the young woman sitting at the desk near the public entrance door. The paper scattered onto the floor, a drawing of Hayden pictured on the front. It appeared as if Máiréad had gotten word about it early in the morning, shortly after she'd just woken up—if she hadn't been woken by the news itself. Her usually perfect hair was a bit frazzled and pulled back into a messy updo. Her clothing had a few wrinkles. Her face was without a spot of makeup, and her regularly bright blue eyes had darkened. She smacked the counter with the palm of her hand out of both impatience and urgency. "Where is my son?" she questioned with demand. "Take me to my son!"

The receptionist had trouble keeping Mrs. Quartermaine calm. She pursed her lips together and stood up. There was inner panic that reflected in her green eyes, and she struggled with finding the right words to say. She tucked her brown hair behind her ear. "He's—um— he's government property, Mrs—Mrs. Quartermaine. Now—now if you would please just—"

"Oh no," she started to laugh, which only frightened the young woman further. "He most certainly is *not* government property," Máiréad snapped. "You better take me to my son. I know he's back there. You've been keeping him here for months—"

"Mrs. Quartermaine, please! I'm going to have to call security if you don't calm yourself!" Her hand was reaching toward the phone, and Máiréad grabbed her wrist.

Agent Dacua witnessed the commotion. She had been Hayden's first official visitor. She typed in the access code as she watched the commotion from the sidelines and walked into the back. Hayden was being kept in room 117. She knocked softly on the door prior to opening it, and her jaw dropped slightly at the sight of him. His hair was a mess, and his face was scruffier than she'd ever seen.

"You look—"

She chewed on her bottom lip. She couldn't finish her sentence.

"Handsome?"

"Awful," she stated, stepping further into the room. She closed the door behind her. "Dreadful—partially dead—"

"Thanks."

"You look like you aren't getting enough sleep—"

"For fuck's sake, Elaina. I got it."

"Sorry, I got carried away." She wandered around the room, looking at the white walls, but she stopped at the radio beside his bed. "When did you get this?" she asked.

Hayden shrugged.

"It doesn't work, anyway."

"Or you just don't know how to turn it on." Agent Dacua fumbled with the knobs of the radio and it came to life, a voice crackling through the speakers. "I Don't Want To Set The World On Fire" by The Ink Spots began to play. She turned it down a little softer. He looked at the radio, noting how nice it was to hear music again. Hayden closed his eyes for a moment and listened.

"I'm guessing you didn't hear about the battle at Midway," she said, looking at the newspapers gathered on the ground. She shuffled them with her feet as she examined the dates on them and noticed the stories involving Corpse Walker. "All of these appear to be at least a few weeks old."

Hayden's eyes shot open, and he immediately got to his feet.

"There was a battle at Midway?"

Agent Dacua made a face. She crinkled her nose and closed her eyes before touching her forehead with the tips of her fingers. "Maybe they were keeping that from you on purpose," she said quietly, as though she just let out a secret.

"What happened?" Hayden moved closer to her and tilted his head. "Who was victorious?"

"Oh, the United States, thankfully. But—they got it," she sighed. She returned the radio to the small table.

"The second piece?"

Agent Dacua nodded, her gaze lingering on the radio still.

Hayden cursed under his breath as he turned around. He slammed his fist against the padded wall, which made no sound and cushioned his hand instead.

"There's a crazy woman—Mrs. Quartermaine, I think—outside yelling at the receptionist," she said in an attempt to change the subject. "It's something else."

"Wait," Hayden said as he turned around, frowning. "What? Mrs. Quartermaine? Are you sure? That's my mom."

"Oh—" she frowned too. "Your mom?"

"How did my mom even get to Harrisburg—she doesn't drive."

Agent Dacua shrugged.

"I don't know, but she was screaming about them not letting her in. To come see you, I guess." It dawned on her. "Oh, okay, that makes sense now."

Hayden sat back down on the bed. He clenched his jaw and rubbed the back of his neck, unsure of what to say.

Agent Dacua rocked back and forth on her feet. She then clapped her hands together.

"Well, I have to head to Baltimore—would you like me to escort your mother back home?"

He nodded. His brows were still scrunched together in a frown.

"Anything you want me to tell her?"

"Yeah—tell her that I love her, and I'll be home soon." He looked up at Agent Dacua from where he sat. "I promise."

Agent Dacua smiled. "Of course."

Hayden nodded a thank you. Agent Dacua leaned down to give him a hug, but turned her head and attempted to kiss him. Hayden turned away and pulled back from her, causing her to end up kissing his cheek instead. He looked up at her, frowning further as he stood up.

"What the hell, Dacua?"

"What?" she asked, perplexed. "I thought—"

"No," he said sternly. "You? No."

"It's Miss Sharp, isn't it," she said, rolling her eyes. "You like Miss Sharp. Of course you like Miss Sharp. Who wouldn't like Miss Dorothea Sharp?" she mocked.

"What? No. And if I did, that wouldn't be any of your business anyway." Hayden shook his head, waving his hand. "I have too much on my mind—"

Agent Dacua let out a small sigh, tucking her hair behind her ear as she stared at her feet. "Fine," she said quietly. "Alright, I understand. I'll see you, Hayden. Good luck."

She didn't wait for him to say anything, nor did she touch his shoulder like she normally did when she wished him good luck. Hayden hummed as he sat back down on his bed, listening to the song playing softly on the radio; "Stardust" by Artie Shaw.

The next person to come brought him dinner, but Hayden seemed to have lost his appetite as he stared at the bland food with lack of interest.

He sat in the same room of the same facility for months without another visitor. While some of the restrictions lightened up as the weeks passed, he still wasn't allowed out. He wasn't allowed to call his mom or have any visitors who didn't work for R.A.V.E.N. directly. He received a few messages saying Sergeant Kamuela had been asking about him, but he wasn't able to respond to anything. It was like they were trying to erase him. While he was there physically, this wasn't living. This was existence. Though, there were some days where it didn't even feel like that.

Through the little window of his door, he saw the hallway decorations change with the seasons. The fake spiderwebs, then cornucopias, and then paper snowflakes.

It wasn't until December that he was finally transported to an actual cell.

CHAPTER ELEVEN

Harrisburg, Pennsylvania, December 5, 1942
1900 — local time

Out in the hallway, awaiting transport, Hayden stared at the doctor, who he knew ordered the collection of his blood samples. His nose was buried deep in someone's file, and he paid no attention to anyone else around him.

"You all sure you won't be needing any more blood?" Hayden asked, his tone dripping with sarcasm. The medical staff only looked at him, barely glancing in his direction. His wrists and ankles were both cuffed to the transport wheelchair he sat in.

"We have more than enough of your useless blood, Corporal," the doctor said, talking down to him. Hayden balled his fists in annoyance. The condescending tone was one he wasn't fond of. "It's gotten us absolutely nowhere, and it's been an absolute waste of my time."

"I'm a sergeant."

He scoffed before a satisfied grin crossed his face. "Not anymore."

Hayden mumbled expletives under his breath before clenching his jaw.

"They really are trying to take everything from me…"

"Hi, Mr. Hayden?" One of the nurses had approached him in the hall. He remembered her; she always donned a friendly yet timid smile on her face. "I'm not sure if anyone's told you, but—sorry, I'm going to move you. I hope you don't mind—" she wheeled his chair over to the small television screen at the nurse's station.

The U.S. Navy stood publicly to address the losses of the attack on Pearl Harbor nearly a year ago to the day. Hayden's expression hardened as he watched the footage. They had video of the harbor being bombed, footage of the USS *Oklahoma*. Hayden wanted to close his eyes, but he also couldn't look away. It was the day he died. He swallowed hard, trying to absorb the lump rising in his throat. He could feel it again, drowning. He exhaled deeply and looked down at his hands cuffed to the armrests of the transport wheelchair. He clenched his fists. "I know it doesn't mean much," she began, her voice bringing him back. "But I'm very sorry for everything you've endured—and I can't begin to imagine…" Her voice broke as it trailed off and she squeezed her eyes shut.

CORPSE WALKER: THE NIGHT PARADE | 187

Hayden looked up at the nurse. Her earrings today were no longer fruit, but were small little gingerbread men. The corner of his mouth twitched.

"It's *dawhee*, by the way."

She opened her eyes again and tilted her head as she looked at him.

"I'm sorry?"

"My last name. It's Irish—it's dawhee. I sorta figured you weren't saying it because you didn't know how to pronounce it—a lot of people don't."

"Oh," she said, and a smile brightened her face. "Mr. Dáithí."

"Anne."

Her eyes widened a little as her brows raised. "You know my name?" She seemed both surprised and delighted by that fact.

"I know all of your names," he said with a nod. He looked around the facility at the familiar faces of the nurses who had come to draw his blood. Eventually, his eyes landed back on hers. "But you're the only one who bothered to learn mine. So thanks for treating me like a person, Anne."

Her genuine smile took up half her face. Though her eyes were glistening from watching the news on the television, they seemed to change from sadness to delight. "It was my pleasure, Mr. Dáithí." Her tears dampened her lashes and instantly he could see now all the reasons she had become a nurse in the first place. To connect with people, to help. Anne was in fact a remarkable nurse who clearly didn't get the recognition she deserved.

"I do hope we run into each other again one day," he said.

Anne only smiled. She opened her arms and stepped forward but then stepped back. "Do you mind if I give you a hug?" she asked.

Hayden raised an eyebrow playfully before finally nodding.

Anne quickly wrapped her arms around him and squeezed him tightly.

"I think you're going to do great things, Sergeant Dáithí." Anne's voice was different now, her lips brushing up against his ear. "My brother trusted you. Don't let him down." As she pulled away, the face of a beautiful Japanese woman adorning a crown that represented the sun appeared where Anne's once was.

"Amaterasu?"

He blinked several times. Surely he was seeing things.

Anne looked up at him now, tilting her head.

"What was that, Mr. Dáithí?"

"Uh—I'm—uh—gonna miss you?" he said quickly, as an agent came to fetch him for transport. "I said I'm gonna miss you."

Hayden looked around, but no one else seemed to have noticed what just happened. Maybe his mind was playing tricks on him. Maybe he was seeing things. He couldn't get it out of his head as they loaded him into the van.

He looked up at the rearview mirror, and saw her again, sitting beside him. But when he glanced to his left, she was gone. Now he was being haunted by a Japanese goddess.

So much for *peace*.

***

For months, Hayden continued to sit in an iron cage in the United States Disciplinary Barracks in Leavenworth. From his window, he watched the seasons change from winter to spring, and then to summer. Every hour, his vitals were taken. Every day, he was fed three meals. It was consistent, but boring. No one had told him where he was being transported to, or why, just that he would not be staying in Harrisburg.

At least the blood draws had stopped.

He also never got another visit from Amaterasu.

There were moments when he thought he saw her— out of the corner of his eye, or out through the window in the reflection of the glass—but every time he would turn to look, she was never there. Perhaps she was there and he just never caught her, but if she could visit him, why not Susanoo?

Hayden sat at the edge of his bed, feet bare and flat against the floor. His eyes were closed. He thought long and hard about the storm god and the sun goddess, convinced that maybe he could manifest them, or summon them somehow. But every time he opened his eyes, he was alone.

He was always alone.

This was surely not the peace he had hoped for. This was a different kind of hell. To be alone with one's thoughts when you couldn't sort them all out was torture, and he hated it. But every time he looked at the wires of his cage, he just sank back and accepted this as his fate.

Some days he was angry.

Hayden punched at the cement brick wall. Once, twice, three times, again and again till his knuckles bled. It only started as a crimson red, and quickly darkened to a mahogany shade. He looked at the backs of his hands, outstretched before him with the thick, dark liquid coating his skin. Turning his hands over, he watched the blood run like sap, slow and steady. He curled his left hand into a fist and took another swing.

CORPSE WALKER: THE NIGHT PARADE | 191

This time, his hand went right through the wall. His jaw nearly hit the cement as his body fell forward. He took a step to stop himself. With a creased forehead and a crinkled brow, he stared at his hand that was still inside of the wall. Slowly, he pulled his hand out. He could see a translucent outline of his hand, but its solidity was gone. Hayden put his hand through the wall again, and then out once more.

Beneath his eyes, he could feel the slight burning of his veins darkening in his face. He looked over at the fence of his cage and stuck his hand through before stepping through it entirely. He crept up the stairs and slipped through the door.

The halls of the United States Disciplinary Barracks in Leavenworth were desolate. For a known maximum security prison, he surprisingly saw no security.

"I'm sorry, you want us to do *what* with him?"

Despite being invisible, Hayden stopped in his tracks and pushed his back flat up against the wall when he heard voices streaming from an office. What he failed to realize was that he would go right through the wall.

There were two men on either side of a desk. One looked like a R.A.V.E.N. officer, while the other behind the desk wore a Leavenworth uniform.

"He's on death row, awaiting execution."

192 | RALYNN KIMIE

The man behind the desk quickly raised his brows, eyes slightly bulging in surprise.

"How exactly do you expect us to kill someone who already died?" he asked, scratching the side of his head. "Can he even be killed?"

Hayden took a step back. They were talking about him.

"I guess we'll find out."

"And if it doesn't work?" the guard asked, crossing his arms. "I don't think that's someone you want to piss off."

"We'll cross that bridge when we get to it."

Hayden couldn't recognize the R.A.V.E.N. officer, only the emblem he wore. Not wanting to hear anything further, he took another step back and left the room. He stood in the empty hallway, looking one way, then the other. He briefly considered escaping—but wouldn't that only make him look guilty of the crimes he didn't commit?

So instead, he returned to his cell on the lower level, and he sat there.

Alone, waiting to die.

About half an hour later, four security guards came down. Hayden was sitting on his bench, the back of his head resting against the wall when they approached his cell. One of them held iron shackles in his hands.

"It's a little early for birthday presents," Hayden said as one of the guards unlocked the gate. He tilted his head.

"Something happened with your security footage," the beefy guard holding the shackles said as he and another man stepped into the cage with Hayden.

"It's just a precaution," the other added. "Strongest we have."

"Sure," Hayden said simply, outstretching his hands. "If that'll help you sleep at night."

The fat security guard holding the shackles raised one of his hands, and Hayden's expression darkened, as did the veins in his face.

The other guard cautioned against hitting him.

Instead, the security guard collected himself and bound Hayden's wrists and ankles with the iron shackles. Noticing the dried blood on Hayden's hands, the guard looked over at the wall.

"Stop making a mess down here," he said, pointing a meaty finger at the wall. "I hope you intend on cleaning that up."

Hayden rolled the back of his head against the wall to look at the bloodstains. He shrugged and redirected his attention back onto the guard.

It wasn't worth his breath.

Leavenworth, Kansas, July 21, 1943
1855 — local time

Hayden sat there for several more months, waiting for his time to come. He'd be lying if he wasn't curious about what would happen during the execution. Could he die again? Would he just get resurrected again?

It was nearing the end of July when Miss Sharp finally came to see him. Over a year had passed since he slipped her the journal in the bar. Upon being escorted to his cell, her eyes widened, but only briefly, and much too quick for Hayden to have seen from where he sat. The guard left the two of them, and she took the liberty of stepping toward the gate of his cage. Hayden's face was scruffy, his unwashed hair stuck up in twenty different directions, and his eyes were sunken into his skull. He was locked away like an animal, deep down in the darkness, as though they were hoping he'd be forgotten.

"Are those iron shackles?"

"The strongest they have." Hayden sat back on the bench. He didn't get up, and he didn't look at her. Instead, he stared at his wrists. "Though I don't think they realize I'm only here because I'm allowing it." He lifted his left arm, and his arm instantly lost its solidity. It slipped right out of the cuff. He glanced back up at her as he moved his wrist back into it.

She was still staring at his wrists like she'd just seen a ghost. In a way, she had. "Well, I would appreciate it if you continued to behave, Sergeant Dáithí, or they'll never release you to me."

"Didn't you hear?" Hayden raised his eyebrows. "I'm not a sergeant anymore."

Miss Sharp pursed her lips together. "You'll be reinstated once you're cleared."

Hayden just shook his head.

"I can leave whenever I want to—"

"Then why haven't you?"

Hayden didn't answer her. Instead, he just looked down.

"I figured running would make me look guilty, and..." He stared at the iron cuffs. "I didn't know what might happen to you and Stolly if that were the case."

Miss Sharp squinted at him.

"Let's do this the right way, please."

Hayden's stare was unfocused, and he leaned back against the wall.

She sighed as she paced in front of the cell. She looked down at her hands holding her cardigan. "You know when you first arrived at my factory, I didn't want to hire you. It was my father who suggested that we did because we'd

196 | RALYNN KIMIE

need all the help we could get. Personally, I thought you'd be more trouble than you were worth."

"And what do you think now?"

"That I was right."

He chuckled, but the amusement faded.

"Did you know they were going to do this to me?"

Miss Sharp shook her head as she turned to face the gate.

"I had no idea." She chewed on her bottom lip as she fished out a comic book from her bag. "It could be worse—you could be on a stage wearing tights and selling war bonds."

Hayden glanced at the Captain America comic book in her hands.

"Well, I'd rather be a celebrity."

"I promise it's not all it's assumed to be." She inhaled deeply and tilted her head as she looked at the comic before returning it back into her bag. "Did you hear about Japan?"

Hayden shook his head.

"No one's told me anything about the war since I got transferred here." He looked down at his hands. He used his nail to dig into his thumb. "There are days where I forget we're even in the middle of one."

"Oh—I figured they'd tell you because—" she smiled. "The Admiral and Commander-in-Chief of the Imperial

Japanese Navy—the architect of the attack on Pearl Harbor—he was shot down by one of our own, an Army fighter pilot."

Hayden slowly stood up. His iron cuffs clanked about as he moved.

She nodded. An eager smile quickly spread across her face. "Naval intelligence intercepted and decoded a message that included the itinerary for an inspection tour the Admiral was making. The tides are turning, Hayden."

"What is today?"

"July 21, 1943."

Hayden sighed and averted his eyes. "I've been in this cell for two hundred and twenty-eight days." He stared at the gate ahead of him.

Miss Sharp could feel her heart sink.

"You counted?"

"Seven months and sixteen days," Hayden said, keeping his attention on the gate. He then shrugged. "I didn't exactly have much else to do."

"Well, it's been two hundred and twenty-eight days too long," she said. "I think it's time to get you out." She placed her hand on the fencing of the door. "Dr. Stolly and I have been working on deciphering the text in the journal. While we aren't Dr. Susanoo, we've managed to make tremendous progress. And with the war and everything else happening—we lost track of time. I—I—I'm sorry it took so long."

Hayden watched as a guard came with the keys to his cage.

"Wait," he said as he took a step closer to the door. "I'm getting out? Right now?" he asked a bit eagerly. The guard looked hesitant to approach him now, but Hayden raised his hands up in surrender and took the same steps backward.

Miss Sharp nodded in regards to his questions and smiled.

"I paid to have you released to me." She looked at the guard and tilted her head toward Hayden. "Let's go," she said, commanding him to open it up.

The guard then did as he was instructed.

"I thought there wasn't a price—" Hayden's voice trailed off as the guard came into his cell and unlocked the iron cuffs. Hayden didn't take his eyes off of the guard, and the guard didn't take his eyes off of him. It was the same guard who cuffed him in the first place, filling Hayden with some satisfaction, though he wouldn't say it outloud.

The cuffs clattered to the floor loudly, and Hayden rubbed at his wrists. The guard then picked up the iron shackles and turned away from him.

"Everything has a price, Hayden." Miss Sharp watched as the guard left the two of them alone. "Just not everyone has the means to pay it." She brushed her hair over her shoulder. "But I'm Dorothea Sharp—and I have a way of getting what I want."

Tired, he asked, "And what is it you want, Miss Sharp?" His blue eyes met her brown ones.

"I want to win the war," she declared sternly.

Hayden nodded. "Let's go win it then."

CHAPTER TWELVE

Clarendon, Pennsylvania, July 24, 1943
0902 — local time

Miss Sharp and Dr. Stolly brought Hayden far north in Pennsylvania to what appeared to be an abandoned lot. There was a small cottage nearby, beside a large wooden barn. Hayden frowned as Miss Sharp opened her car door.

"Aren't you coming?" she asked plainly as she tilted her head challengingly. "Or would you rather go back to your cage in Leavenworth?"

Hayden continued to frown, barely acknowledging what she said.

"Where are we?" he asked.

"My grandparents' place. My grandparents were farmers and enjoyed the simple life, believe it or not." Miss Sharp fondly looked at the old barn. "I used to come here during the summer and spend my days riding horses while my grandparents tended to their animals. Sometimes my grandpa would even let me help him move the cattle."

"Farm girl?" Dr. Stolly asked, eyes wide as his eyebrows rose. "Never would've guessed." He acknowledged her clothing and the way she carried herself. She was always dressed in the finest silks and cottons. Those things were expensive—especially during a war.

"Technically, my dad was a farm boy," she corrected. "But I've never been afraid to get my hands dirty." Miss Sharp looked over at Hayden as she nodded to the barn. "Come on, I have something for you."

"My grandparents left their property to me when they died," Miss Sharp continued as the three of them walked toward the barn. "We've been using it to house experimental research for the Manhattan Project, but since development has progressed rapidly, we were able to move it and the space freed up so now we can use it to house—" she glanced over at Hayden while she spoke, "—other types of experimental research," she finished with a grin as he rolled his eyes. She yanked open the doors. Miss Sharp was a small lady, but she was much stronger than she looked.

The outer exterior gave the appearance that the farm had been deserted decades ago, but the interior was upgraded, reinforced, and well taken care of. Hayden took a step back to look at the cracks between the boards of the barn. He saw himself staring right back. Miss Sharp noticed his observation and went up to him. She watched as he stared at the different spaces between boards, many of which reflected their surroundings.

"Mirrors," she said. "Helps with the abandoned look from afar. People generally just keep moving along. No one really gets close enough to actually look inside."

"Clever. But what if someone does?"

"We have security for that. Now come on."

Hayden furrowed his brows as he looked around for this security. Miss Sharp was clearly full of surprises.

"So what exactly is the Manhattan Project?" he asked as he followed her deeper into the old barn. The tables were made of steel and bolted into the ground. There were shelves attached to the walls that were mostly bare, aside from a few boxes scattered among them.

"All you need to know is that we have a failsafe for the war," answered Miss Sharp with slight hesitation as she turned around to face him. "And it's a button I'd rather not press."

There was a single box sitting on one of the tables. It was long, yet narrow.

"Open it," she instructed, acknowledging the box with a nod.

"What is it?" Hayden asked as he removed the lid.

"It's a whip," she said with a smile as she clasped her hands together excitedly.

"Is that—"

"Yes!" She ran her fingers along the different pieces of the spinous process on the thoracic. "It's a human spine." She took out Dr. Susanoo's journal from her bag and flipped to one of the pages that depicted a drawing of a whip very similar to the one placed on the table in the box in front of him. "It's modeled after the ones the Dullahan carry—Dr. Susanoo called it Marfóir." Her finger then traced along the text written beside it. "Most of his journal is written in Old Japanese. Do you have any idea how difficult it was to find someone who could translate Old Japanese while we're at war with Japan?"

"I imagine very." Hayden's answer was monotone. He carefully picked up the whip from the box. Miss Sharp took a step back as she watched him handle it.

"How does it feel?" she asked, her eyes grew larger. She nearly looked like a child at Christmas time.

"It's lighter than I imagined." He took a few steps back from the table. Tightening his fist on the handle, he cracked the whip against the ground and the joints stretched between the vertebrae, lengthening the whip significantly. Black smoke circled around his hand before disappearing into his veins. "So it extends too? That's pretty cool." He turned it over in his hand as it retracted.

Miss Sharp watched with continued excitement and nodded.

"It also turns into a sword. It's reinforced with vulcanium—stronger than steel, harder than diamond. Corrosion resistant. My dad gave me all he had."

Hayden looked up at her. "What's 'Marfóir' mean?"

"Killer," Dr. Stolly interjected.

Hayden glanced over at him, slightly startled.

"You were being so quiet, I forgot you were here."

Dr. Stolly rolled his eyes.

"But, that's great." Hayden's tone was sarcastic. He looked down at the whip in his hands. "Carrying a human spine whip named Killer will do wonders for my already amazing reputation."

"It's not about reputations, Sergeant."

"Yeah, I know. This just isn't what I had in mind when I agreed to come back."

"I don't think any of us did, except maybe Dr. Susanoo."

"I wonder what made him think of the Dullahan," Hayden said, examining the whip further. "My mom used to tell me stories about them when I was a kid."

"Probably because of your Irish heritage," Dr. Stolly said nonchalantly.

"I never mentioned being Irish."

"Your last name literally screams at everyone that you're Irish, Sergeant *Dáithí*."

Hayden opened his mouth to protest, but then tilted his head as he went over how one might draw that conclusion. Dr. Stolly had a point that Hayden had never really thought of. "Touché." He did flinch somewhat as he said it. Despite how often it might happen, Hayden didn't exactly like admitting when someone else outsmarted him.

"My guess is a lot of this was after his discovery of your existence," Dr. Stolly said, acknowledging how far into the journal the notes were. "He probably figured the beliefs of your ancestors would be your strongest connection to whatever abilities the scythe bestowed upon you, rather than Japanese ones that he would be most familiar with." He acknowledged the whip. "Does it feel like it belongs to you?"

"I'm carrying a human spine—that isn't mine." He furrowed his brows at the realization as he turned to Miss Sharp. "Where did you even get a human spine?"

She gave a pained smile.

"People donate their bodies to science. I'm sure this person would be honored to aid the Corpse Walker in the war against Nurarihyon."

Hayden cringed, closing his eyes at the mention of that title. "You guys are going to start calling me that too?"

CORPSE WALKER: THE NIGHT PARADE | 207

"It is kind of cool," Dr. Stolly said, hesitantly scratching at his chin. "It's almost like having a hero name. Like Captain America."

"Yeah, but he's America's new hope. I'm—"

"The walking dead?"

Hayden scowled, narrowing his eyes at Dr. Stolly.

Dr. Stolly was more than amused with himself.

"Enjoying this, are you?" he asked.

He shrugged and crossed his arms, a smug smile still plastered on his face.

"Anyway," continued Miss Sharp, referring back to the text. "According to the journal, Marfóir can be used to expel demons or even kill them. Dr. Susanoo has a theory that demons or souls get absorbed into the spine, which only strengthens it. Nurarihyon is apparently known for being a demon that cannot be caught. We're not trying to catch him though, are we? We're trying to kill him."

"I don't really want to kill anyone."

"He's trying to end humanity," Dr. Stolly said.

Hayden clenched his jaw and sighed.

"Well, a theory doesn't exactly sound promising." He looked down at the whip in his hand as he turned it over to examine it. He cracked it again, this time a little quicker and swifter, but it didn't solidify into a sword like he had hoped it would.

"He's been right about everything else so far, Hayden."

That was something he couldn't exactly argue with. Dr. Susanoo believed the artifact would make him walk again, along with giving him other abilities he didn't quite understand. All of which were true.

"As long as the only thing it's killing is demons," he began, accepting his weapon and its name. "Then maybe Killer's not so bad."

"It doesn't sound as cool in English."

Hayden and Miss Sharp both looked at Dr. Stolly who only shrugged. He blinked rapidly at the two of them and rubbed his neck awkwardly.

"What? Tell me I'm wrong. Killer and Marfóir just don't have the same effect."

Hayden just stared at him blankly and raised his eyebrows, while Miss Sharp tilted her head in an obviously judgmental manner.

"What's with you and things sounding 'cool'? First his hero name and now Marfóir—did you join the Republic of Letters because it sounded *cool*?" she asked, her glare fixed on him as she crossed her arms.

"Maybe," he answered quickly.

Miss Sharp rolled her eyes, exasperated. "You're unbelievable."

"I'm kidding!" he said. "Learn to take a joke, woman. My family founded the first intelligence salon on American soil in eighteenth-century Philly." He cocked his head and pointed at Miss Sharp. "And you know it, Dottie. Your great-grandmother was an Intellectual. So don't be trying to pull this shit with me."

"Yeah, but it's funny when you get all worked up over it."

"How long have you two known each other?" Hayden asked. His gaze swept back and forth between the two of them.

"I've changed his diapers," Miss Sharp said with a laugh. She then shook her head and closed her eyes, once more thinking about how old she was getting.

Dr. Stolly was now unamused as well. "Yeah, yeah. We're not getting into that. Don't you have somewhere to be?" he asked her.

Miss Sharp checked her watch and gasped. "Oh, no! I'm going to be late." She turned to Dr. Stolly. "Listen, everything you'll need is in the warehouse or the cottage to help Hayden with training." She then turned to Hayden and tilted her head sympathetically. "You will be kept here where it's safe until you are needed. Understand?" she asked, but he doubted she actually expected him to answer that.

"Until I'm needed?" He raised his eyebrows as he began rolling the whip up in his hands. "What does that mean, exactly? Needed? I thought I was supposed to go up against this demon and you want to keep me on a farm?"

"You're not ready!" Miss Sharp insisted.

"That's not the only reason," added Dr. Stolly.

Hayden looked over at him, waiting for him to elaborate.

"She's going to try to talk to the Colonel about your return to O'ahu first."

Miss Sharp shot Dr. Stolly a disapproving glare.

"He's going to say no," said Hayden. "I mean, he had me arrested—he kept me in prison—gave me a dishonorable—"

"That wasn't his decision. He has orders too, you know." Miss Sharp stepped up to Hayden. "We all have our own parts to play in all of this, Hayden. Just focus on yours." She headed for the door. "I'll be in touch."

The two of them watched from the doorway of the barn as she got into her car and hurriedly began driving away.

"She does that, doesn't she?"

"Comes and goes when she pleases?" Dr. Stolly responded. "Yeah…"

Hayden turned around. He had the whip rolled up in his left hand. He raised it and pointed a finger at Dr. Stolly. "So am I fighting you?" he asked, slightly amused.

"No, we are not fighting. I'm training you."

"Sounds like fighting to me."

CORPSE WALKER: THE NIGHT PARADE | 211

Dr. Stolly sighed. "That's what dummies are for—and the only one I see is you."

Hayden grinned. "Watch it, Stolly."

Dr. Stolly chuckled and nodded, standing down. He raised both hands to his chest in surrender before turning his attention to the journal Miss Sharp had left on the table next to the box that formerly contained Marfóir. He returned the cover over the box and pushed it to the top of the table's edge.

"How are you and Dacua?" Hayden asked while he continued to examine the whip in his hand, still having trouble accepting he was holding a human's spine—and as a weapon.

Dr. Stolly's gaze was unfocused, and he seemed to avoid looking at Hayden. "Barely seen her, honestly. R.A.V.E.N. has her running around quite a bit. We were a thing, and then we weren't. Then we were, and then we weren't. Women confuse me, really."

"Exactly why I don't do 'feelings,'" Hayden said dismissively.

Dr. Stolly sighed. "She's from Guam, you know."

Hayden's expression fell as he shook his head. "I didn't."

"Yeah. Can't really imagine how she's been taking all of that. Can't imagine what it'd be like if Pennsylvania was taken over by the Nazis or something."

"Yeah..." Hayden continued to fidget with the whip. "So you're from Philly?"

Dr. Stolly nodded. "I read in the journal that you were born in Pittsburgh." He thumped on the journal. "What part?"

Hayden scoffed. "You read that? You can read Old Japanese?" He stared at him in disbelief. "You're as white as I am," he said in observation as he stuck out his arm to compare skin color.

"I learned. I'm fluent in seven languages," Dr. Stolly said, turning away from Hayden as he looked through the journal. "Better than having other people translate Dr. Susanoo's journal. We don't know who we can trust and that's not exactly information we can share with just anyone."

"So *that's* what took so long."

Dr. Stolly shot him a glare.

"Seven languages, huh?" Hayden continued, slightly impressed. "I'm not even sure if I speak English correctly half the time."

"You don't."

Hayden rolled his eyes. "Braddock."

Dr. Stolly looked surprised. "That's where George—"

"Washington was supposed to die. Yeah, Susanoo mentioned that. During the Battle of the Monongahela of the French and Indian War."

Dr. Stolly nodded before holding up his fingers to measure out an inch with his index finger and thumb. "I was this close to being impressed by your historical knowledge, so good thing you mentioned Dr. Susanoo first before I made that mistake."

"I swear, you're asking for it."

Dr. Stolly chuckled before referring back to the journal.

"Dr. Susanoo wrote about the trials he wanted to conduct with you if Project Reaper worked—which it did. I didn't have the opportunity to translate all of it into English yet, as Dot and I were so focused on making *that* correctly." Dr. Stolly nodded toward the whip. "I'm not a fighter—or a former Marine," he said as he acknowledged Hayden before referring back to the journal, "or a god, like Dr. Susanoo, but I can follow instructions. So I'm going to translate that for you and we'll go over it before we start. I think there are even some scriptures in here about summoning demons—"

"We're not summoning anything."

"We won't know if you can expel them if we don't have any to expel. We need to know this is going to work before we send you after Nurarihyon. So we have to do the trials correctly. Nurarihyon is considered to be a monster who cannot be caught. We have to take this seriously."

"You think I'm not taking this seriously?"

"Are you?" Dr. Stolly asked, his tone changed. "I mean, you came back from the dead, Sergeant Dáithí. The dead. If I were you, I don't know what about life I would take seriously anymore." Dr. Stolly closed the journal. "So I heard about your little magic trick in the cell—and you scaring the shit out of another Marine. What else can you do?"

"I don't know," Hayden said, running his free hand over his blond hair. "Only one way to find out."

"We better get started then."

Hayden looked down at the whip.

"But we're not trying to catch him anyway, we're trying to kill him. We're trying to kill a demon. What if I can't do this? What if I—"

"Fail?" Dr. Stolly pressed his lips into a line, thumping the journal lightly with his thumb. "Well, then the portal opens, demons invade our world, life ends as we know it, and we all die." He finished it with a playful half-smile.

Hayden wasn't amused.

"Dr. Susanoo believed in you," Dr. Stolly continued earnestly. "Think about it. An ancient Japanese god believed in you. I think that says something."

Dr. Stolly's words reminded Hayden of Amaterasu's visit at the medical facility.

I think you're going to do great things. My brother trusted you, don't let him down.

Hayden clenched his jaw as her voice rang in his ears. The pressure was intense, and as he focused on the whip in his hands, he only felt as though it would increase from there. After all, things often got worse before they got better.

But how much worse would they get?

"What kind of demons are we going to summon?" he asked.

Stolly gave him a slightly creepy smile.

CHAPTER THIRTEEN

Clarendon, Pennsylvania, August 2, 1943
0700 — local time

Hayden was sitting beside the radio, listening to updates regarding the war when Dr. Stolly woke up and made his way out of his room. The two men were situated in the small cottage belonging to the Sharp family. Dr. Stolly had the smaller room in the front, while Hayden took the master bedroom in the back. Dr. Stolly's hair was sticking up in all different ways and he rubbed the sleep from behind his glasses. It took him a second to notice Hayden after hearing the radio. He took notice of Hayden's sandy blond hair, still neatly combed through, and frowned.

"Did you sleep at all?" he asked.

Hayden shook his head. His eyes remained on the radio for a moment longer.

"I feel like I should be doing more. Now that I can, now that I can help..." his voice trailed off.

Dr. Stolly turned the radio off. He glanced down at Hayden, who didn't move. Instead, his eyes shifted to look out the window.

"It'd be foolish to send you in before you're ready, Sergeant."

Hayden nodded once before looking down. He picked at his thumb, crossed his arms, and sat back in the chair.

"You can call me Hayden, you know."

"Would that make us friends?" Dr. Stolly asked.

"Aren't we?"

Dr. Stolly furrowed his eyebrows for a second and nodded. There were few people either of the two men really trusted, and in times of war, it was better to have friends one could rely on. Hayden looked back at the window.

"I spent last night setting up a few dummies out back." Using his thumb, Dr. Stolly acknowledged the backyard over his shoulder.

"So how come you aren't standing outside?"

Dr. Stolly stood there with his jaw hanging, taken aback by his friend's remark. Hayden smiled. Dr. Stolly scowled and rolled his eyes.

"Anyway," he continued, "we'll see how you are with the whip."

"I can use a whip—but how do I turn it into a sword?"

Dr. Stolly shrugged.

CORPSE WALKER: THE NIGHT PARADE | 219

"There wasn't really mention of that in the journals, so I'm not going to be much help with that, I'm afraid. You're just gonna have to figure it out." Dr. Stolly ran his fingers through his messy hair. "I'm going to go get changed. Go get Marfóir and I'll meet you out back in half an hour?"

Hayden nodded, and Dr. Stolly excused himself.

He looked over his shoulder as Dr. Stolly closed the bathroom door before turning back to face the radio. There were so many things happening around the world; people dying, a war raging. But looking out of the window, it looked like just another day. Hayden inhaled deeply and got to his feet. He rolled up the sleeves of his white button-up shirt to his elbows and went to his room.

Marfóir remained nestled in the box it had been given to him in. Hayden took off the lid and placed it down beside the box as he took a moment to examine the spine whip. His fingers gently grazed against each piece that made up the whip, and he still had some trouble believing he was using someone's spine as a weapon—a magical and reinforced weapon at that. He wrapped his hand around the handle and lifted it from the box. In one swift moment, Hayden cracked the whip in the air, making a loud snapping noise. As he turned it over in his hand, he noticed the black running through his veins. When he glanced in the mirror, the same thing happened in his cheeks, running up toward his eyes.

Corpse Walker, he thought, observing his reflection as his eyes turned a very shiny black color. He clicked his tongue against the roof of his mouth and turned away from the mirror.

Dr. Stolly was already outside by the time Hayden went to meet him. Though Marfóir was his to use, it still felt foreign in his hand, and his grip was loose and apprehensive.

Hayden counted ten dummies in a row. He pointed at each with his finger as he counted, before pointing at Dr. Stolly.

"Eleven," he said finally.

"You should be pointing at yourself," Dr. Stolly mumbled.

Hayden stifled a laugh, moving his hand to fumble with the handle of Marfóir.

Dr. Stolly had Dr. Susanoo's journal open in his hands. He looked down, reading through a passage on the page, before looking up at Hayden.

"Alright, so the first one. I want you to hit it on the side of the neck." Dr. Stolly patted the side of his own neck with his fingers. "Just by the rope."

Hayden unfastened Marfóir from his belt and cracked it against the ground. He lifted it in the air, veins darkening in his forearm, as he clumsily aimed for the neck of the dummy. Upon release, he smacked the dummy beside the one he intended to hit.

Dr. Stolly sighed.

"We're going to be here a while."

Hayden stared at the dummy and looked down at the whip before looking at Dr. Stolly. "My aim is usually better than that."

"Sure," he said with a sarcastic nod. "Try hitting the correct dummy, will you? The last thing we need is you whipping everyone except Nurarihyon."

"It won't kill them though, right?" Hayden asked with a hint of anxiety. "Just in case I miss."

"No," Dr. Stolly replied. "Not unless they're a demon. Though you may severely injure them, maybe." Dr. Stolly walked over to the dummy, admiring the tear in the wool fabric. It had ripped it so quickly and so harshly that it was smoking. He looked over at Hayden. "But the whole point of these trials is that you don't miss."

He closed the book as he walked away from the line of fire. Once he was in his own marked safety zone, Dr. Stolly blew his whistle.

"Try again!"

Hayden whipped Marfóir at the line of dummies for hours, till his hand was rubbed raw and bloody. He switched it to his right hand for a moment as he wiped his palm against his pants and closed his fist against the material.

"You okay?" Dr. Stolly asked.

"Never better," he mumbled. "There any rituals in there to heal my hand?" he asked, looking down at the wound.

"Based on your records from when you were in custody, I'm sure that'll be healed by tomorrow morning."

"You were looking at my records?"

Dr. Stolly shrugged. "For science."

Hayden rolled his eyes.

"So when are we going to start summoning some actual demons?"

Dr. Stolly waved his hand dismissively. "Not yet."

Hayden tilted his head as he walked toward Dr. Stolly, rolling up his whip. "But dummies aren't exactly going to attack me," he said. "I have to learn how to defend myself, right? Properly? You're the one who said we would."

"Not yet," he repeated. He didn't look up at Hayden and instead flipped open Dr. Susanoo's journal.

Hayden groaned. "Oh, come on."

Dr. Stolly pushed his glasses up the bridge of his nose and looked over at Hayden. "When you do something impressive, then we'll talk about summoning demons."

Hayden's eyes widened in disbelief. "Do something impressive? Stolly, I came back from the dead!"

"Not by choice."

Hayden naturally opened his mouth to argue, but he couldn't really argue that point. He didn't exactly choose to come back. He just woke up at the morgue.

"Yeah," he began as he leaned back against the peeling, exterior wall of the warehouse and fastened his whip to his belt. "I wouldn't have chosen to come back if I knew I'd be stuck on a farm with you."

"I'm a delight," Dr. Stolly said proudly. He closed his eyes and pressed his palm to his chest.

"Delight must mean something else to you."

Dr. Stolly opened one eye before shooting a glare at Hayden.

Hayden, of course, only smiled smugly.

"You want me to be ready, don't you?"

"As long as we stay on track, Hayden, you will be."

Later that afternoon, Hayden poured alcohol over his wound. It stung differently than it used to, at least differently than it did before he had died. He balled his left hand into a fist and glanced up in the mirror, before having to look again. He spun around and acknowledged his visitor.

"I thought you were gone."

The apparition of Susanoo smiled. He looked exactly the same as he did when he disappeared, only now Hayden could see through him.

"I was—I am. I'm not supposed to be here, but I've been on good behavior. Which is not like me and why I was banished in the first place. I've never been very good at behaving."

Hayden wore a look of relief on his face.

"I wanted to see how you were faring," Susanoo continued. "Well, I hope."

"I missed my first target."

"But you improved?"

Hayden nodded.

Susanoo smiled.

"Will you help us?"

"Win? I'm afraid if it weren't for my interference, none of this would've happened in the first place. While I cannot end it myself, I can only hope we can prepare you well enough to take care of it."

Hayden clenched his jaw.

"I don't know if I can do this."

"Then don't."

"What?"

"You have a great fear of failure. It's why you've insisted on wanting *peace*, right? A resurrected paraplegic who insisted on working in a factory, because you still had to help with the war, somehow, right? Even if not on the front lines, you had to do something. You couldn't just sit at home keeping a low profile. But you didn't want to fail. You didn't want to be rejected. You mask that with your arrogance and your insistence on being a jerk to your friends. Like the way you tease Stolly."

"It's banter," Hayden defended.

"It's hurtful, and rooted in your insecurity."

Hayden averted his eyes.

"But I cannot convince you of what you are capable of." Susanoo pointed at Hayden's chest. "That comes from within. That comes from you. Anyone can say anything, but if you don't believe it, what good will it do you?"

Hayden remained silent.

"Unfortunately, I didn't come to make you feel better, Sergeant Dáithí. But if you aren't ready, you will lose. You will lose so much more than your life." He paused and looked down at Hayden's wound. "Your hand?"

Hayden looked down at his hand. It healed. When he looked back up, Susanoo was gone. He opened the bathroom door and peered into his bedroom. The thought crossed his mind of telling Dr. Stolly, but he figured he should just keep it to himself.

Clarendon, Pennsylvania, October 22, 1943
2026 — local time

Over the next few months, as summer turned into fall, Hayden's aim improved dramatically, and his left hand was calloused from using Marfóir. The grounds were coated in a myriad of crunchy red, yellow, and orange leaves that drifted down from the surrounding trees with the winds that rustled them free from the branches.

Hayden's eyes darkened, veins transferring nether energy as he leaped high in the air. Yielding Marfóir in his left hand, his arm moved over his head and crossed his chest as he attempted to strike the dummy as he landed. But Marfóir solidified into a sword and cut the dummy's head clean off.

Hayden dropped to his feet. He blinked rapidly and his black eyes returned to their normal blues. His jaw hung ajar until realization set in. He closed his mouth, and a smirk peeked at the corner of his lips.

Hayden sliced through the air playfully and looked over at Dr. Stolly, whose jaw was still dropped.

"You look impressed."

Dr. Stolly's expression faltered. He quickly closed his mouth. He knew where Hayden was headed with this. "You didn't mean to do that, did you?"

"That's not the point," Hayden said, pointing the sword at Dr. Stolly. "The point is, you're impressed. You said if I did something impressive, we could take things up a notch."

"Do you even know how to use a sword?"

"I've done a little fencing."

"That's totally different."

"It's not *that* different."

"It's *different.*"

"Oh come on, Stolly. Stop changing the subject! I know you want to. I know you've been waiting to use one of these rituals. You can't be part of the Republic of Letters with basically a demon encyclopedia crafted by a Japanese god in your hands and not be tempted."

Dr. Stolly scowled. He hated when Hayden was right.

"Come on, Stolly. I can do this. Just one demon. One."

"Fine," he said. "But we're starting small. I mean, really small."

Dr. Stolly flipped through the pages of Dr. Susanoo's journal and smiled when he found a page he liked. Hayden narrowed his eyes, not liking the look of amusement plastered upon his face. He cocked a brow.

Dr. Stolly performed a small ritual, muttering a few words in Japanese, and a little umbrella appeared before them.

At first, Hayden frowned. Then he laughed.

"You're kidding, right?" Hayden said, staring at the one-legged umbrella that had one eye. It looked at Dr. Stolly, then at Hayden. "That? You want me to kill that? Look at it. It's helpless."

Dr. Stolly used the book to point at the being.

"That is a murderous Yokai you're talking about."

Hayden tilted his head. "Yokai?"

"Monster."

He couldn't help but scoff. "Is this a joke? I can't kill that."

"You better kill it before it kills you."

"Kill me? It's an umbrella, Stolly."

"Kasa-obake," Dr. Stolly corrected.

"An umbrella—*ah!*" Hayden stumbled backward. "What the fuck?" He stared at the long tongue that slithered out of the umbrella. He took a step back, and holding Marfóir firmly with both hands, he pointed the spine sword at the umbrella Yokai hopping around on one foot. As the wind began to pick up, the umbrella opened, and the Yokai lifted into the air. Hayden's eyes widened as he took another step back, waving Marfóir in the air. "Get it away from me! Get back!" he shouted.

Dr. Stolly covered his mouth to stifle the laugh building in his throat.

Hayden missed the Yokai with every swing he took.

"You're not doing a very good job—"

"Shut up, Stolly! I'm trying to concentrate!"

"Maybe you should turn Marfóir back into a whip—"

"I said shut up!"

Hayden finally managed to swing the spine sword right at the umbrella, causing it to break into a million little pieces. Black absorbed into the sword and the small little pieces faded into the wind. He took a step back and lowered Marfóir. He smiled and looked over at Dr. Stolly.

"Give me a challenge next time."

"A challenge?" Dr. Stolly scoffed. "You were scared of an umbrella."

"*Kasa-obake*," Hayden sneeringly corrected. He clenched his jaw and narrowed his eyes. "And I wasn't scared. It *startled* me."

"Get it away from me!" Stolly yelled, mocking Hayden's initial reaction to the Yokai. He raised his arms in the air as he started running back toward the cottage. "Get back!"

"Real mature!" Hayden shouted after him. He looked down at Marfóir and shook the handle. Surprisingly, it released back into a whip. He raised his arm and cracked it in the air sideways, hoping to turn it back into a sword.

It didn't.

Clarendon, Pennsylvania, December 25, 1943
2119 — local time

The Oni had Stolly cornered.

While Hayden was close to mastering his use of Marfóir, the Oni managed to dodge each of his attempts at absorbing it into his whip. It was a black, hulking figure with three horns protruding from its head. Wearing a tiger pelt as a loincloth, it tightly held onto a spiked iron war club. Sharp claws, wild hair, and fang-like tusks, it almost resembled a large boar that walked on two legs.

Storm clouds rolled in. Hayden looked above as lightning stretched across the sky and thunder rumbled, shaking the earth.

"Careful, Stolly!" Hayden warned, his eyes blackening as the thunder continued to roar above them. Stolly scurried backward on all fours, not taking his eyes off of the grotesque Yokai coming for him. Its repulsive mouth watered from the corners as it raised its arm, ready to club Dr. Stolly in the head.

"Will you hurry up?" Dr. Stolly shouted. "This thing can eat me in a single gulp!"

"Okay, you're not *that* short—"

"Now's not the time for jokes! Kill it!"

The veins in Hayden's face darkened, as did the ones in his left forearm. He leaped in the air and cracked Marfóir. The tip of the spinal whip finally thrashed against the demon as it sprang forward, its focus entirely on Dr. Stolly. It exploded immediately as lightning lit up the sky in flashes. The Oni dissipated into thin air just before it had the chance to take a bite. Black smoke absorbed into the spine of Marfóir like it had with every demon before that, and the thunderstorm above began to clear within seconds.

"Merry Christmas, Stolly." Hayden grinned, offering him a hand. "I told you I'd save you."

Still sprawled on the ground, Dr. Stolly looked up at him and narrowed his eyes. His heart was beating rapidly in his chest.

"I hate you," he said bluntly, smacking away Hayden's offer of assistance as he rubbed the fog from his glasses. "You almost didn't get that one." He quickly got up to his feet and dusted the snow off of his body. He shivered beneath his coat and rubbed the sides of his arms. "I was almost an Oni's dinner."

"Don't be so dramatic." There was a smug smile on Hayden's face as he rolled up his whip, clearly quite pleased with himself and his progress. "Wonder what Dot's gonna say when she finds out we've been summoning demons for practice."

Dr. Stolly cleared his throat and shook his head quickly. "She doesn't need to know."

Hayden grinned. "You're not scared of her, are you?"

"Everyone's a little scared of Dot. You're lying to yourself if you think you aren't."

Hayden scoffed. His face donned a smug smirk as a crease etched into his forehead when he scrunched his brows together. "She's like five feet tall."

"She's five-foot-*two*."

Hayden raised an eyebrow.

"Know that because you're an inch taller than her?"

"Shut up." Dr. Stolly rolled his eyes, knowing he was at least three inches taller than Miss Sharp. He tucked the journal under his arm. "Let's not forget you were scared of an umbrella."

"Look, that's old news. I've defeated a lot of demons since then—including that one just now. That Oni. That one was—something."

"Terrifying," Dr. Stolly said, a sigh escaping his mouth. "And to think, that was only a small one."

Hayden tilted his head forward. His eyes bulged slightly out of his head as he raised his eyebrows. "*That* was only a small one?"

Dr. Stolly waved him away dismissively, muttering expletives under his breath as he went back into the cottage.

That evening, the two of them ate a small meal out of the best canned foods they could find in the pantry. Hayden was shoveling corn in his mouth when he looked over at the journal.

"You reading about Nurarihyon?"

Dr. Stolly nodded.

"There's a lot about him, but no weaknesses are listed."

"There has to be something."

"Unless Susanoo just didn't know them."

"Or he just doesn't have any," Dr. Stolly said with a shrug as he shoveled a spoonful of food into his mouth. He took a moment to chew his food and then swallowed before continuing to speak. "There has to be a reason he's the 'demon that can't be caught'. Ah—listen to this: 'Nurarihyon may enter homes in the evening while people are busy, drink tea, and smoke as though he lives there. When he's seen, he's thought of as the owner of the house and is never chased away or noticed as out of place.'" Dr. Stolly looked up from the journal and over at Hayden. "So basically if he wants to be protected—"

"He can hide in plain sight, wherever he wants."

Dr. Stolly sighed and nodded.

"That makes things a little difficult," Hayden said.

"He has no reason to hide though, the Japanese are occupying all of Guam and then some."

"He doesn't have all the pieces of the scythe though," Hayden noted. "So there is a small reason to hide." He turned the spoon between his fingers. "Do you think I'm ready for this?"

Dr. Stolly put his own spoon down. He looked at the drawing of Nurarihyon before looking at Hayden. "That's not really my call to make."

"You're the one doing the trials. If it's not your call, whose call is it?"

"Yours," Dr. Stolly said plainly. "Do you think you're ready? Do you think you can do this?"

Hayden sighed. He clenched his jaw, recalling what Susanoo had said to him only a few months ago. Hayden rubbed his forehead before running his hand down the front of his face. He massaged his jaw for a minute, before looking at the drawing of Nurarihyon.

That comes from within. That comes from you.

"I'm scared," Hayden admitted finally. He had no rude words to say. No usual insults to throw at Dr. Stolly, nothing. He felt defeated by his own insecurities. He couldn't take his eyes off of the picture of Nurarihyon. "I'm scared I won't be good enough and all of this will be for nothing. I'm scared I'll fail, and I'll cause—"

"Hold on," Dr. Stolly interrupted. He pointed at the drawing. "You won't cause anything. This is on him. This is on Nurarihyon. The only thing any of us can ask of you is to do your best." He sat back in his chair. "I would've called you a liar if you didn't admit to being scared. When that Oni was coming after me, I nearly pissed myself. Literally. My mind went blank. But you saved me. You pulled yourself together long enough to make sure you got it. Maybe you don't believe in yourself just yet, but I believe in you—for what it's worth."

"That was really mushy of you," Hayden said with a small chuckle as he pretended to wipe a tear from his eye.

Dr. Stolly rolled his eyes.

"But I really do appreciate it," Hayden admitted. "You've helped me a lot."

"That's what friends do," said Dr. Stolly.

"Well, it's also your job."

"*Really?*"

"Sorry," Hayden laughed. "This was getting a little too emotional for me."

"I was going to say there's nothing wrong with showing your emotions, but I remember—Hayden doesn't do emotions."

"Hasn't failed me yet."

"It will one day."

Hayden shook his head.

"Doubt it."

York, Pennsylvania, March 21, 1944
0726 — local time

Máiréad Quartermaine stood at the window of her home that overlooked the driveway. The grounds were blanketed, and the trees were frosted from the snowfall earlier that morning. Her hands cupped a hot mug of tea as she blew on the surface gently. She stared blankly.

"Are you alright?" Gabe asked, snaking his arm around her waist. He tenderly kissed her cheek and brushed stray blonde hair away from her face. She looked at him with tired eyes.

"It's been two years since Hayden decided he was packing up and rejoining the war," she said softly, her voice breaking as she looked down at her steaming tea. "He was arrested, and when I tried to visit him again, they told me he was no longer there. They wouldn't tell me where he was transported to, or if he was even still alive. Everything is 'classified.'" She ended her sentence in a mocking manner as she leaned into her husband.

"What if he's—" she couldn't bring herself to finish that sentence.

Gabe scratched at his beard and shook his head.

"We would have been notified," he assured. "Hayden promised he'd come back. He'll come back."

Though Máiréad desperately wanted to believe that her firstborn was okay, she couldn't help but worry. She later found herself in his bedroom, with everything untouched and just as he left it as it awaited his return.

One of his wheelchairs was propped into the corner nearest the entryway. She held a picture of a man in her small hands—a man whose blue eyes were a bit darker than hers, whose jaw was strong, and who wore no smile. It was a tattered photograph, worn at the edges, and creased over several times. It was of Hayden's biological father.

She stared at the photo for a moment as she approached his bed.

"I hope you're looking out for him," she said softly as she folded the photograph back up and tucked it beneath Hayden's pillow. "He *needs* you."

CHAPTER FOURTEEN

Hawai'i, June 5, 1944

Agent Elaina Dacua was a very busy woman during the time Hayden Dáithí spent away from the war of the Pacific. Having been stuck on the East coast running what she felt were silly and meaningless errands for R.A.V.E.N., it was nearly the middle of 1944 when she finally made her way back to the Hawaiian Islands after having been gone for so long.

Things were different there.

She could feel it. The whole energy of the islands had changed. The people weren't the same. The military wasn't the same. It made her curious.

"Colonel, you asked to see me?" she said, once finding Colonel Richards in the hall looking through a file he was cradling in his large, worn hands. She was hesitant about their meeting but remained composed.

He looked up in confusion for a moment before realizing who she was. He excused the corporal assisting him and motioned for her to take a seat.

"Ah, yes. Agent Dacua. I haven't seen you in a while."

She only sighed and shook her head in frustration as she sat down.

"Honestly, I feel like a R.A.V.E.N. carrier pigeon. I've been running all over the East coast. Back and forth between Manhattan and Philadelphia. I'm exhausted and tired of the cold weather. But—I'm back now. I was so relieved when they said I was coming back. Hawai'i reminds me so much of home," she finished with a smile. "What did you need?"

"I have someone I'd like you to meet." Colonel Richards sat back in his chair. "He's here to replace Dr. Susanoo with Project Reaper."

Agent Dacua furrowed her brows in confusion. She tilted her head slightly and crossed her arms uncomfortably. "I'm sorry?"

"I don't know if you heard about Sergeant—I mean— Corporal Dáithí, but he's no longer with us. So we have to start over."

"You're joking. Exposure to the artifact tends to kill people… Doesn't it? Everyone who touches it—it absorbs their energy. Everyone except Hayden—"

"Well, yes. But we had samples of his blood and it was as useless as taking blood from a rotten corpse. We were going to try to use that to make a serum, but it was fruitless. So, we figured if we can recreate a small disaster near the artifact, maybe its effects will save another person and we can start over."

She looked horrified.

"You want to recreate the bombing of Pearl Harbor?"

He raised his hands up in surrender. "Not to that extent."

Agent Dacua frowned. "I don't think this is the best thing, Colonel. This seems—this seems wrong. You're going to intentionally kill people to hopefully bring someone back to life? That isn't even a guarantee. What if Hayden was one in a billion?"

"We're at war, Dacua. We don't exactly have the option to always do the right thing. Just the best thing, for the sake of the country."

"I can't agree with this."

"Good thing it isn't up to you." The Colonel got to his feet. "Would you like to meet him now?"

"It doesn't really seem like I have a choice," she said as she stood up and straightened her skirt.

"Good, then come with me."

As she walked with the Colonel, she looked around at the military personnel on base. It was a near ghost town.

She quickened her pace as they approached the facility. She remembered seeing Hayden there in his wheelchair before the second exposure to the artifact. It felt like a lifetime ago. He was different after that. She was almost relieved she wouldn't have to face him again.

"Dr. Stolly always speaks highly of you," Colonel Richards said in an awkward attempt to make small talk. "I think he's got a bit of a crush on you."

"He's a nice man," she said. She turned her head from one direction to the other while looking for him. "Is he here? Will he be joining the project this time as well? I haven't seen him in a while either."

Colonel Richards shook his head.

"I believe he's doing work with the Republic of Letters. They've had some kind of breakthrough with something, I'm told, but not much else. Those Intellectuals are rather secretive."

Agent Dacua nodded, somewhat pleased she wouldn't have to face him either, but she tried not to make that public knowledge.

She followed the Colonel into the facility, trying to contain her excitement about seeing the artifact. She wasn't allowed in the first time, but in the time since, she had acquired the proper clearance with her promotion for doing the tedious work R.A.V.E.N. had given her over the last year and a half. Despite disagreeing with the

Colonel's chosen methods of recreating a disaster, she was still excited about it.

Sergeant Kamuela stood as the guard at the door. He snapped to attention.

"Good morning sir, Sergeant Kamuela reports-"

"At ease, Sergeant."

"Sergeant, it's so good to see you!"

"Dacua!" Sergeant Kamuela grinned and pulled her into a friendly bear hug, squeezing her so tightly that she couldn't breathe. Her feet lifted off the ground as he raised her in the air.

The Colonel cleared his throat.

Sergeant Kamuela put her down.

"I'd do the same to you but I feel you wouldn't like that."

"You'd be right."

Agent Dacua laughed while Sergeant Kamuela just smiled awkwardly.

"Are you working on Project Reaper?" she asked.

"I'm actually going to volunteer for the—disaster."

Agent Dacua frowned.

"You can't be serious? You'll die!"

"Then I'll die for my country. That's why I joined the Marines."

Agent Dacua exchanged glances between the Colonel and Sergeant Kamuela. "There's no winning with you Marines."

The Colonel smiled approvingly. "Come on, he's inside."

When Sergeant Kamuela opened the door, a Japanese man at the counter turned around. Agent Dacua froze. He offered a friendly smile—despite her reaction to being a deer in headlights—and bowed respectfully.

"This is Dr. Akihiro Hashimoto," Colonel Richards said. "Doctor, this is Agent Elaina Dacua with our research division. She's looking forward to assisting you with this project."

Agent Dacua stared at him, dumbfounded.

"Yes, sure," she finally managed, in a rather soft voice. She tucked a few loose strands of her dark hair behind her ear and glanced around the room before noticing a metal rod that lacked an object.

"Is that where the artifact normally is?" she asked.

The Colonel nodded.

"It'll be hauled out shortly."

"When do we begin?"

"Soon," Dr. Hashimoto said.

The Colonel excused himself for other duties, and Sergeant Kamuela followed him out. Agent Dacua's eyes fell back onto the doctor, who had returned to the counter he stood at when she first entered the room.

"What are you doing here?" she questioned with demand and urgency in her voice as she stared at the man whom she knew to be an Imperial Japanese soldier. Her eyes were wide as she tugged on his sleeve. "You could blow my cover!"

Dr. Hashimoto didn't bother turning around.

"You were assigned this mission over four years ago, Elaina." He still didn't offer her the respect of looking at her while he spoke. "When the plans for Pearl Harbor were nothing but a pipe dream. He's been trying to contact you, and what do we find? You weren't even on O'ahu this whole time. All of Orochi's signals went up in smoke." Dr. Hashimoto still didn't look at her. "An invasion fleet headed for Saipan departed Pearl Harbor today. Nurarihyon doesn't want to wait for you any longer."

Agent Dacua furrowed her brows. She missed a lot.

"I had business to take care of! I was still a new agent, and I had to work my way up, okay?" she snapped. Agent Dacua balled her fists as she walked over to Dr. Hashimoto. She moved in front of him and forced him to look at her. He was much taller than her, but she wasn't easily threatened and looked him straight in the eyes. "I can't tell these people 'no' without them getting suspicious. Especially after what happened with Dr. Susanoo and

Sergeant Dáithí. Their suspicions were running high to have such a threat so close."

Dr. Hashimoto smiled in approval. "That was thanks to Nurarihyon," he said. "The things he planted in Dr. Susanoo's old laboratory... Well, it certainly shook the Americans and took care of their dead stalker problem, hm?"

"It's Corpse Walker," she corrected.

Akihiro Hashimoto cocked a brow.

"Has your alliance changed, Elaina?" he asked, tilting his head as he baited her. "I think you're harboring a soft spot for these Americans."

She narrowed her eyes.

"Don't make me kill you, Akihiro. I won't even blink an eye."

"Kill me then, Elaina. It doesn't matter. He'll just send another to do the job you couldn't complete. No one really needs you. Especially not Nurarihyon. You're disposable. Remember that." Akihiro gathered the file that was scattered on the desk. "Complete the assignment tonight, Elaina, or it will be done for you."

"I'll get it done. Today."

"For your sake, I hope so."

Dr. Hashimoto gathered the remaining papers he had been shifting through and looked up through the glass window as the doors opened from the other side.

CORPSE WALKER: THE NIGHT PARADE | 247

Agent Dacua followed his gaze. On the other side of the glass, a few Marines were hauling in a large titanium box. Sergeant Kamuela was assisting with the moving of the artifact. They wore thick, leather protective gloves that went up to their elbows. Using a large metal rod, Sergeant Kamuela moved the toe of the scythe and placed it on the rack before covering it with a black sheet. Dr. Hashimoto looked over at Agent Dacua.

"You better work quickly," he said quietly as he excused himself from the room.

She watched him leave before her attention was directed back to Sergeant Kamuela, who helped the guards move the box back out from where it came.

Agent Dacua walked closer to the glass. She pressed her fingertips against it as she stared at the blade covered by the single black cloth. She could feel the power emitting from it. One of the three infernal artifacts was near completion.

Sergeant Kamuela turned around and saw her standing there.

His grin spread from one side of his face to the other as he playfully pointed at the object like a gleeful child. Agent Dacua met his excitement with a small smile of her own and shook her head. He waved his arm, inviting her into where he stood. Agent Dacua inhaled sharply as she looked around. Crinkling her nose, she exited the small office part of the room and re-entered through the back. She typed in the access code, and the large metal doors opened for her once the light shifted from red to green.

There, Sergeant Kamuela stood beside the artifact.

"It's strange to see you acting like such a child, Charlie."

"This artifact brought Hayden back to life," he exclaimed. "This artifact helped him walk again! How can you maintain composure? It's amazing."

Agent Dacua approached the black sheet as she circled it. "It's terrifying, don't you think?" She glanced back at him momentarily. "The power it holds. Like you said, it brought Hayden back to life. That's not normal."

"What is, though? Normal?" He outstretched his hand as if motioning to grab her, but she was out of reach. "Don't get too close!"

"Don't worry," she said, looking at the black cloth shaping the artifact perfectly. Her fingers brushed along the bottom of the cloth. "I'll be fine." Agent Dacua looked up at him as her eyes flickered to a shimmering gold. There was slight remorse in her voice and in the look on her face. "But you won't be," she said softly. She raised her hand, and just as she was about to close her fist, Sergeant Kamuela tackled her to the ground.

"What are you doing?" she snapped, trying to push him off of her.

"What are *you* doing?" he demanded.

Sergeant Kamuela grabbed hold of her wrist and twisted her arm behind her back.

Agent Dacua, despite being so small in stature, was very strong. Surprisingly strong. She broke free of his hold and shoved him off of her. Getting back to her feet, she pulled the black sheet off of the artifact and dropped it onto the ground. Without touching him, she wielded the air like a weapon and stopped Sergeant Kamuela in his tracks while forcing the oxygen out of his lungs. He gripped at his throat as he struggled to breathe, but no air entered through his mouth or nose. His fingernails clawed and scratched at his skin as he began turning blue in the face.

"I'm sorry," she whispered, her eyes glistening. Agent Dacua lifted her other hand, and the artifact levitated. "I hope you forgive me, Kamuela." She thrust her arm toward him and the toe of the scythe shot directly into his chest. "The perseverance of nature is far more important than the survival of humanity," she uttered softly as he dropped to the floor. Agent Dacua looked directly at the security cameras observing her as she heard the sirens go off. The same sirens that went off the first time she tried to steal the artifact after Hayden's encounter. Effortlessly, she picked up Sergeant Kamuela's limp body and hauled him over her shoulder before darting through the doors just as they bolted shut. Then she vanished into thin air.

Agent Dacua reappeared in an empty airfield. She dropped Sergeant Kamuela on the ground as she dragged him toward a helicopter. Using the air as her wielded weapon, she threw the airmen away from the carrier with nothing but a wave of her hand. A strong gust of wind knocked them off their feet, making them unable to get up. Agent Dacua gripped the front of Sergeant Kamuela's uniform, threw him into the copter, and got in.

"Why are you doing this?"

Agent Dacua clenched her jaw at Sergeant Kamuela's words. He regained consciousness, but barely. She looked back at him for a second. His eyelids fluttered.

"'The perseverance of nature is far more important than the survival of humanity?' What does that even mean?" he asked weakly. His voice wavered both in strength and volume. The blade of the scythe was punctured deep into his body as it drew energy from his life-force. He looked down at the blade. He moved to grip it, and his hand began to shrivel and gray, skin sticking just to his bones, as his flesh deteriorated right before his eyes. "What's happening to me?" Coming from behind her, he sounded horrified.

"Please stop talking, Kamuela. Or it'll only kill you faster. I need you to stay alive..." her voice trailed off toward the end of her words. "Or it'll begin to feed off of me."

"I thought we were friends," he mumbled. He struggled to get up.

Agent Dacua glanced back at him. She lifted her right hand in the air and spun it quickly, cutting off his air supply again. He began to suffocate until he passed out.

"I don't have friends." She kept her focus on the helicopter's controls as she opened up communication to Nurarihyon.

"Please let Commander Mori know we're on our way," she said into the headset. She looked down at the beautiful blue ocean waters below her, fully knowing what lurked deep beneath the surface.

With the help of the wind on her side, the flight time in the copter was much shorter than it normally would have been. Agent Dacua managed to make it to Guam in under three hours. Time was of the essence, but she was also afraid of her potential punishment from Nurarihyon for being so late.

She dragged an unconscious Sergeant Kamuela to the palace and dropped him at Nurarihyon's feet. He looked down at the blade stuck in the Sergeant's chest. Leaning over, Nurarihyon gripped it tightly with his gloved hand and ripped it out of his body. Sergeant Kamuela groaned, covering his abdomen with his hand as he turned over.

"Do you remember when we first met, Elaina?" Nurarihyon asked as he ran his finger along the edge of the long blade. He had his back to her now as he returned to the counter with the other two pieces, meeting Dr. Sauer who stood on the other side, ready to power the portal with the nether energy. Dr. Sauer stepped back a little, with his fingers laced together behind him.

Agent Dacua looked down.

"Of course," she said softly.

"A Diwata from the Philippines, brought to Guam on a little boat with shrubbery and others of your kind, unknown to the sailors who transported you." Nurarihyon recounted what she had told him as he organized the three pieces together, but didn't yet assemble them. "Small woodland nymphs and guardians of nature, able to shape-shift and hide in forests while often disguising themselves as plants and flowers." He looked up at her. "You were so young and so hopeful. Guam was beautiful, right? Until you then witnessed the destruction that came with humanity. The suffering of nature. Having to watch as your own kind perished in flames, unable to protect the forests from human development. They destroyed everything in their wake, and you were left to watch your world die."

He glanced between her and Dr. Sauer.

"You two are a lot alike," he said. "Like you, Dr. Sauer, I found Elaina curled up in a ball. Terrified, small, and full of rage. But there wasn't much a small Diwata could do on her own, much less the last of her kind on a tiny island.

"I offered her comfort. I offered her love." He walked over to Agent Dacua and stroked her cheek with the back of his fingers. She stared at him with water in her eyes. "I offered her a promise. You would get back at them and nature would prosper under my reign after we bring forth the night parade."

She closed her eyes and a few tears ran down her cheeks.

Agent Dacua often thought of it. The memory was one she looked back on fondly. But so much had changed over the years.

The man standing before her was hardly a man at all, and certainly not the one who welcomed her all those years ago. Nurarihyon was different now. He was changed. Or perhaps this was who he was all along, only now his mask had fallen off.

Agent Dacua watched him as he walked back to the counter and began assembling the pieces of the scythe together, being the only person she had ever witnessed able to touch it with his bare hands without injury. But there was something strange happening as he did so. Black smoke emitted from the ancient artifact that seemed to dissipate into thin air once he had finished its assembly.

Nurarihyon now wielded the scythe, and yet—nothing was happening.

He stood at the edge of the portal and tapped the center with the tip of the blade. Still, nothing. What was expected to be a grand moment, an entry for the demons of the night parade, fell flat. There was nothing. Only an uncomfortable silence filled the room.

A chuckle came from behind as the barely conscious Sergeant Kamuela sat amused. He had managed to get up to sit against the wall, though his head was hanging forward as he looked down at the ground. His hand was pressed up against his bleeding stomach. Still, he chuckled, even though it hurt him greatly to do so.

"After all your hard work, years of hard work." He sat with a grin while he taunted. "You're still not good enough for that scythe. It's not choosing you now, is it? You're no one compared to Hayden." Sergeant Kamuela raised his head to look up at Nurarihyon. "How does the rejection feel? Rejection by Death himself? To realize you're unworthy? I bet it hurts, don't it?"

Nurarihyon snapped the Sergeant's neck with a snap of his fingers. He didn't even have to touch him. Agent Dacua gasped and covered her mouth quickly with her hands as Sergeant Kamuela fell completely limp.

She began backing up toward the door.

"Maybe I should go back to O'ahu—" Agent Dacua began, still staring at Sergeant Kamuela's lifeless body. "I—I can retrieve the journal and—" she shrugged. "Maybe the answer to why you can't use the scythe will be in it? Maybe Susanoo knows something you don't?" She regretted her words as soon as she spoke them.

Nurarihyon scowled at the mention of Susanoo being superior to him in any way. But luckily for her, he didn't acknowledge it.

"So I can wait another three years for you to complete your one job?" Nurarihyon asked, then shook his head. "No. I'm afraid you're not going back to O'ahu, Elaina. I have other plans for you."

From a small green glass bottle, he poured sake into a large cup, nearly filling it to the brim. He walked over to Agent Dacua, and raised it to her lips, offering it to her as a drink. She was hesitant, keeping her eyes on him, but he insisted as he raised his eyebrows, urging her.

When she looked down at the liquid, Nurarihyon blew across the top and it set ablaze with bright blue fire, blistering Agent Dacua's face. It didn't stop there. Instead, it spread quickly over her body as she screamed. Agent Dacua tried to put out the fire, but it continued to burn as long as sake remained in the cup. Nurarihyon put the cup down on the table and watched as the flames ate away at her body, reducing her to a pile of ash on the floor.

Dr. Sauer hesitated. He, of course, knew that Nurarihyon possessed a rather unique power, but seeing it in play was always something else. It reminded him of his own mortality, and often he found himself wondering if he was on the right side of war. These moments were often brief, as he would always remember why he had joined Yamata No Orochi in the first place, but when he watched Nurarihyon reduce other beings to ash right before him, he wondered what things would be like when the world was filled with more of his kind.

Agent Dacua was a nice girl. That was her downfall.

"What are we going to do?" Dr. Sauer asked once he found the courage to speak.

"*We* are not going to do anything," Nurarihyon said. He picked up the scythe and the black smoke that engulfed it seemed to vanish every time. Frustrated, he threw the ancient artifact back onto the counter. Dr. Sauer ducked beneath the table and covered his head, but nothing happened. Nurarihyon fixed his cap over his head as he walked over to the call button. Pressing on it, he spoke in Japanese to the Imperial soldiers. When he finally released his finger from the button, he looked at the scythe in disgust before directing his attention toward Dr. Sauer, who was reluctantly standing up straight again. He didn't bother acknowledging Dr. Sauer's cowardice.

"We were told about a resurrection from the Pearl Harbor attack. This… Hayden? I want him found. Now."

Dr. Sauer picked up the bag next to Agent Dacua's pile of ashes. He looked through it for her notes. "I'm sure there's something about him in her notes. Maybe he has a family."

"Find them."

"Yes, sir."

CHAPTER FIFTEEN

Saipan, June 15, 1944
0550 — local time

U.S. ships have been sighted.

The Japanese bomb-carrying Mitsubishi A6M Zero attacked picket destroyer *Stockham*, but was shot down by the *Yarnall* destroyer.

Just a few days ago, approximately thirty U.S. ships set out for Saipan. As they approached, they fired upon the Imperial Japanese military from over five miles out to likely avoid potential minefields that awaited them. The interesting call of action made it clear to the Japanese that the U.S. troops upon those ships were untrained in shore bombardment.

They didn't dare move closer.

A smirk crossed Commander Mori's thin lips as the United States remained far in the water. He watched from the shrine in Guam through Tadeo's ghostly eyes.

Tadeo possessed a Japanese officer in Saipan to properly keep Commander Mori up to date.

"Is this the best the great United States has to strike fear in our hearts?" Commander Mori mocked their attempts as his vision cleared, and he sat back, amused. "Pathetic."

Still in high spirits, he checked in with Tadeo the following day, only to clench his jaw and glare at the sight. Commander Mori had doubted them too soon. Tadeo's vision showed two U.S. naval groups of nearly fifty ships arriving in assistance, and they were quickly gaining upon the shoreline.

Their landings began at seven.

By nine that morning, watching through his Inugami's eyes as Tadeo had a meeting with the higher ranking officers, Commander Mori learned more than eight thousand U.S. Marines covered by fire support ships had landed on the west coast of Saipan.

"We're prepared for this," Tadeo reassured the group, his voice deep. They had carefully placed barbed wire, artillery, machine gun emplacements, and trenches to maximize American casualties. "Many Americans will die today." Tadeo bowed his head slightly, eyes lifting. "Take charge, and remain calm," he instructed as they returned to their posts. Tadeo then hurried back to his quarters where he watched the attacks from his window that overlooked the west side of Saipan.

With the orders to stay calm, knowing they came from Nurarihyon's right-hand man, the Imperial Japanese Navy didn't feel threatened.

Their planning paid off.

Tadeo cocked his head as he watched them destroy nearly twenty American amphibious tanks.

Commander Mori sent Japanese aircraft from Guam to assist and a battle broke out once the U.S. ships spotted them, countering the attack with a group of thirty Grumman F6F Hellcats from the USS *Belleau Wood*. The Japanese began circling to regroup their formations for another attack, but the ten-minute delay was critical. Only one American Hellcat was lost and the United States responded with fury, shooting down thirty-five of the sixty-eight Japanese aircraft.

The Japanese launched every fighter they could. The aircraft that survived were met by other fighters, but sixteen more were shot down. The twenty-seven that remained in the sky made attacks on the picket destroyers USS *Yarnall* and USS *Stockham*, but caused no damage.

One bomb hit the main deck of USS *South Dakota*, causing over fifty American casualties, but failed to disable the battleship.

Tadeo closed his eyes.

262 | RALYNN KIMIE

What do I do? he asked his master.

A Japanese soldier knocked on the door and Tadeo slowly opened his eyes. He looked over at the soldier, whose gaze remained on the floor out of fear.

"Sir, I was told to let you know that we lost more than half of the aircraft from Guam and we were only able to destroy one American Hellcat," he said in one breath. With his eyes still on the floor, he took a step back into the hallway and began to close the door.

"Wait," Tadeo said, finding humor in his body language. It still amused him how different people acted in the presence of a demon than a normal dog. He wondered if they truly feared him though, or just Nurarihyon. "Kill every last American, and make sure all bodies are on land."

The soldier nodded and quickly shut the door.

Tadeo returned to his chair near the window. He had a full view of the ongoing battle. His nose twitched at the smell of iron and he looked down to see a few droplets of blood on his sill. He smeared his fingertips through the crimson liquid and brought his hand to his nose. He closed his eyes and attempted to contact his master again.

There was a continued slaughter and the Japanese losses exceeded three hundred and fifty planes on the first day of the battle. Only about thirty American planes were lost, and there was little damage to the ships. The

Japanese pilots who remained were the small number of seasoned veterans who had survived the six-month Japanese advance early in the Pacific War. They were losing.

By nightfall, the 2nd and 4th U.S. Marine Divisions had a beachhead over six miles wide and half a mile deep.

Tadeo made sure the Japanese used the night to their advantage and waited for complete darkness to counter-attack. Unfortunately, they were repelled with heavy losses as the land of the free fought with fervor.

Japanese planes swarmed overhead. The United States Navy aimed their weapons and shot hundreds right out of the sky, including three major aircraft carriers.

They burned viciously in the waters around Saipan. It was hauntingly beautiful to see the dancing flames reflecting in the dark water and the smoke reaching up at the sky, but it was devastating to witness.

Without resupply, things looked grim.

Units of the U.S. Army's 27th Infantry Division landed and advanced on the airfield at As Lito the following day. The Imperial Japanese Navy Air Service assigned two squadrons to the airfield and were nearly wiped out by the American forces within two days.

Lieutenant General Saitō quickly abandoned As Lito on June 18 after their failure and it was captured by the United States by the end of the same day. The Lieutenant

General organized the Imperial Japanese military into a line anchored on Mount Tapochau in the defensible mountainous terrain of central Saipan after fleeing the airfield. They used many caves in the volcanic landscape to delay the attackers by hiding during the day and making sorties at night.

While the United States advanced quickly, there appeared to be inter-service rivalry between the soldiers and the Marines, and a lack of clear communication, leading the Marines to run right into a solid wall of Japanese fire.

Just when Tadeo thought they might have regained some control, one U.S. battalion held the area while the other two battalions managed to surround them.

Using timed-artillery fire, smoke, and tanks, the U.S. military stormed to the top, bursting in cave entrances and moving down the face of the hills like a stepladder. They tossed grenades and satchel charges of high explosives into well-camouflaged concrete reinforced bunkers and smoked out the hidden Japanese military.

Some attempted to make a run for it but the United States cut them down.

Tadeo closed his eyes.

What will you do? he asked his master.

There was no answer. Tadeo's eyelids fluttered as he looked out the window.

Shortly after the disaster for the Japanese, Commander Isamu Mori arrived.

Alone.

They needed help, and *Nurarihyon* would assist.

He walked through the battlefield, unthreatened by the war that surrounded him.

The air reeked of iron and rotting flesh from the bodies that were sitting in the sun all night and day, their flesh burning off of their bones. Commander Mori took a step further into the battlegrounds. Fire rained around him, but nothing hit him. Nothing came close. Mori took off his cap and held it firmly in his hands as he continued to walk. The flesh of every limp Japanese body he passed seemed to deteriorate much quicker, burning off till there was nothing but bones left.

Many of the Americans muttered to each other at the sight of his elongated head and the way his jaw fell open while his mouth stretched to the high points of his cheeks. Many of them fired at him, but it was like they had all forgotten how to aim. Nothing hit him.

Nurarihyon stopped in his tracks as the bones of the dead began to stir and rattle against the ground. The sun was setting, and night was approaching quickly.

"Are you seeing this?" A soldier stared at the giant skeletal creature assembling from the bones of the fallen Japanese military.

Marine General Smith blinked in disbelief. He rubbed at the tiredness in his red-brimmed eyes to make sure he wasn't hallucinating at the sight. It wasn't an illusion. A giant skeleton made of human bones was assembling right before their eyes.

"Seeing—" he started, "still—still working on believing."

The Americans could hear Japanese civilians shouting 'Gashadokuro!' at the giant building-sized monster with hands rivaling the size of most houses. The Gashadokuro grabbed several American soldiers while being fired at by the 27th Infantry Division.

The Gashadokuro appeared unfazed and unharmed by the human attack, and the soldiers in his hand lay limp from the gunfire as he brought them to his mouth to bite off their heads. Blood dripped down the front of his mouth as he threw the bodies back to the ground and crushed them with his large foot. Their heads hit the insides of his ribcage before dropping out of his skeleton body.

A crackle came from behind the monster. A skeletal whip wrapped around the right ankle of the Gashadokuro and tripped him. The creature hit the ground and broke into a thousand pieces from the impact.

Hayden stood there, Marfóir tightly gripped in his hand.

"Ah, the Corpse Walker..." Nurarihyon spat.

"Surprised?"

"No."

Slowly, the Gashadokuro began to piece itself together.

"You look confused," Nurarihyon taunted as Hayden's eyes grew wide, watching the monster reassemble itself before his eyes. The pieces came back together like a magnetic attraction. "A Gashadokuro is created when people die with anger and pain in their hearts! Look at the agony you have caused my people!"

"Your people?" For a second, Hayden looked away from the monster to turn his attention toward Nurarihyon. "You're not even human!"

"And you are?" Nurarihyon observed, taking a step toward him. "We have the same eyes, Corpse Walker. The same nether energy that flows through my veins flows through yours. You're as much of a demon as I am."

Hayden attempted to hit Nurarihyon with Marfóir but the Gashadokuro grabbed him instead and pulled him away.

"Not so fast," Nurarihyon taunted him with a cackle.

Hayden struggled against the grip of the giant creature, the spine of his whip crushing into his side.

"Don't kill him yet," Nurarihyon warned his monster. "I still need him." He patted the ankle of the Gashadokuro before fleeing the site.

"Well, don't just stand there!" Marine General Smith said, acknowledging the Japanese demon. "Help the Corpse Walker!"

The Gashadokuro vanished into thin air, Hayden disappearing with it.

"Where'd it go?"

Many of the American military members were looking at each other for answers, but none had anything to say. They all had the same questions. Who was that man with the elongated head? What was a Gashadokuro? More importantly, where did it go? Where did the Corpse Walker go? There were too many questions, and no one was equipped to answer them. How were they supposed to hunt and kill something they couldn't see?

They aimed at nothing.

They fired at nothing.

They hit the hills, bunkers, and small, hidden Japanese bases. But the Gashadokuro did not reappear.

Hidden with its own invisibility shield, the Gashadokuro stared intently at Hayden, who struggled in the grasp of its large bony hand. The monster brought him closer to its mouth as the military swarmed around them on the ground and in the sky. Hayden's eyes darkened to black as he stared back at the monster before him. He managed to work his arm free and cracked the Gashadokuro in the face with Marfóir. It stumbled backward, causing a few

Japanese casualties as it accidentally stepped on them. The United States military opened fire at the invisible attack, but the bullets went right through Hayden and the Gashadokuro. The monster opened its hand and Hayden quickly leaped onto its wrist, ran up its arm, and toward its neck.

The Gashadokuro swatted its shoulders, attempting to smack Hayden off. Hayden raised his arm and snapped his whip into a sword as he charged toward the Gashadokuro's head. Right before he was about to stab it in the jaw, he was hit by the giant bone hand and slammed into the hillside.

Hayden sat up and rubbed at his head. The side of his temple was wet with blood. He wiped his fingers on his uniform and blinked several times, but he couldn't see two feet in front of him. He couldn't see anything but darkness. Flashes of green smoke began to appear in humanoid forms around him. Hayden tilted his head back as one figure approached. He narrowed his eyes.

"You appeared before, didn't you," he began. "That night I got my dishonorable discharge?" He looked around as the form lowered its head. Hayden chuckled a little and shrugged his shoulders. "You scared the shit out of that corporal." Hayden noticed the apparition smile. "So you can hear me. Who are you?"

"I'm of no importance," it said, appearing less smokey and more like a person.

"Oh, you can talk too. What are you?"

"Dullahan."

"No shit?"

He looked at the other figures who appeared, many of which were on horses, carrying their heads in their arms. Some still had their heads while riding headless horses. Hayden instinctively touched his own neck.

"Where are we?"

"You don't remember this place?"

He shook his head.

"We're in the Underworld."

He scoffed. "Excuse me? But—"

"No, you're not *quite* dead," the Dullahan assured. "Why did you come here?"

"I—what? I don't know."

With the light emitting from the ghostly Dullahan, Hayden could see his whip on the ground near his feet. He closed his eyes and sighed.

"You doubt yourself." The figure tilted its head. "You can come with us. We've been watching you since your resurrection. You're strong, we could use you—"

Hayden got to his feet and dusted himself off.

"No," he said plainly, shaking his head. "I'm not done with the living."

"Then we will wait until you're ready, my *son*."

Hayden furrowed his brows at his words. He opened his mouth to speak, but his surroundings faded around him as he was transported back to Saipan.

The Gashadokuro was terrorizing the American military, and it appeared to be the only hope the Japanese had left. Most of Japan's aircraft had been shot down. Little damage was done to the American battleships, however, and they continued to hold strong.

Hayden slowly picked up his whip and gripped it tightly in his hand. He cracked it against the ground, catching the Gashadokuro's attention. It dropped the Marines it held in its hand and started coming for Hayden instead. Blood trickled down the side of Hayden's head. He wiped it with the back of his sleeve and waited for the Gashadokuro to come closer. Just as it attempted to grab him again, Hayden leaped onto its hand and ran up its arm toward its shoulder again. He snapped his whip back into a sword and shoved it into the throat of the Gashadokuro. Hayden ripped the sword forward and bones broke away, clattering to the ground.

Pulling his arm back, the sword swayed back into a whip. He cracked it against what was left of the Gashadokuro's neck and tore its head off. Soldiers and Marines were performing the same operation they did in the hilltops. One battalion held the area, while two others surrounded the Gashadokuro. They vehemently attacked until all of the bones had clattered against the earth, many of which were broken and beyond reassembly.

Hayden dropped to the ground as the head of the Gashadokuro crumbled behind him. Both he and his whip were surrounded by the black smoke of nether energy. His eyes were pitch-black, his veins darkening throughout his body. There was damage to his forearm and his abdomen, chunks of his own flesh missing.

The United States military fell silent at the sight. Many of the present military had never seen the Corpse Walker until the Battle of Saipan. They had only read about him in the papers and heard stories through whispers. But there he stood, surrounded by the broken bones of the fallen Japanese.

Marine General Smith nodded once in his direction.

Hayden nodded back.

The battle was coming to a close, but Task-Force 58 had problems locating what was left of the enemy, who were operating at a great distance. Their early morning searches found nothing. It was the beginning of July, and the United States was extremely close to the reclaiming of Saipan. What was left of the Imperial Japanese Navy was still scattered and hidden mostly in caves. The United States attempted to attract Japanese civilians to keep them out of harm's way. They had a civilian prisoner encampment, with electric lights left on overnight, promising three warm meals and no risk of being shot in combat.

Many instead committed suicide, jumping from cliffs in the north above Marpi Point Field, hoping for a privileged place in the afterlife.

"The Japanese have nowhere to retreat and they will not surrender," Marine General Smith said, warning all frontline units as they readied themselves for the last stand. "Prepare for a final Banzai charge."

Saipan, July 9, 1944
1615 — local time

In the late afternoon on July 9, Admiral Turner announced that Saipan was officially secured. While the military had their time to rejoice in their win, Hayden crept along the sides of the volcanic terrain in search of Lieutenant General Saitō and the other commanders that disappeared during the final Banzai charge. Though Hayden had grown accustomed to wielding a whip, he now held a gun instead. Sent to disarm and capture humans, his whip wasn't the weapon he needed, though it remained fastened to his belt. He and several other

Marines advanced on the many caves of Mount Tapochau, formerly occupied by the Japanese.

Hayden lifted his weapon, noticing two commanders dead on the ground, stomachs split open.

Lieutenant General Saitō knelt on the ground, holding his sword in both hands. He lifted his arms and plunged the blade into his stomach, severing his abdominal aorta.

"Wait!"

Saitō's adjutant shot him in the head.

The man looked at Hayden and then shot himself.

The other United States Marines gathered around him at the mouth of the cave, peering in to see the four dead bodies. Hayden lowered his gun.

CHAPTER SIXTEEN

Saipan, July 10, 1944
2315 — local time

What you witnessed was seppuku," Dr. Stolly later told Hayden after he explained what he saw in the cave. They were in a small radio room that the military allowed Dr. Stolly to borrow as his own office, with a desk pushed up against a wall and a small table near the doorway. It almost looked like a small break room, only it lacked a kitchen. "It's a ritual suicide."

"Why?"

"Well, it's a samurai practice," Dr. Stolly continued, pushing his glasses up the bridge of his nose. "Seppuku was used voluntarily to die by honor rather than be captured and tortured. That's also why a lot of the Japanese civilians jumped off of Suicide Cliff. They'd rather die an honorable death."

"Suicide Cliff?"

Dr. Stolly shrugged. "That's what everyone else is calling it." He shook his head. "But there's nothing honorable about suicide."

"It's not really an easy decision to make, either," said Hayden. "I don't think anyone actually wants to die." He glanced up at the map on the wall, staring at the shape of Death's scythe. "I don't think it's exactly as peaceful as people think, either."

Dr. Stolly nodded. Hayden would certainly know much more about death than Dr. Stolly would. Dr. Stolly had never actually died.

Miss Sharp entered the facility. Her large brown eyes searched for Hayden in the busy hallway as the two men were exiting the small room. The second she laid eyes on him, she approached him in a hurry, pushing all of the military personnel out of the way.

"Thank goodness you're alive!"

She looked up at him and touched his shoulder before looking at Dr. Stolly.

"I need to speak to both of you," she said, her voice soft.

Miss Sharp had the unfortunate responsibility of delivering the news of Sergeant Charles Kamuela's death to Hayden Zachariah Dáithí and Ingram-Zander Stolly. The three of them sat quietly at the table, with Hayden's eyes blackening as she spoke. It was a lot for Hayden to

CORPSE WALKER: THE NIGHT PARADE | 277

take in. Agent Dacua was working for Nurarihyon, and his best friend was dead.

His veins darkened in his cheeks, fading in toward his eyes, over and over, as he processed the information Miss Sharp had just told them. Hayden's hands tightly gripped the rolled spine whip, and the veins in his arm blackened as well as if there was energy being exchanged between him and his weapon. The bones dug deeply into his palms.

"I should've known better," Dr. Stolly said finally, breaking the silence between the three of them. Normally it was Hayden who couldn't stand the quiet, yet he remained silent. A few tears fell from his red-rimmed black eyes as he stared at nothing. Dr. Stolly began shaking his head in disbelief. "She was a Diwata, and I didn't even know. She was—I didn't even know. How fucking useless—" Dr. Stolly buried his face in his hands as he sank back in his chair.

Hayden got up from his chair. He leaned back against the edge of the desk and stared at the wall. There was a map plastered upon it, with a scythe drawn over Guam, Midway, and Hawai'i. It was a larger copy of the one Susanoo had shown him. Hayden was at a loss for words and still couldn't string a proper sentence together to speak. His eyes remained pitch-black and his focus blurred to nothing. Sergeant Kamuela had gotten Hayden through everything, and now he was gone.

"You're not useless, Stolly," Hayden finally managed, though he didn't turn around to look at him. Dr. Stolly, however, looked up from his hands in confusion. His own eyes were red and watery. His cheeks were damp and flushed.

"What?" He blinked several times, unsure if he had heard him correctly. It wasn't a question meant to be answered. He said it merely out of disbelief. Dr. Stolly shook his head a few times and took off his glasses to wipe his eyes. Even after he returned them to his face, the look of confusion remained. "Why aren't you mad at me, Sergeant Dáithí?"

Hayden cut him off.

"It's Hayden."

"What?"

"I told you to call me Hayden."

"Well, why aren't you blaming me? I should've—this is my area of expertise. I should have known she—"

"What good would it do?" Hayden asked him simply.

Hayden still didn't turn to look at Dr. Stolly, though. His eyes were still as black as night, and his focus stayed on the wall as his grip only tightened on the whip until the bones of the spine were digging into his palms.

"What good would it do to blame you?" he clarified his question. He finally got up from the edge and turned around to look at Dr. Stolly. "It's not going to change anything if I get mad at you. If I blamed you. It's not going to bring Kamuela back—" Hayden's brows furrowed at his choice of words. For a second, he froze. Bring him back. He looked over at Miss Sharp as his eyes widened. They slowly faded back to their crystal blue color. "Can we?" he asked. There was slight desperation in his voice. "Can we bring him back?"

She sighed and slowly shook her head.

"Elaina took the only piece of the scythe that we had." Miss Sharp clenched her jaw and swallowed. Her eyes mirrored remorse. "I saw the security footage…" Her voice was so shaky. It made Hayden uneasy. "She—um—she—" How could she tell him that Agent Dacua stabbed Sergeant Kamuela with it?

Hayden continued to tighten his grip on the rolled spine whip. The bones further dug into his palms as he did so.

"Can I bring him back? I mean, I have… weird abilities. Stolly and I have been—have been—I mean, we've been mostly killing what we've summoned, but we've summoned—"

Miss Sharp let out a small sigh through her parted lips. She shook her head.

"Even if you knew how to resurrect someone—we don't have his body, Hayden. And even if we did, how do we know it would be him who came back? There's so much that we don't know about the Underworld." She shot Dr. Stolly a rather subtle glare for Hayden's comment about summoning demons, but Dr. Stolly failed to notice. He was too consumed by his own guilt for not knowing what Agent Dacua truly was.

Hayden finally allowed himself to collapse into the chair. He put his whip down on the table and stared at it. What good was magic or being a 'corpse walker' if you couldn't save anyone? What good were abilities if friends still died? His blue eyes grew watery, reddening as the tears threatened to spill. Hayden clenched his jaw and started shaking his head. He forcefully wiped his face.

"It should've been me. I should've been there."

Miss Sharp sighed. The last thing she wanted to be was inconsiderate. She glanced back and forth between Sergeant Dáithí and Dr. Stolly, both of whom were too consumed with their own guilt in the matter to look at the bigger picture.

"Sergeant Kamuela was a great Marine," she said finally and sternly. "He died a great Marine. Don't let his death be in vain." The two men didn't seem to hear her, though. Neither of them looked at her. Neither of them seemed to acknowledge her at all. Miss Sharp smacked her palm against the table. "You two need to pull yourselves together. We don't have time for this. They have all the pieces of the scythe. Nurarihyon could bring about the Night Parade any moment now. He can open the portal."

"He was my friend," Hayden mumbled. He sniffled and wiped his face with the back of his hand. He sat back in his chair and put his hands on the table to fumble with the edge of the whip.

Miss Sharp tilted her head. Her own large brown eyes were red. She placed her hand upon his to comfort him.

"He was my friend too," she said softly, squeezing the back of his hand gently. "And I don't want him to have died for nothing. I don't want his sacrifice to have been for nothing. I'm sure you don't either."

Hayden furrowed his brows and nodded. Miss Sharp had a point.

"Nurarihyon wants to unleash demons on the world," she said. "He wants to wipe humanity out of existence completely and let demons take over. We have to do something. We can't just let him win."

Hayden looked at Miss Sharp, then at Dr. Stolly.

Miss Sharp wiped her face and gathered her composure.

"I saw him," he said, looking down at his whip. "During the fight, he made a giant bone monster."

"A Gashadokuro?"

Hayden looked over at Dr. Stolly again.

"You're a square."

"Yeah, well, it pays the bills."

Hayden sat up in his chair.

"Why didn't he use it?"

"What?"

"He has all the pieces of the scythe, but he didn't have it with him." Hayden scratched at the side of his arm before his fingers returned to fumble with the whip. "Wouldn't he need it to create a gasha—thing?"

Dr. Stolly shook his head.

"Gashadokuro are made from the pain, suffering, and desire of vengeance by those whose skeletons make up its body. Those spirits haven't passed over anywhere—so they had nowhere to come back from."

"I also saw something else."

Hayden had both Miss Sharp and Dr. Stolly's attention. He thought about his quick and unintentional trip to the Underworld where he saw the Dullahan, and one who called him his son.

"What did you see?" Dr. Stolly asked, urgency in his voice.

"I think my dad's part of the Dullahan."

Dr. Stolly's eyes widened as he dug in his bag for Dr. Susanoo's journal.

"Dr. Susanoo knew exactly what he was doing. This makes so much sense!" He also pulled out his own notebook and a pen and sat with wonder in his eyes as he looked up at Hayden. He looked like an eager school kid ready to learn. "What were they like? I need to know everything."

Hayden looked away from him. He closed his eyes and rubbed his temples. The cut on the side of his head had already healed itself. He looked over at Miss Sharp, ignoring Dr. Stolly almost completely.

"When are we going to Guam?"

Saipan, July 17, 1944
1710 — local time

As Lito was quickly renamed Isely Field after United States Navy Commander Robert H. Isely who was killed a month before while strafing the base. The field was quickly repaired and expanded by the Seabees of the 6th Naval Construction Brigade to become Naval Advance Base Saipan.

"There's still persistent Japanese resistance," Marine General Smith said. "It's believed Captain Ōba has less than fifty soldiers who survived after the last banzai charge, but they likely have civilians with them as well."

"Should be easy," one of the captains said. A small smile of doubt appeared on Hayden's face as he watched the two interact.

Smith narrowed his eyes.

"I wouldn't underestimate Ōba. They've evaded us so far—and also conducted several guerrilla-style attacks on us. He's smart. Stealthy. But we now have air and naval superiority," Marine General Smith continued as he started to bring up Guam.

There was a knock at the door. The room went silent.

"I apologize for interrupting," the Corporal said, his eyes zoning in on Hayden. "Sergeant Dáithí, you have a phone call. It's urgent."

All eyes moved from the Corporal to Hayden. He rubbed the back of his neck as he excused himself from the table. Perfect timing, he thought, slightly annoyed by the interruption as he followed the Corporal out of the room.

"Should we wait for him?" the Captain asked. "Nurarihyon is in Guam. We're going to need the Corpse Walker."

"Nurarihyon isn't the only one we have to worry about," Marine General Smith said. "We're still up against Imperial Japan. This is a lot bigger than some Japanese demon with magic tricks."

The Captain raised his eyebrows at the remarks and sat back in his chair.

The Corporal led Hayden down the hall of the Isely Field base.

"That was amazing—what you were doing out there," the Corporal said, only glancing at Hayden once or twice. "That bone monster—"

"Gashadokuro—"

"Yes—that thing. It was terrifying. But you—you were amazing. Running up his arm, breaking open his neck. I saw the whole thing. I wish I could do things like that. It must be amazing. You looked like a superhero."

A small smile peeked at the corner of Hayden's mouth. *This was nice*, he thought. *Recognition.*

Hayden looked over at the Corporal.

"How old are you?"

"Twenty-one."

Young.

Hayden was twenty-three when he was first killed in action. He gave the young man a closed-lip smile as he placed a firm hand on the Corporal's shoulder.

"Take it easy, yeah?" he said, as the Corporal led him to a small radio room. It was the same one where Miss Sharp had told him and Stolly the news about Sergeant Kamuela.

The Corporal nodded.

Hayden went inside alone. He closed the door behind him and looked around for a moment. There was a phone sitting on a desk, and in front of him, the large map with a drawing of Death's scythe across the Pacific Ocean. The room reminded him of Sergeant Kamuela, even though Sergeant Kamuela himself had never been there. Saipan had been under Japanese possession since World War I, when it was captured by their Imperial Army.

He inhaled deeply and picked up the phone.

"Good evening, Corpse Walker."

"Who is this?" Hayden asked. The accent sounded German to him.

"I am Dr. Hans Sauer," the man said on the other end. "You may have met my colleague, Nurarihyon."

Hayden's grip tightened on the neck of the phone.

"How are you this evening?" Dr. Sauer asked.

"What do you want?"

"Nurarihyon requests your presence," he said plainly. "Go to the cave where you witnessed seppuku. Go alone. If you don't, we will kill all those who accompany you."

The phone line went dead.

Hayden hung up the phone. He looked back up at the map before taking a seat in the chair. While the desk was mostly cleared, there were a few files stacked in the corner. He looked over at the pile before picking one up.

It had his name on it.

He sat back in the chair and looked through the newspaper clippings that dated back to the one of him pictured at Sharp Co. Factory in York. Most of them were lies about the Corpse Walker, but he singled out the one at the factory. Hayden was drawn to the smile on his face in that picture, his desire to still do something good with what he had. His hand moved to his dog tags as he stared at 'Howard Davey.' He thought about the teenage boys at the factory, eager to fight in a war they didn't understand. They would've been of age now.

Hayden tilted his head when he noticed the second file beneath his—Charles Kamuela. It had 'volunteer' stamped across it. Hayden closed his own before opening up Sergeant Kamuela's. On the first page, his picture was paper-clipped to the form. Most of it was filled out in Sergeant Kamuela's handwriting. Sergeant Kamuela had nicer handwriting than he did, and Hayden learned more about what they were planning to do with the scythe after his dishonorable discharge.

Sergeant Kamuela volunteered to die.

Hayden looked through the pages at their details for the desire to recreate casualties at a smaller scale than Pearl Harbor and hoped the scythe would choose another. Hayden furrowed his brows in both anger and frustration.

Hayden remembered seeing Sergeant Kamuela for the first time after being resurrected, and he reminisced about the jokes the two shared between them. Sergeant Kamuela didn't even want to go near the scythe or even see it, for that matter. Hayden closed his eyes. He had trouble remembering the last time he saw Sergeant

Kamuela, and he was saddened at how he hadn't known it would be the last.

That all felt like a lifetime ago.

"You're so stupid, Charlie," Hayden mumbled to himself as he closed the file and threw it back onto the desk, pissed that Sergeant Kamuela would volunteer for something so ridiculous. He got up in frustration and shoved the chair. It smacked the edge of the desk and fell backward from impact. Hayden turned around and ran his fingers through his blond hair.

He stopped for a second and closed his eyes, trying to concentrate. He hadn't really thought of anything specific when he accidentally stumbled upon his father in the Underworld, but perhaps he could somehow contact Sergeant Kamuela if he thought hard enough. If he focused on it.

His fists tightened, nether energy flowing through his veins as he concentrated. His physical form faded in and out, between solid and translucent, but when he opened his eyes again, nothing had happened. He was still standing in Dr. Stolly's small radio room. The phone was still on the desk, along with the files. The map was still on the wall. He hadn't gone anywhere.

He was still at the Isely Field in Saipan.

All that training and Hayden still barely had a clue about the things he could do or what he was capable of.

Go alone, Hans Sauer's voice repeated in his head like a soft echo. *If you don't, we will kill all those who accompany you.*

Hayden sighed. There were a million things going through his head but he was certain of one thing. He wouldn't allow any more blood to be spilled because of him. Because of him or his failures. One could argue that his dishonorable discharge wasn't his fault, but his lack of presence in the war could be thought of in that way. He could have trained harder, faster. But he didn't. So many casualties of too many lives that could have been spared.

His hand curled around the doorknob and he left quickly, not bothering to return to the meeting. The United States military could take care of Imperial Japan. Hayden had his own target to worry about.

***

From another realm, Amaterasu stood beside Susanoo as she watched Hayden get ready for his mission. She glanced over at her brother, who remained quiet at her side. The two of them were immaculate in appearance. Amaterasu harbored the beauty of both the sunrise and sunset and just looking at her brought warmth to the faces of those who had the pleasure of seeing her. Susanoo was youthful and ageless, his long hair bound in a tight bun that sat high on his head.

"You have nothing to say?" she asked her younger brother.

"You should have left me there," he answered finally.

She clicked her tongue, her gaze returning to the Corpse Walker. She and her brother stood high in the aether, watching him from a marbled bowl full of silver liquid.

"It is up to them to determine their right to continued existence. If they want to live, they have to fight for it, not you."

"I created this mess."

"The Fates would disagree."

Susanoo rolled his eyes.

"I made Nurarihyon what he is," he said. "He wouldn't have gotten this far if it weren't for me."

"True, but it's up to them to end it." She turned away from the bowl to face him completely. "You believe in them, don't you? You believe in your... Corpse Walker?"

Susanoo nodded. "I do," he said. There was no question or doubt in his mind. "I just hope he believes in himself."

"You have nothing to worry about then. Things have a way of working out."

Amaterasu turned away, and Susanoo followed.

"What is that supposed to mean? You believe in him too?"

She looked her younger brother straight in the eyes.

"I believe in *you*." She looked back on the world. "When I banished you to Terra, this is not what I thought would become of it. Nor did I ever think I'd forgive you for your... transgressions." Amaterasu folded her hands together as Susanoo averted his eyes. "But you surprised me. That doesn't happen very often." She looked at her brother and reached to touch his jaw. "As for your mortal friends, they will be needing all the strength they can get on their side. I worry for their future."

Susanoo looked at her curiously. He tilted his head.

"What do you know?"

"That, I cannot say." She pulled her hand away from his face and laced her fingers together again. "But we'll see how they fare in this fight. It will determine so much."

She left without another word, and Susanoo was left with many questions of his own. His gaze returned to Hayden. Susanoo inhaled sharply through his mouth as he turned his body to face him completely. Hayden seemed lost in thought. Susanoo tilted his head.

"Be well, Sergeant Dáithí," he muttered softly.

CHAPTER SEVENTEEN

Saipan, July 17, 1944
2312 — local time

As instructed, Hayden waited till that evening to return to the cave where he witnessed Lieutenant General Saitō commit suicide, and he went alone. Watching the Japanese lieutenant general stab himself replayed in Hayden's head, along with the loud sound of the gunshot echoing within the cave walls. Saipan was now completely under American occupation, and while he could move about the island freely, Hayden remained on guard with his hand firmly on his whip. There were still the soldiers and civilians led by Captain Ōba lurking about and the cave was far on foot. It took Hayden quite some time to get there.

As he walked, he could see translucent shifts around him, wandering spirits of the recently deceased soldiers. He watched as many rose from their bodies and stared down at their limp physical forms. He wondered if anyone else could see them too. There weren't as many American casualties as there were Japanese, and while they were considered the enemy, they still had families and loved ones who cared for them. They were still sons, brothers, fathers, and husbands.

Hayden thought of them and the telegrams their families would receive to let them know of their deaths as he carefully walked around each corpse. He thought of his mom. First the telegram she received, then the phone call of his resurrection.

He clenched his jaw.

He stepped further in. He looked to the ground first, and at the bodies still lying there. Hayden was numb to the smell.

There was a glint in the darkness.

While he could feel the energy of it emitting from the opening of the cave, it was strange to see Death's scythe assembled before him. The toe of the blade at home with the rest of its pieces. A whole.

What was stranger was the person wielding it.

"Finley?"

The boy looked up at him with cold, dead eyes. His hands were disintegrating, the scythe draining the life from his body.

"I am not Finley," he said. His voice was a low whisper, as if a shadow had taken the sound. He looked like Finley, but he didn't sound like him. He was a few years older now since Hayden had last seen him. Finley had to be about eight years old now, and a few inches taller than he remembered.

Hayden pulled out Marfóir and cracked the spine against the ground. He raised his arm and snapped it into a sword.

"Now, Corpse Walker, you don't want to harm your brother, do you? He is still here somewhere, clinging to his life. Scared."

"Release him."

"We will. I want no harm to come to your brother."

"Who are you—what are you?"

The little boy only smiled.

"Will you come with us?" Finley offered Hayden one of his small rotting hands to hold after peeling it away from the scythe. "My master would like to see you." He looked up at Hayden with black, beady eyes. Hayden had trained against demons and fought a fifteen-foot-tall skeletal monster, but seeing his little brother this way sent a chill down his spine and raised the hairs on the back of his neck. Hayden looked down at Finley's bloodied hand. He shook Marfóir, returning it to a whip, and rolled it back up before fastening it to his belt. He glanced up at Finley's eyes once more before looking back down at his hand.

But then Finley's attention was redirected to the mouth of the cave.

"I thought you were told to come alone," the voice said.

"I did," Hayden said, looking at the cave opening. His hand moved back to gripping the handle of Marfóir. "Whoever's out there, he isn't with me."

"Then you won't care if we kill him."

Finley opened his bloodied hand, his palm facing the ceiling of the cave. He closed his fist tightly and pulled it toward his chest.

"No, don't!"

The Corporal who informed him of the phone call was gasping for air as he was forced to enter the cave.

Hayden stared at the man.

"Let him go," Hayden said, stepping away from Finley as he cracked Marfóir against the ground.

"We told you to come alone," Finley repeated. "Hans told you to come alone. You were warned, Corpse Walker."

"I'm going with you," Hayden assured. "Please, just let him go."

"No."

Hayden looked at the Corporal, who mouthed him an apology. Hayden cracked his whip against the side of Finley's cheek as a warning. Finley touched the side of his face, fingers moistening with the blood seeping through the tear.

"Let him go," Hayden said again. His voice was still calm, but much more serious this time.

The small boy hissed at him.

"You will pay for that," Finley said, wiping his hand forcefully against his pajamas. "This American's blood is on your hands."

Finley twisted his wrist and snapped the Corporal's neck without laying a single finger on him. Hayden flinched at the sight as the Corporal dropped to the ground beside the dead Japanese commanders.

"Come," Finley said to Hayden. "Nurarihyon's patience is wearing thin. As is mine."

Hayden stared at the Corporal's body on the ground. He didn't even know his name. He'd told himself no more would die because of him, and another just did. He sighed in frustration, and his gaze lifted from the body to the decaying hand Finley offered him again. His gaze rose a little further to the cut on Finley's face. It was no longer bleeding, but leaking some kind of silvery fluid. Hayden cocked his head slightly in observation and looked down at the Corporal's body once more.

"I'm sorry," the Corporal said. His spirit lifted from the corpse and looked at Hayden. In death, the man was much more solemn. He only shook his head. "My mom laughed at me," he said quietly, staring at his body. "'You're going to follow orders?' she said when I told her I wanted to enlist. 'You don't even know how to listen.'" Though there was a small smile on his translucent face, it was sad and disappeared quickly. He looked at Hayden. "I guess I never really learned." He faded in and out of sight.

Hayden looked over at Finley. It was clear that whatever was possessing his brother couldn't see the Corporal floating beside him. Hayden took one last look at the Corporal's translucent form, and finally, he took Finley's rotten hand within his own.

It was time for this to end.

Finley gripped Hayden's hand tightly, while still firmly grasping onto the scythe with his other. The small boy leaned forward, tucking his chin toward his body, and the two of them vanished from the cave.

They reappeared at the governor's palace in Guam.

It was a rough landing, and Hayden immediately let go of Finley's hand. He stumbled away and rubbed at his temple. He still firmly held onto his whip which had once more solidified into a sword. Pointing the tip at the ground, he steadied himself.

"Ah, Sergeant Dáithí. So happy you could join us."

Hayden didn't open his eyes, not yet.

"You look pathetic, stumbling about like a drunken fool."

Hayden scowled and looked up at Nurarihyon. The demon looked much worse than he recalled. His head was still badly misshapen. It was twice, maybe even three times, as long as a normal person's. His jaw hung ajar, with his mouth opening extending toward his ears. His long, boney fingers had nails that were even longer than his fingers themselves. Black, beady eyes stared at Hayden. His own stared back.

"Let my brother go," he said, pointing the sword at the demon. Hayden's veins were darkening. "Don't make me kill you."

"Kill me? Now, now… let's not go around making promises we can't keep. You can barely stand. And *you're* the one *I'm* supposed to fear? How sad that this was the best the Americans could do." Nurarihyon waved his hand dismissively. "It's amazing you managed to defeat my Gashadokuro." Nurarihyon looked over at Finley. "I'll let your brother go."

Hayden frowned.

"You will?"

"If you do something for me."

"What?"

"Open the portal," Nurarihyon commanded.

Hayden gripped at Marfóir. Nurarihyon noticed Hayden's hand moving in defense and the corner of his mouth twitched.

"Why can't you do it?" Hayden asked.

Frustrated, Nurarihyon grabbed the scythe from Finley's hands and touched the center of the portal. Hayden took a step back, his hand still tightly gripping his sword.

Nothing happened.

"It won't work for me," he said plainly and pointed the scythe at Hayden. "But you, Corpse Walker, came back from the dead. Handpicked by Death himself from perdition. It wants you."

Hayden slowly made his way around the room, inching closer to his brother.

"And if I say no?" he asked, his hands up in surrender.

"Tadeo will kill your brother," Nurarihyon said plainly. "It would be a true shame for your mother to lose both of her sons."

"You're making a lot of assumptions," Hayden said. "We don't know if it'll work for me."

"We don't know that it won't."

Hayden's attention swept over toward Finley. Somehow his little brother looked even worse than he did in the cave in Saipan. He returned his sword to its whip form and started rolling it up before fastening it to his belt. Hayden held both hands in the air in surrender again before acknowledging his little brother.

"Release him first," he said. "My brother is dying. Tadeo—whatever that is—let my brother go, and I'll do it."

Nurarihyon paced the floor, slowly moving the scythe back and forth between his hands. He looked at Finley, before looking at Hayden. His gaze then dropped to the whip.

"Throw it on the floor," Nurarihyon said.

Hayden followed his opponent's gaze and looked down at the whip fastened to his belt. Without hesitation, he immediately unlatched it and threw it at Nurarihyon's feet, who kicked it far away from the portal. He turned back to Tadeo and nodded.

"Release the boy," Nurarihyon commanded.

Tadeo's spirit fled from Finley's mouth. Silvery smoke filled the air and took the form of a ghostly Akita dog. Nurarihyon handed the scythe to Hayden.

Hayden watched as Finley fell limp to the ground now that the dog spirit was no longer inside of him. Tadeo still remained beside Finley though, as if ready to possess him again should Hayden not obey Nurarihyon's orders.

Nurarihyon stepped aside to allow Hayden access to the portal.

Hayden observed the metal plates of the structure and the metal that covered the ground. He stepped right up to it and looked down. He wasn't sure what type of metal it was made of, but it looked indestructible. It was welded, bolted, and pieced together with care. He might've admired it, had it not been about to release a hundred demons into their world.

"Touch the center," Nurarihyon commanded. He walked around the portal and watched Hayden attentively from the other side. "With the toe of the scythe."

Hayden's eyes were completely black now. His left hand, which held the scythe, was burning as Hayden's flesh began rotting away. Chunks of his flesh were deteriorating in the same spots they always did—first his arm, then his stomach. The gaping holes not only hurt, but they exposed Hayden's bones. He winced a little, but he had grown accustomed to the pain of his rigor mortis and his constant fight against it.

Nurarihyon noticed this.

"Curious," he observed. "Your Corpse Walker form starts to mirror how you looked when you were dead the first time, I presume." Nurarihyon nodded. "Do it now before the scythe consumes you!"

Hayden glanced back at Finley, who stirred on the ground. Relief washed over him at the realization his brother was still alive. Hayden wrapped his other hand around the neck of the scythe and gripped it tightly as he lowered the blade toward the circle in the center.

Across from him stood Nurarihyon, whose hands were in the air. He was chanting something in Japanese.

"Hayden! No!" .

The familiar voice came from behind as the toe of the scythe touched the center of the portal. It exploded. He flew backward and collided with a wall. A myriad of colors streamed out of the opened portal from hell.

Finley sat with eyes wide as the ground began shaking. Colors continued to spill out of the portal and rip through the roof of the governor's palace. He pulled himself with his arms and slowly crawled over to Hayden, who lay unconscious.

Dr. Sauer stood at the door, watching from afar as Nurarihyon picked up the scythe again. He raised it in the air and watched as the demons continued to escape. They were ripping through the portal at such velocity, it was beginning to tear itself apart while the palace began to crumble around them.

"It is upon us," Nurarihyon said, noticing Dr. Sauer in the doorway. "The moment we have been waiting for." A creepy grin stretched far across his face, as his mouth reached straight across, revealing his razor-sharp teeth. "The night parade will march tonight." He nodded toward Dr. Sauer. "If you want to run," he warned. "Do it now."

Dr. Sauer didn't wait for him to speak again. Though he wasn't sure if Nurarihyon was going to spare him, he took the opportunity in case it didn't happen again.

Finley sat against his brother as he tried to wake him.

"Hayden," he said softly, pushing against his chest. "Hayden, wake up!" Finley gripped the front of Hayden's uniform. "Please." The governor's palace was falling apart. Finley looked around for Hayden's whip. Once he spotted it, he crawled over toward it and brought it to his brother. "I need you to get up." He wrapped Hayden's left hand around the handle of the whip. The deterioration from the scythe slowly began to repair as the nether energy flowed through his veins.

Just as Hayden opened his eyes, Finley gave him a small smile. Finley was bleeding from his ears, and he collapsed against his older brother as he fell unconscious. Hayden quickly sat up to catch him. It took him a second to realize what he had done when he noticed the portal breaking apart. He fastened his whip to his belt and quickly scooped Finley up in his arms as he looked for an escape.

The walls of the governor's palace were shaking. Japanese soldiers were running in chaos, fleeing from the site to avoid being crushed by the debris falling from above. Some were taken over in possession by the demons that escaped the portal and walked without a care in the world, almost like zombies, to follow Nurarihyon during the night parade. Hayden backed away, careful to not be seen by them. He could not defend himself while holding his brother.

He had trouble navigating around the palace as he had appeared directly in the lab with Finley when he had initially arrived.

"Pst!" a voice came from behind.

Hayden quickly spun around.

"Who are you?" Hayden asked.

The older white man pulled his dog tags from beneath his shirt.

"Name's Tweed—Radioman of the United States Navy," he said over the noise of the collapsing building. "Let's get you two out of here! Follow me!"

There weren't many he could trust, but Hayden wasn't about to stand in a building that was near demolition. He quickly followed Tweed to his escape.

Hayden frowned once they were outside.

It should have been nearing morning, but the sky remained dark overhead. Light was nowhere in sight.

"What's going on?"

"The demons are keeping the night," he said, checking his watch. It was nearly five o'clock in the morning. "I watched as one flew up to the sky. We're done for, Corpse Walker."

Hayden tilted his head, looking at the older man curiously.

"You know me?"

Tweed tucked his chin down toward his chest, raising his eyebrows in the process as he looked up at him. "I know the Imperial Japanese military don't like you."

Hayden shrugged, shifting his brother's weight in his arms. "The feeling's mutual."

Tweed's smile remained on his face.

"You need help?"

Hayden took a step back, bringing Finley closer to his body.

Tweed raised his arms in surrender.

"I understand." He nodded toward the bridge. "Follow me."

Hayden could feel Tweed's eyes burning holes into his sides with his stares. He glanced over at him once, and then twice.

"Is there something you want to say?" Hayden asked.

Tweed scratched at his ear.

"What happened to you?" Tweed asked finally. His voice was low, in almost a whisper. While they were alone, the Japanese could be anywhere.

"I died," Hayden said, keeping his focus ahead of him. "During the bombing of Pearl Harbor. I was on the USS Oklahoma."

Tweed stopped in his tracks. Hayden stopped too when he looked behind him. He turned around and his brows raised, creasing his forehead to acknowledge Tweed's expression. His eyes were large, and while he looked surprised, he also looked worried.

"I suppose I should've made the connection with your name—Corpse Walker."

Hayden shrugged.

"I wouldn't call it a name."

"What would you call it?"

"A moniker?"

Tweed grinned. "What's the difference?"

"Informality."

Tweed waved his hand. "Ah, technicalities."

"How did you know where I was?"

"I got a message from Miss Sharp. I saw the portal open—I put the two together and there you were."

Hayden looked around as they approached the Chamorro village. Even from what he could see in the dark, much of it was damaged. He looked up at the sky as lights continued to fill overhead with swarming spirits.

"Nurarihyon occasionally came through these villages, stepping into their houses, asking for me. They have no choice but to obey him. I stay in secrecy, and most of them turn a blind eye when they hear a thump in the night. The less they know, the less they have to hide. The less they have to tell him."

"Have you seen him? As... himself?"

Tweed glanced away for a moment before looking at Hayden.

"Only from afar. I try not to get too close."

"Are there any others who escaped?"

Tweed pursed his lips together. "Six of us managed to evade being captured. We fled into the forest and—" his voice trailed off. Hayden glanced over at him. His smile had faded from his face.

"How many are still in hiding?"

"I'm the last," he said with remorse. "The rest were caught and beheaded." He patted a heavy hand on Hayden's shoulder. "Come on, Miss Sharp's coming."

Hayden tilted his head.

"Miss Sharp?"

CHAPTER EIGHTEEN

Guam, July 18, 1944
0527 — local time

Hayden ran toward one of the landing aircraft, holding his brother in his arms. Marines and soldiers filed out of the open door, followed by Dr. Stolly and Miss Sharp. Tweed disappeared with the military while Hayden met the other two at the door.

"Please get him to a hospital as soon as you can," he shouted to Miss Sharp as he handed his brother over to Dr. Stolly, who was much stronger than he looked.

Miss Sharp nodded in assurance.

"Hayden," Dr. Stolly said, almost breathlessly. "What—what did you *do*?"

Hayden looked up at him, still on the aircraft. Dr. Stolly was looking past him at the demons being released into the world through the crumbling governor's palace. A silent fireworks show flickered against the dark sky. Hayden turned around to face the portal as the governor's palace began collapsing into it. He gripped onto his whip with a firm hold.

"I had to save my brother," he said. "But—but I'll fix it." He looked over his shoulder at the two of them. "Please get him to safety."

He didn't wait for a response before he disappeared back into the night.

"You're going to be alright," Miss Sharp said to Finley. She tenderly touched the side of his face, wiping the blood from his ears and mouth. "Do you hear me? You're going to be alright."

"Where's my brother?" he mumbled, before slipping out of consciousness again.

Dr. Stolly did his best trying to make Finley comfortable. He noticed similarities between Finley and Hayden. The same black veins running up toward his eyes. Every time Finley's eyes fluttered for a few seconds at a time, they showed nothing but black. The rotting of his arms and hands reminded him of Hayden's first encounter with the toe of the scythe at the office.

The artifact seemed to have had its own effects on the young boy, and Stolly wondered what would become of him.

Dr. Stolly clenched his jaw and wrapped Finley in the blanket.

Miss Sharp piloted a silver Beechcraft Model 18, which was a twin-engined, low-wing, tailwheel light aircraft manufactured by the Beech Aircraft Corporation. It was one of the most widely used aircraft and the majority of the Air Force bombardiers and navigators trained in them.

***

Susanoo watched with an eagerness that made Amaterasu uneasy. She looked over at her brother, who stared at the waters intently.

"You wish to help them," she said finally, breaking the silence between them.

"I could." He looked up at his older sister and held his hands out. "I could just create a small storm—just a small one," he said, looking back down at the water. "Get the plane back safely faster. Maybe help the military in the process." He stepped away from the seeing waters and walked over to Amaterasu, who looked away from him.

"We are *Japanese* gods," Amaterasu said, keeping her gaze away from him and the water.

"What they're doing is wrong."

She didn't say anything, nor did she look at him.

Susanoo tilted his head.

"They could reach us here, you know. The Yokai."
Still, she refused to look at him. Susanoo narrowed his
eyes at his sister's reaction. "This isn't just about them, is
it? What aren't you telling me?"

Amaterasu finally forced herself to look over at
Susanoo. She remained poised, even though something
was clearly bothering her.

"This is a lot bigger than them," she said finally.
"There is something coming—stirring—from the depths
of the Underworld. I can feel it." Her eyes glistened as
though she were near tears, but nothing came from them.
Instead, she blinked once and looked down at the mortals.
She pursed her lips together and tilted her head as her
gaze returned to her little brother.

"I could never control you, *brother*," she said, her voice
calm and serene as always. "Don't patronize me now by
pretending as though you answer to me." She placed her
hand on his. A very small smile appeared on her face.
He barely noticed it. "We both know Susanoo has always
answered to no one but himself." She gave the back of his
hand a gentle pat. Her eyes glanced over to the waters,
watching the aircraft struggle to get back to Saipan safely.

Amaterasu closed her eyes and bowed, disappearing
into a bright light.

Susanoo looked back down at the war and at the
demons flying through the air. His gaze shifted to the

aircraft. Gently, he blew against the surface of the water, pushing the aircraft further along to land much faster in Saipan.

He then closed his eyes and bowed, his physical form disappearing into a small tornado.

Saipan, July 18, 1944
0550 — local time

The winds picked up, pushing them faster to Saipan. What was normally an hour-long flight took less than fifteen minutes. Miss Sharp landed the aircraft in Isely Field and looked up at the sky curiously for a moment. It was a little brighter in Saipan, but not by much. She quickly took off her headset and bolted out of her seat.

Dr. Stolly still had Finley cradled in his arms.

"How is he doing?" she asked.

"How did we get back so quickly?" he questioned, checking his watch.

"Your guess is as good as mine."

Miss Sharp opened the doors of the aircraft and Marines came in to assist. They picked up the small boy and hurried him to the medical facility.

Colonel Richards boarded.

"Where is he?" he asked the two of them. "Where's the Corpse Walker?"

"He's in Guam, and he could use all the help he can get."

Colonel Richards looked at the two of them. He narrowed his eyes before nodding. He put a cigarette to his lips and fished a lighter out of his pocket.

"I want you two to stay here."

Miss Sharp opened her mouth to protest, but the Colonel silenced her.

"Let me finish," he said. "I want you two to keep an eye on the boy. I saw his wounds—you two know more about that whole thing than anyone else. Monitor him. We'll go in and assist the Corpse Walker. Is there anything I need to know?"

"The portal," Dr. Stolly said. "It's open."

Colonel Richards lit his cigarette. He took a drag and closed his eyes as he dropped his lighter back into his pocket.

"So you're sure Dáithí's still alive?"

Dr. Stolly shrugged and waited a moment before answering.

"If you consider *what* he is to be *alive*, then yes." He looked over at Miss Sharp. "After giving us his brother, he went back for Nurarihyon. He did it to save his brother. Open the portal, I mean."

CORPSE WALKER: THE NIGHT PARADE | 315

"I hate Marines," Colonel Richards said as he exited the aircraft.

"Sir, you are a Marine—"

"Still hate 'em." He looked back at the two of them. "And get this aircraft off the field, Sharp!"

"Yes, sir!" she said with a smile on her face.

"Well, you look cheerful," Dr. Stolly noted as they closed the door.

"They're going to help him," she said.

"They're going against demons," Dr. Stolly added. "This isn't just the Imperial Japanese military."

"Well, they took down a Gashadokuro."

"That was only one. This is Hyakki Yagyō—this is one hundred demons under a command."

Miss Sharp fished through her bag and brought out a newspaper. She quickly rolled it up and smacked Dr. Stolly on the top of his head.

"Will you believe in Hayden?"

"I do," he said calmly, rubbing the top of his head. "I just—how did Nurarihyon even find Finley?"

"Elaina," Miss Sharp said suddenly. "It had to have been Elaina. There's a record of her visiting Hayden shortly after he was arrested. There was also a record of Máiréad Dáithí Quartermaine visiting the facility as well. She must have led Elaina right to their home."

Dr. Stolly sank back in his chair.

"Stop feeling guilty," Miss Sharp said, putting her headset on. "It won't make you feel any better."

Miss Sharp did as the Colonel instructed and moved the aircraft off of the field and tucked it away into the hangar. The two of them collected their things from the Beechcraft.

"We're going to find Finley, and then we're going to contact the Quartermaine family to make sure they know he's safe." She looked over at Dr. Stolly, who seemed lost in his own thoughts. "Are you with me, Zander?" she asked.

He looked over at her and nodded slowly.

"I'll find their number," he replied, nodding a bit quicker this time.

"They're probably going to want to see him as soon as possible," Miss Sharp said as they walked toward the medical facility. "We'll have to figure out when we're able to transport him to Hawai'i and then back to Pennsylvania."

"I know you don't think so," Dr. Stolly began, "but I think you would've been a great mother." His bag was slung over his shoulder and he stuffed his hands into his pockets. "You should give that guy a call when this is all over. What was his name again?"

Miss Sharp rolled her eyes.

"It doesn't matter. This is about Finley."

"A child. That you care about."

"I also care about you."

He shrugged.

"One could argue that I am also a child—compared to you at least. You're very maternal."

"Oh, shut up," she said, shoving him in the arm. Miss Sharp may have been little, but she was certainly strong for her size. Dr. Stolly stumbled away from her a bit before managing to regain his stance. "I'm not *that* old," she huffed.

By the time they reached Finley, he was fast asleep in a hospital bed that was situated in a row with several other wounded military men. He looked peaceful in his sleep, and Miss Sharp didn't want to wake him. She looked over at Dr. Stolly.

He nodded.

"You stay here," he said. "I'll go find their information."

Miss Sharp pulled up a chair and sat beside the young, sleeping boy. A nurse came by to check on him and informed Miss Sharp he was doing just fine and that he would be okay. She nodded and put her hand on the child's upper arm, fondly rubbing against his skin with her thumb.

"You poor thing," she said. He was so young, caught up in something he had no business being in. "But I bet you're going to grow up into someone remarkable one day," she whispered. "You'll go on to do great things and become a great person, just like your older brother."

318 | RALYNN KIMIE

Finley stirred in his sleep and smiled a little.

She wondered then if he could hear her. Her hand moved down to gently squeeze his bandaged hand, and he softly squeezed hers back.

Dr. Stolly went back to his small radio room to look through Hayden's file and find Mrs. Quartermaine's contact information. He sat at the desk and stared at the file. All of the newspaper clippings were piled inside and he went back to the one at York. It was strange to have watched Hayden become who he was. From that man in a wheelchair to a decaying corpse wielding a human spine. The stories in the newspaper were fascinating regarding the creepy Corpse Walker, but Dr. Stolly kept them mostly for his own amusement, as the majority weren't true. One day the truth would be out there once the war ended, and all of these reporters would look foolish.

Dr. Stolly finally picked up the phone and dialed the number from the file.

A frantic woman answered the phone.

"Finley? Finley? Is that you?"

"No, ma'am, this is Dr. Stolly—we found your son—"

"*Oh.* Oh no!"

"No! No, not like that. We—Finley's alive. He's fine, he's here—in Saipan."

"He's *where?*" her voice screeched through the phone, reaching a pitch he didn't know humans could make.

CORPSE WALKER: THE NIGHT PARADE | 319

Dr. Stolly winced. His ear was now ringing.

"Ma'am, we—"

"When can I see him? I have to see him—"

"When the skies are safe, we will bring him back home as soon as we can. I assure you, he's in good hands."

"I was so scared when that Japanese man came for him. I couldn't do anything. I had to obey." Dr. Stolly knew she was talking about Nurarihyon. "But he was with Hayden's friend—"

"She wasn't a friend, Mrs. Quartermaine."

"She? No, he was with Kamuela."

Dr. Stolly nearly dropped the phone.

"Hello?"

"Sorry, Mrs. Quartermaine. You said the Japanese man was with *who*?"

"Sergeant Charles Kamuela. He was the one who brought Hayden back to Hawai'i."

Dr. Stolly blinked several times, trying to process what exactly Mrs. Quartermaine was telling him.

"I'm sorry, Mrs. Quartermaine, but I have to go. I'll call you when I have updates on your son. Your sons, I mean. Take care."

"But—"

Dr. Stolly quickly hung up the phone. He moved Hayden's file out of the way and opened Sergeant Kamuela's. He rubbed at the back of his neck as he started shaking his head. He picked up the files and quickly left the room, going to find Miss Sharp as quickly as his feet would allow.

"Dot—"

"Shh!"

All of the nurses immediately shushed him.

"Dot—" he said again in a strained whisper.

She got up from Finley's bedside and hurried over toward Dr. Stolly who looked so tense his face was red.

"You look like you're about to pass out."

"You said Elaina killed Kamuela."

"I watched the security footage," she said. "Elaina stabbed him with the scythe."

"And we're positive he couldn't have been a double agent too? Maybe both of them were in on it?"

"They were arguing."

"Maybe over who was going to make it back alive."

Miss Sharp shook her head.

"No, this—no. This is *Charlie* we're talking about."

"I just got off the phone with Hayden's mom and Charlie was with Nurarihyon when he kidnapped Finley."

Miss Sharp cupped her mouth with her hands as she took a step back. She started shaking her head.

"No, this can't be. This can't—" she continued to shake her head. Her large eyes were beginning to well with tears. "I don't believe it. I can't—I won't. Are you sure it wasn't Elaina?"

"I verified. Mrs. Quartermaine brought up a friend of Hayden's, and I thought she meant Elaina too. I told her she wasn't a friend, and she brought up Kamuela. She saw him, Dot. She saw *him*."

"We have to tell Hayden."

"How?" Dr. Stolly shrugged, defeated. "We can't."

CHAPTER NINETEEN

Hagåtña, Guam, July 18, 1944
0603 — local time

The portal in the governor's palace was well on its way to collapsing in on itself and was going to take the entire structure with it. Cracks veined through the walls, causing them to crumble down to the foundation as the palace shook from the force. Demonic spirits continued to stream through the mouth of the portal like an upside-down waterfall and a myriad of color pooled into the dark sky. While Nurarihyon called it the night parade of one-hundred demons, it felt like there were thousands. More and more flew into their world with nothing to stop them or hold them back.

Hayden looked up at the constant stream and tightened his hand against the handle of his whip. Running toward the portal, he cracked Marfóir at one of the spirits, then another. Each exploded like glass before their remnants got sucked into the spine of his whip. His chest rose and fell as his blue eyes fixed upon the portal. None of this would matter if he couldn't find Nurarihyon and the scythe to close it. His grip remained firm on the handle of Marfóir as he turned around to search for Nurarihyon. He cracked his whip at another demon, and then another, but as they disappeared into his whip, others just took their places.

He quickly slipped through the halls of the palace, hiding in the sounds of the crumbling walls. Just as he was about to move around a corner, he stopped when he caught sight of Imperial Japanese soldiers. Peeking around the edge, he watched as some of the demons found homes in their mouths. The soldiers' heads were driven back to face the ceiling, mouths wider than what appeared to be humanly possible as the spirits forced their way down into their throats. Each soldier twitched with the possession, bones cracking. Hayden leaned back flatly against the wall. When he was finally daring enough to look again, he was staring with both eyes down the barrel of a gun.

It shot him square in the face before he had the chance to move.

One after another, the Imperial soldiers had aimed their weapons at Hayden before firing. The bullets made holes in his corpse, allowing them to pass through the decay with ease before dropping to the ground all around him. His feet shuffled backward before his limp body hit the floor after the clatter.

His eyelids fluttered. He looked up at the holes in the ceiling of the palace as his fingers moved to touch the new hole in his cheek from getting shot directly in the face and at such a close distance. He sat up from the floor and looked up at the soldiers, a small smirk lifting at the corner of his mouth.

"You shot me in the face!" he snapped, and as he did so, his cheek began to repair itself. Upon seeing the regeneration, the soldier fired at him again, as did the rest. But the bullets only continued to pass right through him.

Hayden chuckled.

"Can't kill what's already dead, I guess." He was partially amused himself. Touching his face again, even Hayden didn't understand nor know the full extent of his abilities. Quickly, he got to his feet and cracked his whip against the ground.

Still, the soldiers guarded Nurarihyon and continued to fire at him, even if it didn't do anything. Some of the souls of the soldiers allowed the demonic possession to take the reins of their bodies while others were clearly fighting against it, as their aim would suddenly jerk in another direction and they'd accidentally shoot one another. Some of the soldiers disappeared altogether. Others jumped higher than humanly possible. One leaped up and punched the ground as he landed, cracking the floor of the governor's palace. Hayden paid no attention to them. They weren't who he was after. While he would capture as many as he could, he only had one real target in mind. If only he could get to him.

"Give me the scythe, Nurarihyon!" Hayden shouted as he slayed the demons around him while the Imperial soldiers continued to fire their weapons at him. He felt every single bullet—even if they did pass through his body like nothing. Though the bullets didn't exactly do anything, they were an inconvenience and even stung a little. Despite this inconvenience, Hayden was focused on trying to get to Nurarihyon while driving the other demons out of the bodies they possessed. His whip would wrap around their necks and extract the demon in a shatter before pulling what was left of them into the whip's spine.

"So focused on me—" Nurarihyon taunted as he started for the door, holding tightly to the scythe. He made a tsk noise with his tongue against the roof of his mouth as he tilted his elongated head. "When someone has been dying to see you. Where are your manners, Corpse Walker?" he asked.

A man stepped out of the shadows as if on cue. Hayden turned around and narrowed his eyes as he took a step closer to whatever it was now making its presence known. Hayden tilted his head forward, tucking his chin

CORPSE WALKER: THE NIGHT PARADE | 327

down toward his chest, and raised his eyebrows before coming to a halt. He couldn't believe what he was seeing. He blinked several times and furrowed his brows.

"Kamuela?" he asked, confused. He remained frowning at what he was staring at. "It's not possible…"

"Kill him, Tadeo," Nurarihyon commanded just before he slipped away into the darkness, with several of the Imperial soldiers quickly following behind to remain as his guards. Others stayed to fire their weapons at Hayden.

"Tadeo?" Hayden didn't take his eyes off of his old friend.

It was the same dog spirit who possessed Finley.

Hayden wondered if Sergeant Kamuela's soul was clinging to life in his body, fighting against Tadeo.

"Are you still in there, Charlie?" he asked loudly. Parts of his body turned translucent as the Imperial Japanese soldiers continued to fire at him. The bullets went right through him as if he weren't really there. No longer making holes in his body, just zooming through the air till they hit the walls. "I'll get you out."

The veins in his face darkened toward his eyes, and his blue eyes turned black.

"He's not in here," Tadeo said through Sergeant Kamuela's mouth. "Nurarihyon killed him long ago." Sergeant Kamuela lunged at Hayden as the rest of the possessed Japanese soldiers filed out to follow Nurarihyon.

Hayden dodged the attack, and Sergeant Kamuela jumped toward the wall. His hands and feet hit it both at the same time as he pushed off of it and leaped around the room like a dog without touching the ground. It was then Hayden noticed Sergeant Kamuela's twisted and bruised neck.

Sergeant Kamuela *was* dead.

Hayden's eyes watered, watching Tadeo create a perversion of his best friend.

"Why would you volunteer for something so stupid?" Hayden asked, whipping Sergeant Kamuela's arm with the tip of Marfóir. Sergeant Kamuela hissed at Hayden as he winced. He looked down at the cut on his arm and shook off the pain. Hayden cracked his whip again, and this time Sergeant Kamuela caught it. He wrapped it around his hand and yanked it out of Hayden's before throwing it to the side.

Hayden looked at the fresh slice in his hand. He curled his fingers closed over the wound and tightened his fist as Sergeant Kamuela lunged at him again. He gripped the front of Hayden's uniform and threw him into the crumbling wall with ease.

"You should've seen it," Sergeant Kamuela mocked. "Nurarihyon snapped his neck like a toothpick."

While it sounded like Sergeant Kamuela, it clearly wasn't. Sergeant Kamuela's voice was smooth and friendly. Part of the reason why people were often drawn to him was the undertone of warmth and welcome in the resonance. His voice was there, but the geniality was gone. This was cold and rigid. It was dead.

The rims of Hayden's eyes were red. His pale face was flushed with the blood left in his body.

Sergeant Kamuela got closer and laughed maniacally in Hayden's face. Hayden punched him in the jaw and got up from the rubble.

"You're pulling your punches," Sergeant Kamuela said, rubbing his chin. "Unless that's the best the feared Corpse Walker can do? *Pathetic*."

Even though Hayden knew Sergeant Kamuela was dead, it was still his face. Hayden couldn't shake that. His mind was overwhelmed with everything the two of them had been through, stemming from bootcamp so many years ago. He remembered the look on Sergeant Kamuela's face when he saw Hayden alive again for the first time since Pearl Harbor. His eyes continued to water as he looked at Sergeant Kamuela, unable to fight him. Hayden shut his eyes and turned away.

Sergeant Kamuela punched Hayden in the face again and again, cracking his cheek and brow bone. Sergeant Kamuela kicked him square in the chest and flung him right into another crumbling wall.

"Fight back!" he shouted at Hayden, stalking after him with his fists balled up. "You didn't deserve another chance at life."

Those words triggered Hayden's memory of drowning. His memories of dying from the bombing of Pearl Harbor on the USS *Oklahoma*. The searing water burning him from the inside and out. His eyelids fluttered, and through his watery sight, he could see the handle of Marfóir in the surrounding rubble.

"Get up," something whispered in his ear. "Get up, Dáithí."

Hayden looked to his left and saw a green-tinted translucent corporeal form of Sergeant Kamuela beside him. He closed his eyes and turned away.

"Get up, Hayden!" he urged. "Kill him for me. Please."

Hayden looked back at the ghostly form. Sergeant Kamuela turned to face his body, just before he took another swing at Hayden. He managed to duck out of the way just in time. He tumbled across the ground and grabbed Marfóir as he got to his feet.

"Finally," Tadeo said through Sergeant Kamuela's mouth. There was blood leaking from the corner of his lips. Tadeo's possession was destroying what was left of Sergeant Kamuela's body. Hayden glanced over at Sergeant Kamuela's spirit, who nodded at him. Sergeant Kamuela's ghost attacked Tadeo as a distraction, causing him to split from his body for just a moment. While it only lasted a few seconds, Hayden could see the ghost of the dog. He raised his arm and cracked his whip.

In a swift movement, Hayden wrapped Marfóir tightly around Sergeant Kamuela's neck. It forcefully dragged Tadeo's spirit out of the body and latched onto the spine of the whip as Hayden pulled it off of his old friend. The lifeless body dropped to the floor.

He looked Tadeo's spirit in the eyes.

"*Fuck you,*" Hayden whispered.

The dog's spirit shattered. Its remnants seeped into the whip as the tip of Marfóir fell lifeless to the ground. Hayden dropped to his knees next to Sergeant Kamuela. He felt Sergeant Kamuela's neck for a pulse, but he couldn't feel anything. His body was cold to the touch. His friend was long gone.

He looked around, but Sergeant Kamuela's ghost was nowhere to be seen.

Hayden roared in agony, gripping onto his friend's uniform. His black veins protruded from his forearms and neck as the nether energy rippled through his body with rage. His eyes were pitch-black as his skin and flesh began to rot away again, showing his bones and decaying insides. There was a faint forest-green glow emitting from his skin as his left hand pulled the whip across his body and whipped it toward the left. It cracked violently against the ground.

"Nurarihyon!" the Corpse Walker bellowed, cracking Marfóir again.

The ground trembled beneath him.

Existing within Hayden was an unfamiliar rage he had never felt before. He was angry at Sergeant Kamuela for volunteering for something so stupid, angry at Agent Dacua for bringing him to Nurarihyon, and angry at Nurarihyon for his transgressions—for using Sergeant Kamuela's and Finley's bodies in such a cavalier manner.

Everything was piled on top of one another, increasing Hayden's anger to a level he had never once reached in his life. It had always been important to his mom to keep himself calm and collected, but at that moment, he was having difficulty. He cracked Marfóir against the ground again, causing it to break the floor beneath it. His heart pounded wildly in his chest as his eyes remained pitch-black. The nether energy in his veins continued to seep toward his eyes.

CHAPTER TWENTY

Hagåtña, Guam, July 18, 1944
0733 — local time

Agents of R.A.V.E.N. arrived on Guam with the requested backup of the United States military. Dr. Hans Sauer was quickly found and taken into custody while the United States continued a search for Nurarihyon and the Corpse Walker.

Dr. Sauer was kept in a small room aboard one of the destroyers sitting in the water off Guam's shores. His blond hair stuck up in several different directions but remained smoothed down in the front where his goggles had sat tightly on top of his head. He sat in the dimly lit room alone and twiddled his thumbs as he waited. He wasn't sure what for, but he smiled smugly to himself, knowing the night parade was already upon them. There was nothing the Americans could do now.

Colonel Richards opened the large metal door. He held a file in his calloused hands and looked over the data they had collected on the doctor seated before him.

"Are you German?" he asked, looking down at the blond man.

"I'm Polish," Dr. Sauer answered without looking up.

"So why do you work for Mori?"

Dr. Sauer sat back in his chair as he pondered the question. He was facing forward, not acknowledging the Colonel's presence at all.

"He killed my family," Dr. Sauer said simply and monotonously, only after a prolonged silence between the two men. His gaze remained fixed on nothing before him, and he didn't bother to look up at the Colonel still. "Murdered them on the street, right before my very eyes."

"Who? Mori?"

"The Nazis," he corrected. "When they invaded Poland."

Colonel Richards tilted his head, trying to comprehend what Dr. Sauer was telling him. His meaty hand gripped the top of the metal chair and pulled it out for him to sit across from Dr. Sauer. He took a seat with a grunt and dropped the file onto the table between them.

"I'm not following any of this," he admitted. Colonel Richards sat back and crossed his arms, his eyes remaining fixed on the doctor seated before him.

"I hate *humans*," Dr. Sauer answered plainly, still staring at nothing. His gaze never lifted to meet the Colonel's and instead, his expression remained blank. "Don't you?" Dr. Sauer then laughed, amused by his own question. "No, of course you don't. You're a colonel. You like war, don't you, Colonel? It's people like you who probably enjoy that us humans don't know how to exist with one another without greed and hate."

"You don't know what I like or don't like."

Colonel Richards got out of the chair and pushed it into the table. He gathered the file and headed for the door. The corner of Dr. Sauer's mouth twitched, lifting into a slight and gentle smile.

"You will lose," he added.

Colonel Richards turned around. His hand was already grasping the knob. His thick, graying brows furrowed below his wrinkled forehead.

"America?" he asked. His voice was a lot deeper and more gruff than Dr. Sauer's. It was harsher to listen to.

Dr. Sauer swept his gaze over to him without turning his head.

"Humanity." Dr. Sauer finally turned his head as well. "Humanity deserves to perish." The small smile remained on his face.

"You know that means you perish with us, right?"

"A small price to pay," Dr. Sauer said, tilting his head. "Humans have grown into a perversion of what God had intended. Life should start anew."

"I don't think life starts anew with demons," the Colonel said as he opened the door. Two Marines stepped in.

"Perhaps not, but they will rid a plague."

"Guess that makes you a villain."

"Under the right circumstances, anyone can become a villain, Colonel."

Colonel Richards stared at Dr. Sauer for a few seconds longer. He narrowed his eyes, already squinting from age, before leaving the doctor alone. The two Marines who came to meet him exchanged glances with one another before their eyes focused on the Colonel.

"Did Sauer say anything?" one asked. He was no older than twenty. In addition to his dark brown hair, he had a very sharp jaw and a slightly crooked nose which gave his face character.

"Having him in custody is useless," the Colonel said.

"At least we know he's still loyal," the other Marine said.

Colonel Richards cocked a brow just as the two of them had an exchange in Japanese. He leaped back as their faces distorted from human to monstrous. A translucent arm reached out from the body of one and toward the Colonel as he took another two steps back with the shuffling of his feet. He then snarled a little and regained his composure as he cracked one of the Marines in the face. The demon split from him for a second before becoming one again. He shoved the Colonel up against the wall without even touching him. Colonel Richards could feel his airways restricting as the demon began to suffocate him. He gripped at his throat, nails clawing at his own skin as he struggled to breathe.

Two small black stones hit both of the Marines in the faces—one stone slogging each of them in the eye. They floated in midair after impact, and the demons were extracted from the bodies and sucked into the stones. The Colonel dropped to the ground. He gasped for air, hands still at his throat as he watched the stones fall. He looked up at the two Marines who both appeared discombobulated.

"They were possessed," said a corporal as he caught up to the Colonel.

"Yeah, no shit. What was that you hit them with?"

"Black tourmaline," he said, picking the crystals up from the ground. "My sister's into—weird stuff—crystals and tarot cards and whatever. She said they swallow negative energy. I wasn't sure it was going to work." He looked down at the two in his hand. "I'm never going to be mean to her again."

"So you just threw pebbles at my possessed Marines with the hopes it was going to do something?"

"I mean, it worked."

"That's beside the point, Corporal." Colonel Richards looked at the small stones. "What are you gonna do with those?"

"Drop them in the ocean. If they crack, they'll just be released again and you know what they say, the oceans are the doors to the Underworld."

"Is that right?"

He shrugged.

"That's what my sister says, anyway."

"Where can we get more?"

"I don't know, Sir—I only have—"

A sergeant came running from around the corner. Slightly out of breath, he inhaled sharply and his eyes met the Colonel's.

"Colonel? You're gonna wanna come see this."

The two men followed the Sergeant with no time to spare. From the destroyer, they could see the beach and the demons that were gathered upon it.

"Do we know how many there are?" he asked.

The Sergeant shook his head.

"There's at least a hundred—but that guy," the Sergeant said, acknowledging the one with the misshapen head. "I'm assuming that's gotta be Nurarihyon."

Colonel Richards focused his attention on him. There was no doubt in his mind. He hit the Corporal for his pair of binoculars and adjusted them so he could see him better. Nurarihyon. His misshapen head could be seen from anywhere, along with those sharp teeth, and his long, boney fingers that were choking the neck of the scythe. Colonel Richards looked above at the thundering storm clouds over them in the night sky. He checked his watch. It was nearing nine in the morning, and yet it looked as though it were nine at night.

The ground forces began firing at Nurarihyon and the night parade. Colonel Richards adjusted his binoculars to get a better view. They were killing everything in their wake, from the surrounding United States military, to the very earth they walked upon. The trees shriveled, and the grass grew dry and stiff. Colonel Richards pulled the binoculars from his eyes and inhaled deeply.

"You don't have more of those pebbles, Corporal?"

"Not nearly enough," he said.

"What?" the Sergeant asked, but the Colonel only shook his head. Despite all that they've seen, how could he explain stones extracted the demons through the eyes? He furrowed his thick and unruly graying eyebrows and tightened his grip on the binoculars. The destroyer they stood on was in chaos after what was happening on the shore, not too far from where they stood.

"Sir—" another corporal came running toward him. "Stolly's on the phone. He's got news from the Republic of Letters. Something about exorcism scrolls."

Colonel Richards sighed as he looked up at the sky. "God, help us."

***

Hayden had been searching for Nurarihyon since he'd been sent to fight his dog demon. He managed to evade the Japanese military, both possessed and not, and the spirits in the air seemed less than concerned with his presence. Even as he hit and trapped several of them, the rest were unfazed.

He made his way through Chamorro villages, and while he was focused, eyes black, and veins darkening in his face and throughout the arm that wielded his whip, he turned his head when he heard screaming. He looked ahead, where he could see Nurarihyon just a little further, but the screaming was pulling his attention.

Hayden quickly ran through the rubble of the destroyed homes, searching for where the sound was coming from. It was only after he slowed down that he began to take in his surroundings. His chest tightened as his boots crushed debris beneath his feet with every step. While he did his best to focus on the screaming that had jerked his attention, he had a hard time numbing himself from the ruin of the village. He remembered what Tweed had told him as the Chamorro people did their best to protect him. Innocents, civilians, who had given everything. Who had lost everything.

Smoke had found home in his nose and lungs, along with the powdered smell of the burning wreckage. He thought of his own family. He clenched his jaw and shook his head as if to shake the thoughts from his mind.

He hadn't even realized he had stopped walking.

Hayden nearly dropped his whip when another scream ripped through his ears and jolted him free of the thoughts he had gotten lost in.

Just up ahead, he approached a small shack with the roof caved in. As quietly as he could manage with his boots crushing over the wreckage, Hayden patrolled along the side of the wall on defense. He turned his head as he listened carefully.

There were murmurs, cries, and infrequent screams growing hoarse.

Hayden rolled up his whip and fastened it to his belt as he attempted to move the door, causing the roof to sink in further. Someone inside shrieked and he stopped immediately, not wanting it to collapse in on itself.

"Hold on!" he shouted.

He ran around the small shack, observing the foundation and structure as he looked for an entry point. Through a small window, he saw a Yokai terrorizing the family inside. A small girl was crying, trying to get it away from her. It was an extremely ugly, naked old woman, dropping down from the ceiling with a long snake tongue flicking from her mouth. A man was trying to hit her with a broom, while a woman cradled the young girl. Hayden pulled his whip from his belt, crossed his body, and cracked it against the ground before whipping it at the old woman. He grabbed the Yokai woman by her neck and she broke just like the rest, shattering into pieces with its remnants and black smoke seeping into the spine of his whip.

Hayden quickly ran toward the small window and reached for the little girl to help her out before helping her parents.

"I've never seen one of those before," the woman said, not looking Hayden in the eyes. "Tenjō Kudari," she whispered, looking back at the window from which she crawled out of. She held tightly onto her daughter before glancing up at the Corpse Walker. "We're all going to die, aren't we?"

His eyes widened, and he immediately began shaking his head.

"No, of course not. I'm going to stop this. I'm going to—"

"You're just one person," she said quietly. Her voice came out defeated. She averted her dark brown eyes, no longer wanting to look at him while his skin faded between black and its normal blue hues. "How can you alone stop the night parade?"

The family of three didn't wait for him to respond and quickly ran off into the forest, far away from their burning village. Hayden remained standing there, dejected. He looked down at the small doll the girl must have dropped. Hayden reached down to pick it up—her hair was frizzy, burnt, and the side of her face was charred. He tucked it into his uniform and looked up for the family that had just fled, but they were already long gone.

He was only one person, and he needed help. He looked up at the sky before looking down at his hands and at his whip. Hayden tightened his grip onto the handle of Marfóir and cracked it once against the ground. He inhaled deeply, his veins blackening up his arms and in his face toward his eyes. He tilted his head and cracked his neck before exhaling his breath.

Hayden finally closed his eyes. He thought of the dark place he visited accidentally and he concentrated hard.

Help me. It was a silent plea, but it was heard.

Within seconds, hundreds of green ghostly forms began to materialize from the ground.

The Dullahan were coming.

CHAPTER TWENTY-ONE

The Dullahan arrived at Hayden's request, assisting with not only keeping many of the demons at bay but also driving them out of the Japanese soldiers they possessed and chaining them to their horses. Their own spine whips worked similarly to Hayden's when it came to expelling the demons from the bodies, but they didn't absorb them the way Hayden's could. He did his best at catching the ones that tried to flee and trapping them in the spine but watched as some headed for the shoreline. He could see it out in the distance. He and the Dullahan stood like a wall between the early formation of the night parade and the portal itself.

The demons began to line up behind Nurarihyon. While some remained in possession of the Japanese military, others were beginning to solidify into their own forms. Hayden recognized several as Oni—and Dr. Stolly hadn't been lying when he said the one he fought during his training had only been a small one. These were large, some bigger than houses. Further, Hayden could see a few types of demons he recognized, after having fought similar ones that he and Dr. Stolly summoned, but there were much more he didn't know of—and what they were capable of. There were Japanese lanterns and floating heads flying about as the wind picked up. Giant spiders with bodies larger than bears crawling across the beach.

Hayden clenched his jaw and looked above at the continued night sky—storm clouds began to roll in as it thundered overhead. As more of the Oni began to materialize, the storm worsened. Lightning crackled as it lit up the sky, and rain began to pour heavily, quickly drenching the troops and creatures upon the beach. He wiped the water from his face and smoothed his dampening blond hair back.

"Hayden, none of this will matter unless we destroy the portal," his father said in a gruff, deep, and commanding voice while wielding his own whip. He steadied his translucent and headless horse. Hayden watched as the raindrops went right through them. He didn't get a good look at his father up until that point, and it was then he realized just how much he looked just like him, and how little he looked like his mother. Only his father had a stronger and more defined jawline, with dark, sullen eyes that appeared to have seen too many wars. Hayden hadn't known much of his dad aside from the stories his mom used to tell him as a child. She mentioned his dad serving in some kind of force, but couldn't recall the branch she mentioned, if she mentioned one at all. Maybe the Dullahan was what she had been referring to. But then she would have known… Hayden shook his head, trying not to get lost in his thoughts. They were at war. "The more we slay," his dad continued, "the more come through."

Hayden nodded, trying to focus. "I thought about that too." He looked back at the portal's stream of demons and the crumbling palace around it. What was once quite beautiful, although overrun by the Japanese military, was now reduced mostly to rubble and continued to crumble down to the foundation. A white three-arched gate remained standing, but even that had its own cracks within it, and would likely fall before this was over.

Gunfire and raids rang in his ears as he stood in observation. His eyes grazed over his surroundings, from the palace on fire, to the smoking trees, and the demons fleeing to the shoreline. Finally, he spotted Nurarihyon at the front, the wet scythe glinting under the moonlight in his hands as the rain continued to pour. He held it up in the air and began chanting in Japanese.

Hyakki Yagyō, or the night parade of a hundred demons, was an eruption of supernatural demons let loose upon the mortal world. It wasn't until that moment that Hayden realized they had been taking it much too literally. It wasn't just a *hundred* demons, it was thousands. Demons continued to possess soldiers, now both Japanese and American, while others materialized into their own monstrous forms. Hayden could feel the ground swaying beneath his feet as he watched the march at the shoreline.

The night parade began.

It was unlike the individual attacks by demons, who could only do so much damage as they took possession and adjusted to their time in Guam. Some adjusted faster than others, being able to use their abilities, but the parade struck a different kind of force. It erupted throughout the island of Guam with such fervor everyone could feel the trembles, and nature died beneath their feet with every step they took. They moved like a disease, killing everything in their path as their upsurge over the landmass kept on. The Oni maintained control over the weather and thunder boomed as it rolled in ahead with lightning striking in flashes throughout the sky.

"Looks like he got what he wanted," Hayden mumbled softly. He still maintained a grip on Marfóir but it loosened, and the spine was resting lifelessly on the ground. He didn't even know where to go from there. "I failed."

Hayden's heart pounded ferociously in his chest as he looked over at his dad, who was looking curiously behind Hayden.

"Are you waiting for him to kill everyone in Guam, Sergeant Dáithí?" asked the familiar voice.

Hayden immediately turned around and saw Susanoo standing there. His pained expression melted into one of relief.

"I need help. I can't-"

Susanoo smiled.

"You can," he said, and then nodded. "But I created this mess," he said, leaping high in the air. He levitated above while Hayden and the Dullahan watched. "And the least I can do is help end it. Leave the weather up to me." Susanoo looked up and headed straight into the dark, thundering sky. Hayden looked back at his father as he once more wiped the water from his face.

"I'll join the Dullahan," Hayden said finally, blinking through wet lashes as he looked at each of the ghostly members before his gaze returned to his dad. "But I need your help first."

His father's expression remained stern, but he agreed.

"You have our strength and our numbers," he said reassuringly. "We will follow you, Corpse Walker, till your end."

Hayden nodded as he turned around. He crossed his arm over his chest and cracked his whip firmly against the wet earth. It struck the earth with such velocity that the ground split beneath it. His eyes blackened, and his gaze fixed upon Nurarihyon.

"Let's finish this."

Hayden began running, with the Dullahan following closely behind. His veins were darkening, and as he blinked, he managed to slip into pockets created by the portal. He would disappear in one, and reappear through another closer to Nurarihyon, appearing almost as though he were teleporting across the island.

Nurarihyon was unfazed by him and the oncoming force. He could feel the energy from the demons who were now under his command, thousands of them to do his bidding—the strength of all at his disposal.

Above, Susanoo worked to clear the skies, blowing away the storms that he was usually the cause of. When he stopped the rain, the Oni just caused another downpour. A silhouette of his giant face could be seen in the clouds as they roared above and battled against one another—his own storm against that of the Oni and the sky demon shielding Guam from the sunlight.

Agents of R.A.V.E.N. moved in with scrolls for exorcism, handwritten by an Onmyōji spell-caster. They went after the possessed American troops and drove the demons out of their bodies when they could get close enough with the scrolls and the protection chants. The agents came to aid those who were badly injured, while others who still had the strength rejoined the fight.

Hayden just had to get close enough to Nurarihyon to be able to reach him with his whip. He lifted his arm in the air and pulled it down across his body toward the ground, solidifying Marfóir into a sword. The demons that had taken their own form were the ones he aimed for, slicing thighs to cause them to lose their balance and be trampled by the Dullahan. The Yokai were shattering all around them, going up in smoke. Their spirits would get sucked into Marfóir while Hayden continued to make his way toward the front. He ran straight down the parade.

A blow to the gut surprised him and knocked him right off his feet, driving the air right out of his lungs. He coughed and inhaled sharply, his hand moving to his stomach as he looked up at the Oni standing over him. He held a bloody arm, and Hayden didn't want to know where he had gotten it. Once he noticed it though, he was overwhelmed by the smell of iron—an unusual thing to take notice of when he couldn't even smell the rot of his own body. Hayden slowly got to his feet as the Oni smacked the arm against the palm of his claw, ready to strike him again. This one was much larger than the first and last one he encountered up close. He was blue with four horns growing out of the sides of his head, three bulging eyes, sharp claws, and fangs protruding from his mouth.

Hayden glanced at the ground, but he couldn't spot his whip. He slowly got to his feet, not taking his eyes off of the Oni as he did so. It grunted and growled at him before taking a bite of the arm he held in his claw. Hayden clenched his jaw and looked away for a second. He took another deep breath and concentrated.

His body began fading in and out of its corporeal form just as the Oni tried to strike him again with the severed arm. Instead of smacking him, it went right through him. Hayden swiftly moved behind the monster with a quick shuffle of his feet and grabbed hold of the Oni's skull. His fingers dug deep into his temples just beneath his horns as the Oni's eyes widened. He clouded the Oni's vision and induced a fear into his core. The Oni reached behind, trying to club Hayden with the arm, but soon his own arm fell limp. He dropped the severed limb and fell to his knees. Hayden then jabbed his finger into the Oni's third eye as hard as he could, popping the eye out of its socket. The second he spotted Marfóir, he leaped off of the Oni, tumbled on the ground, and grabbed it. Still solidified into a sword, he swiftly cut the Oni's head clean off. Hayden landed on the ground harshly and rubbed at his knees.

"Are you alright?" a member of the Dullahan asked as he pulled a demon from a body with his bare hands and bound the spirit with some kind of ghostly cuffs. Hayden watched with eyes wide and nodded.

"I should've stretched," he mumbled, still rubbing his knees.

The ghostly form only smiled before nodding ahead.

"Now's your chance—" he said, acknowledging Nurarihyon who was just up ahead. "Go!" he urged. The Dullahan grabbed another spirit and began chaining them to his horse.

Hayden didn't hesitate. Raising his arm, he shook Marfóir back into a whip and used the pockets created from the portal to move closer to Nurarihyon undetected.

Just as he raised his arm, a Japanese woman with long, flowing black hair stepped in front of him. Hayden stopped in his tracks.

"Ma'am, you're going to get hurt!" he said, urging her to get off the beach. The woman tilted her head. She held a small hand fan over her face and peered over at him with small eyes.

"Watashi, kirei?" she asked in a small voice. He could barely hear her over the commotion.

Hayden furrowed his brows and shook his head.

"I don't speak Japanese—" he began as another Oni charged at him. He quickly slipped out of the way and cracked Marfóir between its shoulder and neck. It shattered. "Please, ma'am, find a—"

"Pretty?" she asked. Her slender, pale hand was wrapped around her fan, but she used her index finger to point at herself.

"Yes—" Hayden said, just as she pulled her mask down to reveal the mutilation of her face, her mouth sliced open from ear to ear and her jaw fell open.

"Now?"

She was a Yokai. They really did just look like anything.

Hayden took a step back.

"No," he said firmly.

Her gaze narrowed. She pulled out large scissors with the hand hiding behind her back and sprung at him in an attempt to slice open his face. Hayden stepped back, knocking the scissors out of the way with Marfóir but she was extremely fast. Before he had the chance to blink, she was at it again, the scissors nearly slicing his face as he landed on his back against the beach. He caught the metal with his hand and pushed it away from him, but she pushed further with her weight. Hayden lifted his leg and shoved her shoulder with his foot. He scrambled to his feet and cracked Marfóir at her.

She caught the spine with her hand fan and yanked it from his grasp.

The woman tilted her head.

"Pretty?" she asked again, now wielding her own weapon and his.

"Maybe in your *own* way," he said. He tried to focus on her, but at the same time, caught sight of a few flying Japanese lanterns that were draining the souls from American troops. They weren't ordinary Japanese lanterns, but split open at the bottom as a mouth, with two tired eyes and hair growing around what appeared to be a face between two pieces of split bamboo. The more souls they stole, the more human in appearance they became.

He could feel his anger rising again as the bodies dropped to the ground, and the lanterns flew around for more souls.

Hayden tightened his fists and cracked his knuckles as she hissed at him again.

"Give me my whip back," he snarled and ran toward her as she ran at him with her giant scissors. Hayden jumped right in front of the scissors, allowing her to stab through his abdomen. The scissors slid through his decaying body with ease, and as she tried to free it, he was close enough now to rip Marfóir from her hand. He quickly wrapped the spine around her neck and choked her till she shattered. The black smoke absorbed and the scissors in his body disappeared.

Hayden dropped to his knees and groaned. His hand covered his stomach as he doubled over in pain. That was a lot different than getting shot in the face.

He gripped at the wound, and his other hand, still firmly holding Marfóir, began to tremble. The black nether energy began to encompass him and his whip. Bellowing in pain, an earthquake erupted from where he knelt, immediately downing thirty demons that were coming his way. The bones in their bodies all began to misshapen and crack in toward each other as they folded into themselves like origami before absorbing entirely into the back smoke that crept over the earth like fog.

Hayden looked down at his body as the nether energy began to sew him back together. Breathing deeply, he took a second to gather himself.

He felt a tickle at the back of his neck.

It was one of the lanterns. The energy of draining surrounding spirits to repair his wound had drawn the attention of the Yokai lanterns. He smacked the tongue away with his hand before quickly getting to his feet.

Hayden looked back at the bodies of the American troops whose lives the lanterns had already stolen. With all of his anger and might, he cracked Marfóir and ripped its paper face open. Dozens of tiny white balls of pure light were released as the lantern drifted toward the ground. He watched as they floated toward the sky while the pieces of the lantern shriveled up and the smoke seeped into his whip.

Another lantern came flying toward him. He grabbed it with his other hand and tore it apart. The same thing happened. Several little tiny balls of light were set free. Hayden forced himself to harden his expression. He dropped the paper pieces of the lantern on the ground and turned back toward Nurarihyon.

He felt stronger now after absorbing the energy of the surrounding demons. Hayden gripped tightly to Marfóir and his body drifted between a solid form and a translucent one. He darted toward Nurarihyon quicker now, again using the small pockets between the living and the dead that now existed on their plane created by the portal to move closer to the commanding demon.

The very tip of Marfóir smacked Nurarihyon in the head at such velocity that the bones of the whip tore the side of his face open. It was this that caused Nurarihyon to shake from his delusion of grandeur. When he turned around, he watched in horror as the Dullahan came in full force, trampling over his demon parade, while the United States military fired from a distance at the human Imperial soldiers who remained loyal to him. Nurarihyon watched as the agents of R.A.V.E.N. continued to free their own from possession, and he snarled. He shoved the end of the scythe into the ground before lifting it in the air, hoping to regain control of the chaos.

Nothing happened this time. Any control he had with the scythe was gone.

The parade began to dissipate, and Nurarihyon fell back.

His large, bulging eyes grew larger in his defeat, and he quickly retreated back to where it all began. Hayden followed, slaying demons left and right who still attempted to defend Nurarihyon even as he fled. Hayden did not hold back when it came to his chase. He was faster now, both in speed and precision.

He didn't miss another target. Not once.

While his confidence in his abilities grew, Hayden wasn't sure what he would find when he re-entered the palace. Most of it had been reduced to rubble, with the limbs of corpses peeking from the debris.

It didn't take him long to find Nurarihyon at the portal, watching the demons continue to stream through and into the world. His head was badly bleeding from the altercation, and he stood at the portal, appearing defeated. He was quiet. Sullen. Hayden remained apprehensive.

"You've come to mock me," Nurarihyon said quietly, noticing he was no longer alone and that he was now in the company of the Corpse Walker. "Because it doesn't work on you."

"What?"

"My... control," he admitted, though rather unwillingly. "I can slip into places, homes, and no one bats an eye. That's how I captured your brother. Your mother couldn't do anything about it. None of them could. But you—my powers... They don't work on you."

"I've been known to disappoint."

Nurarihyon smiled a little and shook his head at the comment.

"I don't scare you, do I."

"It's hard to be scared when you've already killed me once. Guess I have you to thank for this." Hayden looked at his decaying arm that held the whip. There was still a faint smoky layer of nether energy encompassing his body.

Nurarihyon didn't acknowledge it.

"You know what's funny about humans," he continued instead, looking past the portal and at Hayden. "Even when things seem grim, you find a way to persevere. You don't give up." Nurarihyon's voice trailed off. "Why not?" he asked, tilting his elongated head.

"You wanted to end humanity," Hayden said, not taking his eyes off of him. "I think anyone would fight for their own survival."

"But you are no longer *alive*, Corpse Walker."

"No, but my family is—my friends are—" Hayden watched as Nurarihyon fiddled with the scythe. "I noticed it helped you command your company."

Nurarihyon looked at the scythe. His long, boney fingers were loosely grasping onto it. "Barely, and with great resistance. Even Death is on your side—but I suppose I should have already known. He brought you back, after all." Nurarihyon ran a long fingernail down the length of the handle. "What do you know of the Infernal Artifacts?" he asked.

"Not much," Hayden admitted. "I know there's at least three but—"

Nurarihyon nodded approvingly.

"The scythe, the book, and the sand."

Hayden furrowed his brows.

"The sand?"

"Dream," he said quietly. "Dream." Nurarihyon closed his eyes, but Hayden remained on edge, refusing to let his guard down. "You wake up and rub the sand from your eyes—the sleep—the dreams."

Nurarihyon pressed a hand against his wound. Hayden saw it as his chance. He used Marfóir to grab the scythe and ripped it free from Nurarihyon's grasp. Holding onto it tightly with both hands, he hammered the toe of the scythe right into the center of the metal plates. Screeching, demons howled and shrieked as the portal sealed itself shut.

Nurarihyon watched with eyes wide as his stream of demons all but disappeared instantly. He took a step back and attempted to run, but Marfóir was whipped around his neck before he had the chance to move.

Hayden pulled the Japanese demon toward him and shoved the toe of the scythe into Nurarihyon's chest. What was once a terrifying creature now appeared to be a frail old man with a misshapen head.

Hayden refused to have sympathy for him.

He murdered Sergeant Kamuela.

He was responsible for hundreds of deaths.

"You're going back to whatever Hell you crawled out of," Hayden said, pushing the scythe further into Nurarihyon's body. He didn't bother to writhe, even as the whip tightened around his neck.

Nurarihyon looked down at the scythe. He looked back up at Hayden, and a smile eerily crept across his face just as the scythe began to stir.

"And you're coming with me," he whispered, and his long, boney hands grabbed Hayden's shoulders. Nurarihyon's nails cut into Hayden's frayed military uniform. Hayden looked down at the scythe, his eyes growing wide. Before he had the chance to let go, the scythe imploded, causing all three to vanish into thin air.

Without a commander to guide them, the remaining demons in the world started to flee Guam.

Susanoo had cleared the skies and his face disappeared into the clouds between the rays of sun shining through them. The Dullahan, feeling no duty to the remaining fight between the living, stayed to slay a few more demons before disappearing. Hayden's father was the last to stay behind, overlooking Guam and the humans that stood to defend it. Many of the possessed Imperial Japanese soldiers were released willingly as the spirits left the humans to fight their own war.

The Battle of Guam officially began on July 21, less than three days later.

CHAPTER TWENTY-TWO

York, Pennsylvania, August 11, 1944
1325 — local time

Weeks later, the radio in a hospital room announced the victory of the United States reclaiming the territory of Guam from Japanese rule, thirty-two long months after their hostile takeover in 1941.

Máiréad was at Finley's bedside as he stirred in the hospital bed while Gabe paced the floor, listening to the news. Hayden had gone to Guam during their preinvasion, and he never came back out. Gabe wiped his cheek forcefully as a single tear slid from his eyes before it had the chance to reach his beard. He turned around to turn the radio off. He couldn't listen to it anymore. He had his doubts that Máiréad wanted to keep listening to it either.

While it was a victory for the United States to reclaim the territory of Guam, it was a great loss to their family.

"As much as I'm thankful he saved Finn..." Gabe looked over at Máiréad, whose eyes were still red. "I wish they both came back out." He clenched his jaw and shook his head. "I should've—"

"Should have what?" she asked tenderly.

He just shook his head.

"Gabe, Hayden could do things that weren't normal— that were unnatural. He came back from the dead once..." she started, frowning a little before looking up at her husband. "I have to have hope that maybe he'll find his way home again one day."

Gabe sniffled violently and nodded. He clenched his jaw, still nodding. He had to agree. Hayden was a remarkable young man for their time, and perhaps he needed to believe in him a little more. He didn't fully understand, but maybe no one did for sure. Hayden was ahead of their time. Gabe scratched at his beard as he sat down beside Máiréad, and she leaned into him while still holding onto Finley's hand. Her thumb gently grazed the back of his hand fondly while she snuggled into her husband.

The little boy stirred again, his eyes fluttering. Máiréad gasped as she sat back up when he opened his eyes. Finally, her little boy returned to her. Finley blinked a few times, his vision a little blurry. A small smile appeared on his face, looking at his mom and dad, but then turned his head to look around the room.

Finley frowned.

"Where's Hayden?" he asked as he began sitting up in bed. There was a bit of demand in his voice. Máiréad tried to stop him from getting up.

"Please rest, Finley. You need to rest."

"No, where's Hayden?" he demanded, his voice growing panicked. "Where is he, Mom? Mom?" His voice grew softer the more he addressed his mom, fearing what she could possibly say.

Máiréad looked over at Gabe, whose expression grew more solemn. He averted his gaze to avoid Finley catching the look on his face. She turned back to her youngest son and got up from her seat to sit with him on the bed. Máiréad clenched her jaw as she fought the tears threatening to gather in her eyes. She forced a smile as she looked down at Finley.

"Your brother—he's a *hero*," she began as she rubbed the back of his knuckles before brushing his cheek with her hand. She pushed his blond hair out of his eyes, distracting herself a bit as she tried to find the right words to say. "And sometimes, heroes have to make sacrifices to do what's right for everyone, even if it's not for their benefit." She swallowed hard. Finley's bottom lip quivered as tears streamed down his face. Máiréad held his face in her hands and wiped his cheeks dry with her thumbs. "And they don't always come home." Her voice cracked, despite how hard she tried to maintain composure.

Finley crashed into his mom as he cried against her shoulder. Máiréad hugged him tightly, consoling the small boy as she rubbed his back. Her own hand moved to cup her face behind him, trying to stifle her own sobs. Gabe turned away and looked out of the window, hardening his expression. He steadied his breathing and stuffed down his emotions.

Their son cried until he physically couldn't. The weight of his sadness grew too heavy for him to stay awake, and he eventually fell back to sleep with his lashes still wet with tears. Máiréad brushed the damp hair from his face. His pale cheeks were flushed, nose pink and runny. She wiped his nose and tucked him back into bed. She steadied her breathing and threw the tissue into the small trashcan next to the chair behind her.

"He would've been twenty-six this month." Máiréad stared at nothing while she thought of her older son. Her hands trembled. "He spent his twenty-fourth birthday in jail, his twenty-fifth who knows where, and now his twenty-sixth—" She cut herself off with a sigh. "Dead. *Again.*"

Gabe hesitated.

"What should we do about a service?" he asked, not meaning to be insincere. "For Hayden." He had still been looking out of the window when he finally turned around, but he had heard Máiréad shifting around behind him.

Máiréad sighed, exhaling deeply as she got up from Finley's bed. She knew she'd have to do something eventually. She straightened her dress, smoothing out the wrinkles before fiddling with her thumbs.

"I'd like to wait," she said finally. "At least until the end of the war." Máiréad clasped her hands together and tucked them beneath her chin. "Maybe they'll find him. Maybe he'll find us. I just... I don't want to rule anything out or jump to any conclusions, but I also don't want to give Finley false hope." She glanced over at her sleeping son before looking up at Gabe, tears gathering again in her already reddened and glistening eyes. Her voice softened as she said, "He promised. He promised he'd come back home."

Gabe nodded slowly. "I'm sure he meant it," he said. He took hold of Máiréad's hand and pulled her into his embrace as she fell apart. She tried her best to silence her whimpers to keep from waking Finley. Her breathing was harsh and jagged. Gabe just held onto her small frame tightly. Though Máiréad was small in stature, her presence was always very loud in a room. For some reason, at that moment, she had never seemed so small.

Máiréad pulled back a little to look up at Gabe.

"I can't believe I lost him twice and I can't even bury him."

There was a gentle knock at the door. Dr. Stolly slowly opened it and popped his head into the patient room.

"I'm sorry to interrupt, Mr. and Mrs. Quartermaine. We need to debrief your son, Finley." Dr. Stolly took a few steps further in and closed the door behind him. "When he's awake and has had the chance to process the loss and everything that has happened, we need to talk to him about what happened with Commander Isamu Mori when he was kidnapped. Can you please let me know when would be a good time?" he handed a business card to Gabe.

Máiréad nodded. "What will it entail?" she asked.

"I'm afraid that'll be classified, Mrs. Quartermaine."

"Classified? With my eight-year-old son?"

"What happened in Guam with Commander Isamu Mori is something that the public can't know too much about. We'll need to speak with him privately. For safety reasons."

"For whose safety, exactly?"

"All of yours, actually. What happened with your son—both of your sons," he said, correcting himself immediately, "is highly classified, and there's a lot even we don't know yet. We don't want the wrong people poking their heads into it and potentially getting hurt—and the less the two of you know, the better for you and your family, and everyone you know."

"I have a bad feeling about this," Máiréad said, looking up at Gabe. "One of us can't go with him?" she asked, looking back at Dr. Stolly. "Just to make sure he'll be okay?" she asked.

"I'll be okay, Mom."

The three of them looked over at the little boy sitting up in his bed.

"It's about Hayden, right?" he asked, looking at Dr. Stolly. "And the bad man?"

Dr. Stolly nodded. His expression was sympathetic.

"I'm sorry about your brother. He was a good man."

"You guys shouldn't have taken him in the first place," Finley said. He then turned around on his bed so that his back faced the three of them.

Dr. Stolly sighed. His focus shifted between Máiréad and Gabe. He chewed on his bottom lip for a second and adjusted his glasses.

"This is probably the wrong time to bring it up, but Miss Sharp would like to cover the cost of his funeral arrangements. Whatever you guys want, she'll make sure it's taken care of." Dr. Stolly frowned a little behind his glasses as he glanced at Finley's back. "I'm sorry there wasn't more we could do."

"Me too," Máiréad said sternly.

Dr. Stolly nodded and excused himself from the hospital room.

Máiréad exchanged glances with Gabe before hiding her face in her hands. Despite wanting to be optimistic, Dr. Stolly's appearance and his words made her feel like Hayden wasn't coming back.

Once she gathered herself again, she sat down on Finley's bed beside him. He turned around to face her, and she stroked his cheek.

"You don't have to do it," she told him.

"I want to," he said. "For Hayden."

Máiréad pursed her lips together before forcing herself to smile.

"I still remember when they came," he said, pulling the hospital blanket up to his neck. "It wasn't Charlie."

"Do you want to talk about it? Saipan?"

Finley stared at his hands gripping onto the blanket before looking at the door.

"I don't think I'm allowed," he said softly. "I have to be strong."

Máiréad stroked his hair, before fondly rubbing his cheek with her thumb.

"You are," she assured. "You and Hayden both are—stronger than I could have ever hoped you'd be." She leaned forward and gently pressed her lips against his forehead.

Finley closed his eyes again and snuggled into his warm blankets.

Máiréad looked over at her husband. The two of them could remember clearly what it was like when Nurarihyon came for Finley. How they were hypnotized by his presence and had to obey him without question. Gabe then looked away and walked over toward the window. It was a harrowing feeling to be a parent and to be helpless in protecting your family.

He wondered then if things with Miss Sharp and Dr. Stolly would be Finley's greatest chance in being able to protect himself. Gabe looked back at his son. His hands were bandaged, but he could see the damage to his fingers peeking from them and over the blankets. Maybe it was the only choice they had at this point. Trusting. Gabe looked at his wife, who continued to stroke Finley's face.

York, Pennsylvania, August 18, 1944
2036 — local time

It wasn't until later that week that Dr. Stolly phoned Miss Sharp, who had gone back to Guam for further investigation. R.A.V.E.N. put together a team to search for the whereabouts of Sergeant Hayden Dáithí, as she was positive he was still out there somewhere. She hoped he would show up, or at the very least, his whip or Death's scythe.

"Any luck?" Dr. Stolly asked, holding the phone against his cheek with his shoulder while he looked through the files he had gathered on the Iroquois Theater fire over forty years ago in Chicago.

"We've searched the entire laboratory that belonged to Dr. Sauer and there's just nothing," she said, her voice expressing defeat. "There's no trace of him, the whip, or the scythe, or even Nurarihyon. There's just nothing here. We can't even detect any of the same energy the artifact emitted or that affected Hayden. The portal doors are open, but it just leads to earth, like a hole someone filled— except it's hard earth, like it's never been disturbed. It's like none of them were here at all." She sighed, clearly frustrated. "How about your end? Did you find more regarding the fire?"

"A little," he said, shifting through the papers. "It says people were killed because the theater lacked proper fire exits, but there's reason to believe it was started on purpose, and people were just locked inside."

"Are you serious?"

"Yeah, the Elves and the Fey were involved. I don't really want to tangle with either of them, if I'm being completely honest."

"Elves?" she asked in disbelief. "Like the little creatures who make toys and help Santa Claus?"

"No," said Dr. Stolly sternly, shooting down her silly question. "The Elves are much different. They're an ancient race entrusted with the Book of Fate. I'm tracing it to Chicago, where it vanished. In 1903."

"I thought the Republic believed it was in Poland?"

"It was."

"So we've lost two of them. One before our time and one slipped right through our fingers."

"Don't forget that there's more."

"Sure, but only two ever made it out of the Underworld."

Dr. Stolly sighed and dropped the papers onto his desk. He took off his glasses and rubbed his face with his sleeve.

"What does the Republic say about all of this? What's happening?"

Dr. Stolly shrugged initially, before realizing she couldn't see him.

"It's been pretty quiet since we reclaimed Guam," he said. "But I'm going to head to Illinois and see what I can see."

"Are you going alone?"

"I'm sure I can arrange for company, but I doubt anything's there anyway. It's been over forty years."

"Well, it's been even longer since Death dropped his scythe off in pieces, and look what happened. Do you even know what's with the resurfacing?"

"No, but honestly? I'm terrified, Dottie. I'm terrified for the future. I'm terrified of what will become of humankind. Nurarihyon let demons into our world. We don't even know if Hayden and the Dullahan got them all, but we lucked out."

"You can't think like that," she said.

"It's hard not to. Especially because we lost Hayden. He could do things not humanly possible."

"I know."

There was a pause on both ends. Miss Sharp gripped the phone tightly. She pursed her lips together as she looked up at the people helping with the search. They were all shuffling around her, and careful to not bump into her. Her finger tangled with the cord of the phone.

"Did you talk to his family?"

There was no answer.

"Stolly?"

"Sorry, I forget you can't see me. Yeah, I did. Mrs. Quartermaine isn't thrilled about us talking with Finley."

"Think it'll be better if I do it?" she asked.

"Probably not. Finley's not too happy that we took Hayden in the first place. Since he worked at your factory, I don't think you'd make it any better because you sort of… gave him up to the government."

"I did no such thing."

Dr. Stolly chuckled on the line.

"I feel bad for him," she added.

"Me too. I feel for all of them."

"I gotta go—will I be seeing you in Harrisburg?"

Again, there was no answer on the line.

"Stolly!" she shouted.

"Sorry! I forgot again. I think I'll be there—not sure when. After I grab someone and head to Illinois."

"Keep me posted, will you?"

"Same to you."

"Be well, Stolly."

"You too, Dot."

Miss Sharp hung up the phone. For a moment, she continued to stare at it as though waiting for it to ring, and on the other end, there'd be good news.

"Miss Sharp?"

Miss Sharp blinked a few times and looked up from the phone.

"Yes?" she asked the agent who had come in.

"We—uh—we found something we think you should see."

Miss Sharp furrowed her brows as she got up. She followed the man who had come to get her. The room was full of other R.A.V.E.N. agents and military personnel who were surrounding something they found in the rubble. Much of the governor's palace had been destroyed during the battle of Guam and the opening of the portal, but she could see what the agent had been hinting at.

Miss Sharp cupped her mouth with both hands. It was Sergeant Kamuela's body. Her large brown eyes began to glisten as she quickly turned away.

"Please get him back to Hawai'i," she said, immediately wiping her rosy cheeks. "He deserves to be with his family—he deserves to be buried."

"We have to do some tests first," the agent informed her.

Miss Sharp's lips parted slightly, appalled by his words. "Excuse me?"

"I understand you knew him," he continued, as agents covered the body and zipped Sergeant Kamuela up in a bag, "but he was stabbed with the artifact, and believed to have been possessed by a demon. It's his dead body, or the kid."

"The kid?" She tilted her head, furrowing her brows.

"Hayden's brother. We have reason to believe he was also possessed and held onto the scythe."

"You don't have proof of any of this."

"Miss Sharp, we're just trying to understand something that is much greater than we are."

Miss Sharp stared at the body bag as a few men carried Sergeant Kamuela out of the rubble of the governor's palace.

"Hasn't he been through enough?" she asked, not taking her eyes off of the bag. Her large brown eyes were glistening still, red-rimmed. "He's eight!"

"Haven't we all?"

Her lips parted as her attention was redirected to the agent speaking to her. His lack of empathy toward the situation was disgraceful in her eyes, but she kept her mouth shut, not wanting to trivialize his own trauma from the war. Instead of saying anything, she turned on her heels and walked the other way toward the portal itself.

Miss Sharp blinked away several tears from her wet eyelashes and dabbed her eyes with a handkerchief.

Despite having seen the stream of demons coming from the portal, the earth was as solid as it could be, nearly hard as rock. The metal plates were broken around the circle, and she closed her eyes, trying to imagine what could have possibly happened between Hayden and Nurarihyon.

"Ma'am?"

She sighed and opened her eyes.

"Yes?"

"We're heading back now," he said. "Are you ready?"

"What about Hayden?" she asked.

He shrugged.

"I don't know what you're expecting us to do, Miss Sharp. There's nothing here but debris. Wherever the Corpse Walker is, it's not here." He nodded toward the door. "Come on. I hear your dad's been asking for you."

CHAPTER TWENTY-THREE

York, Pennsylvania, September 29, 1945
1000 — local time

The United States citizens were celebrating all throughout the country.

The war was finally over.

Thousands of families were welcoming their loved ones who returned from war, and even more than that, were burying them in loud silence.

It was the end of September in 1945. Autumn had begun. Leaves on the trees in Pennsylvania were changing to a myriad of oranges, yellows, and reds that would rustle violently in the cool breeze, some releasing from branches to float to the ground. The Japanese had officially surrendered World War II only a few weeks earlier, and the streets were filled with a constant celebration that the long war was finally over. In the bigger picture, it was an amazing feat, but when brought to a smaller scale, not everyone had something to celebrate.

Over a year had passed since the United States reclaimed Guam and destroyed what was left of Yamata no Orochi in the process. Without Nurarihyon and his allies, Imperial Japan no longer stood a fighting chance—not that they ever had one with him to begin with. Commander Isamu Mori had never been on the side of the Japanese people but followed his own agenda to end humanity as a whole with his parade.

The service for Hayden Zachariah Dáithí had an open casket that lacked a body, to allow mourners to give their last gifts and letters containing their final words.

Finley was now nearly ten years old, and as he looked up at his mom, she nodded at him. He chewed on his bottom lip before looking out at the many people who came to his brother's funeral. His blond hair was brushed back, and his eyes were red but without tears. Though he stood before many people mourning the loss of his brother, Finley stood proudly by the empty casket to honor him. He tightly gripped the notecards for his speech his mother helped him with.

"My brother first died when he was twenty-three in 1941, on the USS *Oklahoma*," he said finally, and everyone quieted down, stopping their side conversations they had with one another to listen to the young man. They all looked at Finley as they awaited what he had to say. He knew a few of them personally, but not the way his brother did. "He joined the military when I was a baby. Him being a Marine was all I ever knew." He sniffled a little but tried to hide it as he glanced at the cards. "He was well-liked too. He was kind—mostly to people who weren't me—" there were many laughs in the crowd. "He was caring and giving, and while he had a general dislike for people, no one cared more than he did when someone needed him." Finley inhaled deeply and pulled on the sleeve of his suit anxiously. "I didn't want him to go, you know. I didn't want him to go back to war, and I was upset with him for wanting to leave again. He'd already died once, and by a miracle, we got him back. I didn't want him to die again—" his voice cracked.

Máiréad fondly rubbed his shoulder for encouragement.

"He would've been twenty-seven this year. He should be here, celebrating with us. If it weren't for him, there's a good chance all of you wouldn't be here." Finley looked over at Miss Sharp, who stood with Dr. Stolly and Colonel Richards. He knew what he wasn't allowed to say, so he stopped himself. "My brother deserves to be here. My brother deserves to be alive. I wish it was him who survived instead of me." A few people gasped, and Máiréad just looked down. Gabe closed his eyes. "I'll never be half the man that Hayden was. Never."

Not too many people knew that Finley had been kidnapped by Commander Isamu Mori and possessed by an Inugami, or that he once wielded Death's scythe, and some of the ones who did, agreed with Finley's statement, whether they were verbal in their agreement or remained silent. Hayden had a lot to offer, and Death chose to bring him back for a reason. Finley had mere exposure to the artifact, and while it affected him, it wasn't the same, nor to the extent. Sometimes his eyes would flicker black and the veins in his face would darken with nether energy, but nothing else happened. His skin never deteriorated or changed color, and he possessed no other otherworldly ability than to slightly terrify people when he was angry.

Many people came to pay their respects to Hayden and his family. Many people had crossed the country just to attend the funeral held for the mighty Corpse Walker. There were hundreds of faces, though most blurred together in the background. Finley didn't really notice those. He didn't really pay attention to any of the faces aside from the ones he was already familiar with.

The rest didn't matter to him.

When the crowds had mostly cleared, Colonel Richards finally approached the casket, not wanting to be amongst the commotion. He looked down at Hayden's casket and while it lacked a body, it was hardly empty. It was full of flowers, trinkets, gifts, and letters saying thank you and paying tribute to him and his sacrifices for their country. While Colonel Richards' face was dry and absent of any tears, there was clear devastation on his face.

"I didn't think it would end like this," he said, mostly to himself. Colonel Richards placed a letter in the casket from the Board for Correction of Military Records containing the official upgrade of Hayden's discharge. "I hope you'll be at peace now, Sergeant Dáithí." His continued voice was nothing but a mere whisper.

He turned around to rejoin Miss Sharp and Dr. Stolly, who were now in the company of Captain George McMillin.

"Captain," Colonel Richards said as he approached them.

"Colonel," McMillin said, before looking at the other two. "What'll become of the boy?" he asked curiously.

Miss Sharp chewed on her bottom lip as she looked over at Dr. Stolly.

"We're going to keep a close watch on him," he said with a shrug as the four of them stared at Finley with his parents. "The Inugami didn't seem to leave any lasting effects on him, but we're unsure of what the scythe might've left behind. He was severely weakened, but men have come into contact with just a piece of it and had their lives completely drained right out of their bodies. Finley's the only living human to have wielded it— possessed or not." Dr. Stolly inhaled deeply and shrugged his shoulders. "There's not much we can do right now, but he's just a child. He deserves somewhat of a normal life."

"A normal life?" Colonel Richards scoffed, shaking his head. "Stolly, his older brother was the Corpse Walker," he said plainly, not taking his eyes off of the small nine-year-old boy who looked so innocent with his parents. "He'll be lucky if he knows a normal day in his entire life." He looked over at McMillin. "What do you think?"

"If he's anything like his older brother, I hope he joins the military."

Máiréad fixed the tie Finley was wearing. Though his eyes were red, they were absent of any tears. She wiped his rosy cheeks with her thumbs, and a small smile peeked at the corner of her lips.

"Your brother would be so proud of you," she said softly with a reassuring nod. "You're so strong, Finley." She straightened the front of his jacket a little roughly to make him stumble and pay attention to her. Finley forced a smile.

"I wish he was here," he said quietly, averting his eyes.

Máiréad nodded.

"I know, baby."

York, Pennsylvania, October 2, 1945
2108 — local time

Hayden's absence was loud, especially in their home. Ever since Finley had returned home from the hospital, he spent every night sleeping in Hayden's room. The wheelchair he briefly used was still kept in the corner by the door, and aside from the disheveled bed, everything else remained neat and untouched since the last time Hayden had been there.

Finley rolled around in the bed, legs tangled in his bedsheet. His eyes were shut tightly as he tossed and turned against the mattress. Sweat beaded on his forehead, dampening his hair and the pillowcase beneath his head as his fists tightened. When he woke up abruptly, hovering above him was a ghostly form of an older man he had never seen before. He screamed. His heart beat rapidly in his chest as he turned on the bed. He grabbed the pillow and swung at nothing.

Máiréad and Gabe quickly descended down the stairs with their husky leading the way, only to find Finley sitting propped up on the bed. He held the pillow under his arm and a photo in his hand.

Máiréad could feel her heart sink.

"Mom, who is this?" Finley asked, looking at the man in the photo.

She didn't have to look at the picture and instead remained standing by the door as Gabe went to investigate while their husky licked sweat off of the side of Finley's face. He smiled a little and pushed the dog off of him playfully.

"Hayden's father," she said finally as Gabe looked down at the picture. She had left it beneath Hayden's pillow so many years ago, she had forgotten all about it.

"I saw him," Finley said softly.

Máiréad's eyes lit up.

"Hayden?" she asked, taking a step further into the room.

Finley shook his head and held up the photo.

"Him."

Máiréad inhaled sharply.

"He was here," Finley continued, running his fingers through the fur of the dog. "I saw him. He scared me."

"What did he want?" Gabe asked. "What did he do to you?"

"Nothing. He's looking for him," Finley said. "He's looking for Hayden."

Gabe furrowed his brows as he looked up at Máiréad. She was leaning back against the wall, trying to steady herself.

"What does he mean?" Gabe asked her.

Máiréad only shook her head.

"The only peace I've found was believing Hayden was with his father, and now that I know he isn't—" she chewed on her bottom lip, unsure of what to think. Her eyes moved to Finley. "Did he say anything to you?"

Finley shook his head.

"But I just—just knew I wasn't who he was expecting. He was disappointed. I could see it on his face." Finley furrowed his brows and brushed his messy hair out of his face. "Does this mean—do you think Hayden's alive somewhere?"

Máiréad continued to chew on her bottom lip, unsure of how to respond to that. Gabe's eyes were fixed on her, burning holes in the side of her head as she kept her gaze locked on her son.

"I don't think so baby," she said finally. Her gaze fell. She looked to her side at the wheelchair next to the door. A lifetime ago. Máiréad sighed and touched the handle of the chair. "I never should've let him go," she said quietly.

"He would've gone without your permission anyway," Gabe said, watching her fumble with the handle. "It's better he went with your approval than without it."

Gabe stared at Máiréad for a moment longer.

"Is your ex going to be a problem?" he asked finally.

"I told you, he's dead."

"Yeah, but—that's before I knew about spirits still lingering and him being part of the Dullahan."

"We were both only ever concerned for Hayden," she said. "We have no interest in or want anything to do with one another." A small smile peeked at the corner of her mouth as she looked up at her husband. "Don't worry, you aren't in any kind of competition with a ghost." She finished with a small chuckle.

Gabe looked at his son and patted his knee.

"You gonna be okay down here, or do you wanna sleep in your room tonight?"

"I'll be fine," Finley said, nodding in reassurance.

Gabe nodded and got up. He kissed Máiréad and told her he'd meet her upstairs before whistling for the dog as the two headed back to bed.

Máiréad stayed at the door for a moment longer.

"I'm sorry you had to see that," she said.

Finley shrugged. Briefly seeing the dead father of his older brother was the least of his concerns.

"Something's wrong," he muttered quietly. "I'm not the same." He closed his eyes, and when he opened them again, his eyes were black. He blinked, and they returned to their hazel color.

Máiréad's breath caught in her throat at the surprise.

"I wish Hayden was here," he continued, pulling the blanket up to his neck. "He'd know what to do."

CHAPTER TWENTY-FOUR

Pearl Harbor, Hawai'i, September 19, 1962
1044 — local time

Years after the end of World War II, Research, Analysis, Verification, and Endorsement of the Nonsensical, or R.A.V.E.N., was restructured and expanded to the Sector of Managing Obscure Knowledge and Eccentricities & Maneuvering Irregular Rehabilitations, Removals, Obliterations, and Regulations Subdivision, also known as S.M.O.K.E. & M.I.R.R.O.R.S.

The founders were Miss Dorothea Sharp, Colonel Norman Richards, and Dr. Ingram-Zander Stolly collectively. It was Dr. Stolly who had grown fond of the acronyms and liked the symbolism that could come with whatever word or phrase the name would make up. S.M.O.K.E. & M.I.R.R.O.R.S. represented much more than R.A.V.E.N., and was something he came to agree with that they stood for—a problem he initially had with the division.

Dr. Stolly and Miss Sharp oversaw the creation of the Pearl Harbor Memorial on O'ahu before it opened in 1962. They made sure Sergeant Hayden Dáithí and Sergeant Charles Kamuela were properly honored for their sacrifices, despite their covert nature. Very few people would ever come to know the extent of Dáithí and Kamuela's contributions, but those who did knew the war on the Pacific would have ended much differently.

The memorial was crowded for a long time once it first opened to the public, as people were eager to learn about the details surrounding the bombing of Pearl Harbor. Many military personnel and their families came to pay their respects to the fallen military servicemen and citizens who died during the attack. There was a section roped off for those who wanted to learn about the man who supposedly returned to the land of the living, or the Corpse Walker, as the media branded him. Once an enemy of the country and dishonorably discharged for desertion, he gained his status as a war hero.

A scruffy, young blond man in a white suit stood in front of it, looking up at the statue modeled after the Corpse Walker. Beside Hayden Dáithí, were statues of Dr. Susanoo, whose name was also cleared and returned in good standing, and Sergeant Charles Kamuela, who died a terrible death on Guam, but was eventually brought back to Hawai'i and laid to rest after the United States reclaimed the territory. The section was roped off, with a short description of each, their place in the war, and a few notable public details on the secret Project Reaper. What was shared at the memorial was extremely minimal compared to what went on behind the scenes on base and in Pennsylvania—at least from what he was aware of.

A young Hawaiian lady approached the man. Her thick, sun-kissed black hair was bound tightly in a bun on her head with a few fresh plumeria flowers pinned to it, and her tanned golden skin seemed to glow. Similar to his, she also wore a white suit, tailored perfectly to fit her body. A brown leather book bag hung from her shoulder, and she gripped the strap tightly when she stopped before him. She glanced up at the memorial of the Corpse Walker he stood in front of and then turned to him.

"Alexis," he said softly, acknowledging her presence.

"Did you know him?" she asked.

The young man tilted his head, staring at the statue.

"A little, but not well enough," he answered plainly. The statues were made of marble and he didn't take his eyes off of Hayden's face. "Though I'm pretty sure he was a little shorter than this." A small, barely noticeable smile lifted at the corner of his lips.

"Well, Agent Quartermaine, we need your assistance," Alexis said. "Dr. Stolly says there may be recent activity surrounding another of the Infernal Artifacts in

Chicago, but he isn't entirely sure. Something about an old fire. Apparently, there's been some strange activity." She maintained composure, but her dark brown eyes demanded his urgency, which he noticed when he glanced at her. Alexis looked back at Dorothea Sharp, who stood off to the side. He glanced over at her too.

She wasn't looking at either of them, though. Miss Sharp looked past the both of them and at the memorial of her fallen colleagues. Finn remembered the first real conversation he had with Miss Sharp. She had sat in when he was being debriefed with Dr. Stolly. She was a kind woman who was aging gracefully. Finn wasn't exactly what one would consider tall, but Miss Sharp was shorter than almost everyone. The only person he knew to be shorter than her was his own mother.

"I'll be there in a minute," he answered finally. Alexis responded with a nod as well and returned from where she came. She passed Miss Sharp, nodding in her direction, and left the memorial.

Agent Finley Quartermaine took one last look at the picture of his brother whose memory was now preserved and immortalized at Pearl Harbor forever. Finley Quartermaine went on to work for S.M.O.K.E. & M.I.R.R.O.R.S. not long after his own military service in the Army when he was drafted during the Korean War. Toward the end of his active duty, Miss Sharp and Dr.

Stolly recruited him as an agent. Finn knew that one of the only reasons he was there, was because of his brother. His eyes turned a smoky black before returning to their hazel color. The corner of his mouth twitched into a subtle smile.

Turning on his soles, he strolled over to Miss Sharp.

"How's your son doing?" Finn asked. His chin was tucked down toward his chest as he looked up at Miss Sharp.

Miss Sharp sighed, clearly exasperated with motherhood.

"I'm ready to give him away." She looked at him with tired eyes as she blinked slowly. "Would you like to watch him for a few days?"

Finn laughed, holding his hands up in surrender as he took a step back.

"Definitely not," he said and rubbed at his scruffy chin. Similarly to his older brother, Finn couldn't really grow much facial hair either, but he cherished what he did have. "I'll admit, I'm not all that great with kids."

"It was worth a shot," Miss Sharp said, looking at the memorial. "The world knows that these Infernal Artifacts aren't just myths. We've tried to cover up what happened in Guam as much as we could but—" she glanced at Finn before looking back at the memorial. "You can't hide something like that. A man returning from the dead and demons being released in our world."

"So, which one is this one?" Finn asked, acknowledging the briefcase she was holding. She pursed her lips together and thumbed her finger against the handle.

"The Book of Fate," Miss Sharp answered finally. "The myth was that it was left with an ancient civilization in Poland."

"What kind of ancient civilization?"

"Elves."

He grinned. "Elves? Like Santa's elves?"

"If Stolly was here, he'd be giving you the nastiest glare right now. I remember when I said nearly the same thing to him almost twenty years ago."

A smirk stretched further across Finley's face as he chuckled. "If it was supposed to be in Poland, then what was it doing in Illinois?"

"I wondered the same thing."

She fished an old newspaper from the pocket of her briefcase. A handbill for the Mr. Bluebeard Musical was paper clipped to the front. He flipped it over and looked at the article. "The Iroquois Theater fire. This was nearly sixty years ago, Miss Sharp. If you guys have been looking into this for the last twenty years and nothing's happened, it sounds like a dead end."

"I know how it *sounds*," she said softly as he handed her the newspaper back. "But I never said nothing's happened there." She tucked the newspaper away. "Back to the point—we figured Chicago would be a good place for another office location in the meantime." She offered him the briefcase. "And I want you to oversee it."

"You want *me* to do what?"

"I've known you since you were—what—eight years old?" she said, waiting for him to take the briefcase. "I've watched you grow into who you are today. You're a remarkable young man, Finley. I want you to have this opportunity. You deserve it."

Hesitantly, he accepted the case from her.

"Your brother doubted himself too, you know," she said, rubbing his shoulder fondly. "But he never had any doubts when it came to you."

Finn glanced back at the memorial.

"I miss him," Miss Sharp said, stepping up beside him. She let out a deep sigh. Finn glanced over at her before his gaze swept right back to the statue of Hayden.

"Me too," Finn whispered. He listened to her heels click against the ground as she walked away, while he stayed for a moment longer. "Rest easy, brother." Finn, even after all these years, couldn't help but wish Hayden was still standing there with him. He wished he would have known him longer. Known him better. He wished for something more. There were a million things he wanted to ask him, and a million things he never got to say. "I hope I would've made you proud."

Rest easy.

EPILOGUE

Of course, little did anyone know, Hayden was not resting easy and hadn't been since Guam. Hayden wasn't dead, at least no deader than he already was. He had been pulled through a hole in the universe that dragged him right down.

All the way down.

He had awoken in a dark and damp place. So dark, he could barely see his hand two inches from his eyes. The ground was wet and covered in something he'd rather not think about. He'd been there before; he remembered. Not intentionally, but still, he didn't know where. He tried to get up, but someone held him back down.

Or something.

Immediately on the defense, the thing leaped away from him when he reached for his whip, their hands up in surrender.

"I don't mean you harm," the eerie voice whispered from the darkness, as though coming from the darkness itself. "Just be careful."

"Where am I?"

"Underground."

"How far underground?"

"You're in the Underworld, sir."

"Oh, for fuck's sake."

The figure leaned in close, but Hayden could still barely see it.

"If I were you, I'd stay away from the water."

His eyes narrowed out of curiosity. "What's in the water?" Hayden frowned. "Hang on—what water?"

The figure pointed behind him.

Hayden turned around to see a giant wall of ocean water before him that reached up higher than he could see, even as his eyes adjusted to the darkness. He tilted his head back so far, his chin pointed at the sky. The wall of water flowed up and down, like the surface of the ocean. He reached his hand out to brush against the watery wall, only to pull back when something larger than a building swam by—lights flickering along its spine.

"What's in the water?" he repeated again, his voice a bit shaky. His hand tightened against the handle of his whip.

He was met with silence.

CORPSE WALKER: THE NIGHT PARADE | 399

Hayden was alone.

"Well, I guess I'll just go fuck myself."

Turning around again, there was something else—or someone else. Hayden narrowed his eyes, and his grip on his whip tightened as he took a step closer.

"You're not going to use that on me, are you, Corpse Walker?" she asked, and almost immediately, Hayden recognized her voice.

"Elaina."

It didn't take him long for his whip to be wrapped around her neck. Her Diwata form blurred with her face as she struggled against the whip.

"Let me go! It wasn't my fault! I didn't kill Kamuela!"

"No, but you led him to his death. You were responsible for it—you may as well have murdered him yourself."

"I can help you find him—down here. I can help you escape!"

"Your words don't mean anything to me, Elaina." He watched as her form shifted back and forth. "What are you?"

She struggled to breathe.

Hayden sighed and released her.

Agent Dacua dropped to the ground. Holding her neck, she coughed.

"I wasn't helping Nurarihyon because I wanted to bring the demons to earth," she said. "I didn't want that.

I wanted to preserve nature. Your kind is—" she inhaled sharply as she looked up at him, her eyes were full of anger. "Your kind is a disease to Terra. I just wanted to save it and sometimes sacrifices have to be made. I chose a side, and I died because of it."

"Terra—" he repeated after her, paying no mind to anything else she claimed. "What are you?" he asked again.

"I'm Diwata," she said finally.

He vaguely remembered Dr. Stolly mentioning it, but the word really didn't mean anything to him.

"You still wanted humankind to die."

"For the right reasons!"

Hayden rolled his eyes as he rolled up his whip and fastened it to his belt.

"Where are we?" he looked around. It was so dark he could barely see two feet in front of him and he wasn't particularly interested in looking at the ocean again.

"Sasalåguan," she replied softly.

"Where the hell is that?"

"Well, *Hell* actually," she said, matter-of-factly. She tilted her head, attempting to gauge his reaction. "Welcome to the Underworld of Guam, Corpse Walker."

He sighed as he looked around and groaned.

"*Fuck.*"

THE CORPSE WALKER WILL RETURN

If you enjoyed this novel,
please consider leaving a review.

Thank you.

Q&A with
THE AUTHOR

What are the Infernal Artifacts?

The Infernal Artifacts are artifacts that belong to the Infernals and believed to be the strongest artifacts in existence. Infernals are the first beings, and children of the Creator. In my universe, the Creator and his children existed before all else, including prior to the existence of Gods and Goddesses.

What inspired Corpse Walker?

I get this question a lot when I've talked about this novel and there wasn't really one thing that inspired it. My ideas usually come to me fully formed.

I started this project building the Underworld and didn't really think of the plot. As briefly mentioned in the epilogue, there are different 'countries' in the Underworld similar to the way we have different countries in the world, or the land of the living. I wanted the Underworld to almost mirror our world, influenced by different cultural beliefs, and that helped develop the idea for the Infernals, and so on.

World War II also inspired Corpse Walker. Being born and raised in Hawaii, there aren't really a lot of things set here in fiction, aside from maybe romance. There also isn't a huge focus on the Pacific War for fiction. I used these things as a starting point, and the more I researched, the more everything fell in to place, including the placements of Guam, Midway, and Hawaii. It was all too perfect to not use. I'm also of Japanese and Irish descent, and I've always been fascinated by both Yokai and by the Dullahan, both of which have been creatively adapted to appear in this novel and will appear throughout the entire collection.

I also didn't know about York, PA's involvement with the war until I had the opportunity to go there in February and March of 2021. Pennsylvania was rich with history, like the connection Susanoo makes about George Washington and Braddock, so a lot was changed about Hayden as I continued to research. I'm not a huge history person—my history teachers would tell you I was terrible at the subject, so I apologize for any errors I might've made, but I did do my best to be as historically accurate as the story would allow.

I guess a lot of things inspired this book. A lot of things inspired the collection itself.

How many books will be in the Infernal Artifacts collection?

I don't know. I could give an estimate, but I don't want to give a definite answer and change my mind later on—but there will be a lot. I have it all planned out and I know how it ends, I just don't know how many books it will take for me to tell it in its entirety. Generally, there are several different book series that all connect for an overarching plot. So the next book that will be released won't be a Corpse Walker sequel, but the first book of the next series.

Will we learn more about Hayden's time in the Underworld?

Absolutely. Just not right away. I promise it'll make more sense as more novels are out and the overarching story comes together. The way I am releasing the books makes the most sense from a storyteller's point of view, but there will be a Corpse Walker sequel.

What made you want to write military and historical fiction?

I didn't! I absolutely did not want to write military or historical fiction! Haha. Those most familiar with my creativity know that if I didn't have to, I wouldn't have. I personally hate following rules when it comes to telling a story. By that, I don't mean the technicalities of writing, (well, I hate that too, actually) but research. I don't like limiting myself to the rules and history and mythology of our world. I like to make everything up and use other things as inspiration.

It's safe to say this novel was a huge struggle for me. Not only did I try to be historically accurate, but I also had to outsource help for military jargon and 1940s slang. It was so much research, and I hate homework. But you've read the book. It just had to be told this way. There was no other way for me to tell this story. I'll admit it's safe to say there's a good chance I will never write military, war, or historical fiction ever again, haha. Personally, I can't wait to dive deeper into more of the fantasy and supernatural elements. Corpse Walker was the introduction.

Did Hayden become the Corpse Walker because of his Dullahan heritage?

No, he didn't. The Infernal, Death, chose to bring him back to life and would have done so whether his father was part of the Dullahan or not. It was about Hayden and what kind of person he is, not because of his background. This is a theme that will happen frequently throughout my books. I tried to subtly show this with Finley, as they do not share the same father and yet Finley also retained abilities from the scythe but this answer is just to provide a little more clarity on the matter. Susanoo linked Hayden to a spine whip because he's Irish, not because his dad is part of the Dullahan. Stolly just assumes the connection because he gets overly excited.

Why did Nurarihyon seemingly give up in the end when Hayden confronts him?

I wouldn't necessarily call it giving up. Nurarihyon became what he was because of Susanoo's guidance. He had plans for the Night Parade for a very, very, long time.

He is very old. He reached a point of acceptance that Hayden would defeat him. Nurarihyon was just a demon guided by a god. Hayden was chosen by an Infernal. The odds were against Nurarihyon.

However, let's not forget, Nurarihyon still partly got what he wanted. He released demons into the land of the living. He may not be commanding them the way he planned to, but they're still there, lurking. That's an important thing to keep in mind.

Just in case I don't like the next book in the collection, will I be able to finish the Corpse Walker series and still understand his story?

Yes. I am writing the novels in a way that you will either be able to enjoy them as a collection or as individual series. You will not have to read all of them to enjoy the stories.

This project is intimidating for me as a writer, so I'm sure from a reader's perspective, it can be a lot to take on.

About the Author

R alynn Kimie was born and raised in Honolulu, Hawai'i. She would spend her days eating sushi all day every day with her miniature dachshunds if time (and her wallet) would allow it. She maintains awful relationships with both coffee and sleep, and forgot what it's like to have a social life as she constantly buries herself in her hobbies. Never satisfied with the limitations of her own humanity, she has found a way to exist in worlds she'll never truly get to live in and gets to share them with others through her writing.

For more information, check out her website below:

www.ralynnkimie.com

ACKNOWLEDGEMENTS

Thank you to everyone who worked on this novel and helped make it what it is today. Thank you for always providing me with amazing, high quality work.

Thank you always to Rachel Fernando, Heather Hanson, and Kristen Vasquez, who have been with me from the very beginning of my writing journey for nearly two decades now. Your unwavering and unlimited support has been the spine of every project I've completed.

Special thanks to my fantastic friends, Sgt. Jack Huber of the Marine Corps, Chez Maae, Sgt. Lucas Morgan of the Marine Corps, Sunshine Pregana, and Spc. Austin Travers of the Army. Without your daily encouragement through all of my doubts in myself and in my work, I would not have finished this.

Lastly, thank you to all the veterans and the men and women currently serving in our military.

Made in the USA
Columbia, SC
26 April 2023